TIME QUEST

GERI HAWTHORNE

Geri Hawthorne

PAGE PUBLISHING
Conneaut Lake, PA

First originally published by Page Publishing 2023

ISBN 978-1-6624-8136-9 (pbk)
ISBN 978-1-6624-8137-6 (digital)

Printed in the United States of America

I dedicate *Time Quest* to my father, Edgar Deschambault. He taught me to never give up.

SYNOPSIS

IN THE YEAR 2599 AD, time travel is not done for anthropological research, or to alter the future, or even entertainment. It is done for the survival of mankind. The earth is barren and males are sterile. Technology is highly advanced, but society has regressed to a dictatorship. It is a time ripe for revolt.

Shari 12101918 prepares for a mission. She is a transporter. She travels back in time to rescue male children doomed to die, and she brings them back to the future to mature and repopulate the human race. Her mentor, Helaine, warns her of the assignment's danger, but Shari feels her bigger threat is being forced to mate with a male not her choice. Shari dreams of antiquated love and passion.

Shari transports to December 1890 to save Crow Foot, son of Chief Sitting Bull of the Lakota, and bring the boy to her time. She is attacked and knocked unconscious during the uprising at the camp. She awakens, in the cabin of a handsome physician-rancher. Shari has amnesia.

John White Wolf Mackensie lives with his two-year-old son, Danny, and his maternal Lakota grandmother. He intends to help his pretty, mysterious patient regain her memory. He names her Sorrel because of her hair color.

Shari struggles to be useful as she waits for her memory to return. But she fails at every attempt. She adores Danny, but she feeds him too many cookies which make him ill. She doesn't know how to pump water. She doesn't know hot water is heated in the stove reservoir. She doesn't know how to cook or even what a potato looks like. She is afraid of horses. And her attraction to John grows. Where is John's wife?

John has been a widower since Danny's birth, and Shari (Sorrel) intrigues him. She awakens emotional needs and physical hungers he has suppressed. Although he senses Shari's innate goodness, he finds her strangely out of place, and he is mystified by an indestructible bag he found when he rescued her.

Grandmother doesn't like Shari. She tells John Shari has him under a spell.

When John opens the strange bag, he discovers a non-decomposing, second corpse of Crow Foot. An autopsy proves the second corpse is not a corpse at all. What is it? Who and what is Shari (Sorrel)?

He takes Shari (Sorrel) to Fort Yates because he wants to help the destitute Lakota people from Sitting Bull's camp, and he desperately needs to find answers explaining Shari (Sorrel).

At the fort, Shari interacts with a newborn baby and sick Lakota children with the measles. She would love to have a baby. Shari aids Doctor Cynthia Pingree. She meets an elderly warrior and a tormented young couple. She makes friends with the newborn baby's mother who is a rape victim. At the fort, Shari is harassed by a cavalry officer.

Doctor Pingree tells Shari John is a widower. Shari's self-confidence begins to return. Maybe there is a chance for her and John?

John argues with the Fort Yates commander and the territory Indian agent about the Lakota people's blight. He becomes embroiled in a conflict over Sitting Bull's burial, and then John and the elderly warrior attempt to steal Sitting Bull's body. John, Shari (Sorrel), and some Lakota warriors are captured and jailed. John is beaten and loses his knife. When Shari is harassed again by the cavalry officer, John threatens to kill him.

John, Shari and the elderly warrior escape with the help of the tormented young warrior who loves the rape victim. John is wounded. Shari shoots the harassing cavalry officer chasing them.

Shari remembers who she is and what her mission was. She takes John to the future, her time, to save his life. Helaine helps Shari trace John's history. Shari learns John is convicted of murdering the cavalry officer she shot.

President Artemis orders Shari to take John back to his time, and then immediately return to her time for mating and reproduction with a male the council has chosen. Shari abhors the order. She is torn between duty and love. She wants to be with John. She knows John will never stay in her time because Danny is in the past and needs his father. What will she do?

John wakens in his own time and he is healed. No gunshot wound. He knows he should be dead. He demands answers. Shari tells John about herself and her time. John believes her. The strange bag, the fake body, and he is not dead. And he has fallen in love with her.

Shari asks John to make love to her. He refuses. He cannot make love to her, and then let her go. They spend the night wrapped in each other's arms. In the morning, Shari becomes ill. She has the measles and cannot return to her own time.

John nurses her back to health. The next time Shari asks John to teach her passion, he cannot resist. However, before they consummate their love, they are found. John is captured for the cavalryman's murder. John is jailed in Bismarck in the Dakota Territory.

Shari returns to Fort Yates for Doctor Pingree's help. Grandmother's opinion of Shari changes. However, even the Doctor cannot sway the jury. John is convicted.

As John walks to the gallows, the elderly warrior involved in the theft of Sitting Bull's body, confesses to killing the cavalry officer because of the rapes he committed. The elderly warrior admits suffocating the cavalry office, and he has John's missing knife, taken by Walker, and again taken during the murder. John is freed.

John and Shari marry and return to the ranch where they consummate their love. Shari hopes she soon conceives John's child.

One morning, Danny is kidnapped by a robot. John and Shari follow Danny to 2599. They are met by revolutionaries who live far outside the dome city. This meeting was arranged by Helaine. The revolution leader gives Helaine's necklace to Shari, proving Artemis killed Helaine.

Upsetting John, the revolution leader removes a tracker from the back of Shari's head, which John though was a cyst. Shari and John go willingly with the rebels. In Freedom Land, there are families. There are children who have been conceived and born from males of the future. Another of Artemis's lies. Man is not sterile.

John helps the rebels fight the robots that hunt them. The rebel leader agrees to show John and Shari the way to the dome city so they can rescue Danny. John and Shari make love.

The rebel leader guides them to an abandon city where they get weapons and where they find young people who have recently escaped from the dome city. One of the young women is very pregnant. John delivers her baby. Shari wishes the baby was her and John's. The revolution leader heads back to Freedom Land, with the young people, while the newborn baby's father continues on with John and Shari.

John and Shari rescue Danny.

Danny is ill. On their way back to Freedom Land, John and Shari are met by a group of rebels. Danny's stomach ache gets worse, until he gets diarrhea and expels a tiny tracking devise.

The rebels rush back to Freedom Land and are attacked by Artemis's robots. Shari is captured.

At the dome city, Artemis beats Shari because she has conceived John's baby. Artemis plans to impregnate Shari and put his brain in the child he has fathered. Thus he can live forever and rule the world.

John and the rebels attack the dome city. The people of the city help the rebels fight for freedom. John finds Shari and kills Artemis. Shari is still pregnant with John's child. They return to Freedom land and decide to stay in Shari's time to help build a free future.

PROLOGUE

AD 2751

"WHY ARE YOU risking your life again?"

"Someone has to."

"Don't you think it's time you retired?"

"I'm not ready to retire." Shari 12101918 smiled as she wrapped a beaded hide belt around her waist. She was only twenty-five and definitely not ready for retirement or what came after. She rubbed her hands over the skirt of the blue-and-gray checkered dress she wore. "Do you think real cotton clothing was this soft?"

Helaine 06021948, senior propulsionist of the Dome City Survivalists, unblinkingly returned Shari's gaze and ignored her overt attempt to change the subject. "You really don't need to do this."

Shari arched her brows. "Yes. I do." She reached out and touched Helaine's forearm. "The others don't care like I do."

The older woman patted Shari's hand. "I know that. It's just dangerous."

"Not as dangerous as not going. Besides, I'm the best."

"I know that too, and I give you full credit for the Lincoln boy and the Davis boy."

"I just want to make a difference."

Helaine fidgeted with the necklace she always wore, making the blue and red stones twinkle. "You do make a difference. But perhaps you can make a bigger difference, just not in the way you think."

"What do you mean?"

Helaine shook her gray-haired head. "We'll talk later. You just concentrate on this assignment so you return safely." She looked up at the glass dome rising above their heads. Dawn lightened the sky. "It's time."

Shari thoughtfully regarded Helaine's words. Her mentor's angst concerned her. "Whatever you need, you know I'll help."

Helaine nodded. "I have no doubt. You just remember to follow the rules."

"I will."

Helaine chuckled.

As they walked through the vaulted white room, toward the ten-story crystal launch tubes, Shari wondered why she felt no fear. She knew she should. Anything could go wrong during teleport or during her mission. Then she admitted to herself, she loved these adventures. She always thoroughly researched before she teleported.

"Shari?" Helaine slowed her step. "Are you using this assignment as an excuse to avoid committing to the mate the presidents' council has chosen for you?"

Shari rolled her eyes. "I suppose I am. I know what my duty is, but this mating edict disgusts me. I think our society needs to regain some of its lost freedoms."

"Like mate selection?"

Squaring her shoulders, Shari nodded and met Helaine's blue gaze. "Yes."

"My dear Shari, I appreciate your romanticism. Unfortunately, the human race lost that option centuries ago. I hope for your sake that your dream doesn't get you hurt."

"It's more a quest than a dream, and it can't hurt to dream."

"Thorne 06031913 is an appropriate choice. His age and education complement your own. And he's handsome. Do you know his lineage is of Scandinavian royalty?"

"Yes. I know."

"You should be honored the presidents chose him to reproduce with you."

"I am," Shari admitted. "But I still didn't choose him." She thought of the mindless, sterile laboratory conception she'd been offered and had refused, and she knew she couldn't tolerate an emotionless sexual performance no matter how appropriate the male. She yearned for the thrill of unbridled physical passion spawned by antiquated love.

When Shari and Helaine reached the crystal launch tubes, Shari looked up and saw the sunrise reflected in the cylinders. A new day awaited her. A new beginning awaited mankind.

She was destined to be a part of it.

She knew she hadn't been selected to reproduce because of her intelligence, and her appearance had nothing to do with being chosen. She was chosen because she was one of few women who carried fertile eggs. Reproduction was her duty.

Fertile men of her time were nonexistent. Male babies were born sterile. For viable sperm, she and a small group of select time travelers risked teleporting into history to retrieve male children and bring them to the future to mature and repopulate the human race.

Shari and Helaine approached the towering teleport structure and ascended the four steps to the navigation platform. Helaine glided her hand across the multicolored flashing lights on the quartz console. Shari watched the machine lights blink and felt a rush of excitement course through her. Impatience tugged at her heart because once again she was leaving her suffocating, predestined existence and escaping into the past.

Helaine rested her palm on a pulsating green light, and Shari watched a gold-trimmed panel open. She saw Helaine reach inside the panel and slowly withdraw a large brown bundle.

"You'll need this apparel," Helaine said. "It's December there, and it's freezing." She handed the folded bundle to Shari.

"It's heavy. What is it?"

"An imitation buffalo hide coat."

"This could keep me warm on Pluto."

"It's not just for you, Shari. The boy will be badly wounded. Hold him close and keep him warm."

Shari understood.

"Did you take your nutrition capsules?"

"Yes." Shari wondered if she would be in the past long enough to eat. Probably not. But it would be a welcome experience if she was so lucky.

Helaine glanced at Shari as she continued working the controls on the console. "You'll find your return disk in the left pocket."

Shari slipped her hand into the coat pocket and felt the disk. "I'm ready for the simulative."

"Almost. But first." Helaine reached up and pulled her gold chain necklace over her head. "Take this." She held the necklace out to Shari.

"Your talisman. I can't." Why did Helaine want her to take the prized jewelry? Helaine wore it all the time.

"Please. I want you to have it. It will bring you luck, as it has me." Helaine dropped the necklace over Shari's head. "Be careful, dear."

Shari saw moisture in Helaine's eyes. Something was wrong. "Helaine, tell me what's wrong."

"Not now. Just promise me you'll be careful."

"I will. I promise." Shari hugged Helaine as she swallowed a lump of melancholy. Helaine was the reason she'd become the woman she was and why she loved the past. History was magic. Helaine had taught her everything she knew about archeology.

Shari believed in the past, people really lived. They experienced joy and sorrow. Success and defeat. It was life as life should be. Free. "Helaine, you're scaring me."

Helaine smiled. "When you get back, I promise we'll talk," she whispered.

Shari averted her face, avoiding the cameras everyone knew watched everything. "Are you in trouble?"

"I'm just an old woman worried about her favorite time traveler. That's all."

Shari didn't believe her best friend. Something was wrong. She intended to make this a fast mission.

Helaine turned back to the control panel and pressed a pulsating red light. Her touch triggered a six-foot platform to slide out the end of the console.

On a quartz slab lay a black body bag. Shari's gaze searched Helaine's, but Helaine merely responded with a slight nod. Shari stepped forward and pressed her palm against the bag. "Bag, open." The bag split down the center, revealing its contents. "It looks real."

"Yes."

"It's handsome."

Helaine nodded again. "The boy will mature to resemble his father."

"I didn't know that." She gently touched the face of the replicated body of an adolescent Native American boy. The artificial corpse's skin felt supple, like a youth's flesh. Even the stomach wounds appeared authentic. Synthetic blood smeared the abdomen, where false bullet wounds revealed incredibly authentic body organs.

Only an autopsy could prove the body never breathed. Historically, that never happened.

The presidents of the council knew they were safe to perpetrate their repopulation scheme by kidnapping. There would be no paradox. This simulative appeared to be the teenage boy Shari sought.

She resealed the body bag and picked up the simulative. The buffalo coat she wore was overly warm. Beads of perspiration broke out on her brow as she carried her burden down the steps of the console and walked toward the nearest launch tube. She awkwardly maneuvered through the opening of the towering cylinder, and as she turned around to face Helaine, the tube sealed with a whooshing sound.

Standing on the circular teleport disk, Shari closed her eyes. Her heart drummed in her ears. All she had to do was make the switch without being discovered.

A brilliant blue light engulfed her, and she felt the teleport disk beneath her simulated leather shoes begin to spin. The disk spun faster and faster, and the centrifugal force increased until it painfully pulled her hair and skin. Her stomach contents rolled. The force held her rigid, paralyzed.

Still, Shari trusted Helaine's skill and the technology enabling her to make this journey. She knew she would survive. If mankind were lucky, it would too.

CHAPTER 1

SHARI AWOKE SHIVERING. Daybreak surrounded her as she lay prone on snow-covered ground in a grove of barren winter trees. She pushed the simulative, which lay on top of her, to the side.

Her breath frosted the air, and when she inhaled, the frigid crispness burned her nose and lungs. Letting her senses assimilate, she listened and heard the wind and the scurry of small animals in the trees. Looking up, she watched snow-covered tree branches sway. Every time she teleported, she felt impressed anew. The past exuded hope.

In her time, life existed in an antiseptic dome. War and pollution had destroyed the earth's atmosphere.

Her fingers tingled in the snow, inducing her to lift her hand and gaze at the white power. In the early morning light, the frozen moisture twinkled like midnight stars. Bringing her fingers to her lips, she licked the snow and sighed. It tasted delightful. She wished she could take some of this winter enchantment back with her.

Shari shivered again, this time convulsively. Helaine had warned her about the cold. She had no more time for self-indulgence. Her mission awaited accomplishment. Rising to her feet, Shari peered through the trees and saw a group of small cabins dotting the ice-encrusted prairie. Smoke drifted from each cabin stovepipe. The scent of burning wood made her wrinkle her nose, but she actually found the smell pleasant.

She reached into her coat pocket and touched her return disk, and then she pulled an artificial hide mitten from each pocket. Helaine thought of everything.

Bending down, Shari struggled until she managed to pick up the simulative and drape it across her shoulder. Then she headed out of the trees, stepping cautiously over snow-hidden branches and brush. An injury would endanger her mission's success and possibly her life, especially if she needed to make a quick escape.

Her fake fur-lined moccasins crunched the snow as she felt ice chunks through the soles. Shari's heartbeat echoed in her ears. As she carried her burden, she felt an adrenaline burst of strength. She believed in the need for her mission. But the last thing she wanted was to die because of it.

Shari slowly approached her destination, the rear of the cabin of Chief Sitting Bull of the Lakota Indian Nation. She put the simulative down at the base of a snowdrift and covered the bag with the frozen moisture. Hunkering down to stay warm, she waited for the historical tragedy to unfold.

As the sun's orange glow reflected off the glacial prairie, the sound of barking dogs warned Shari the time had arrived. She heard horses huffing, bridles jingling, and saddles creaking, announcing the arrival of the Indian police.

Creeping to the corner of the cabin, she peeked around the little dwelling. The forty-three Indian policemen's blue uniforms looked black. They resembled wraiths. She wondered why so many were needed to arrest one man.

Shari stayed low to the ground, holding her mitten-covered hand over her mouth to conceal her exhalation as booted feet stomped to the cabin and a fist thumped on the door. In fascination, she saw Chief Sitting Bull step out of his cabin.

Wrapped in a buffalo robe, Sitting Bull stoically asked, "What do you want here?"

An Indian policeman, Lieutenant Bull Head, squared his shoulders. "You are my prisoner. You must go to the agency."

Sitting Bull replied, "The meadowlark told me you would come. Let me put on my clothes, and I will go with you." The chief asked to have his horse saddled, and Shari saw two Indian policemen leave to fulfill the chief's order. Then she watched Lieutenant Bull Head walk into the cabin.

2

Shari saw dark figures emerge from other cabins, and she watched the camp people silently approach Sitting Bull's home. She sensed their animosity thicken the air, like fog. The people surrounded the mounted Indian police, making the policemen nervously glance around. Their horses neighed and fidgeted.

Indian policeman Sergeant Red Tomahawk rode his horse through the gathered camp dwellers, forcing them to part or be trampled as he brought Sitting Bull's horse to the front of the chief's cabin. When Sitting Bull and Bull Head appeared in the doorway, the people tightened their circle surrounding the policemen.

The people chanted, "Do not leave us. Do not leave us."

Catch-the-Bear, an older warrior, ran up to the cabin. "You think you are going to take him! You will not do it!"

"Go!" Bull Head pushed Sitting Bull out of his cabin and toward his horse. Shari heard the people gasp.

Catch-the-Bear threw off the blanket covering his shoulders, exposing a gun. He fired his revolver at Bull Head, and the shot hit the Indian policeman on the right side. As Bull Head fell, he fired his pistol, and the bullet struck Sitting Bull in his lower body, making the chief stumble forward.

Red Tomahawk jumped from his mount and shot Sitting Bull in the head as the chief fell to the ground. The camp people's screams resonated into the frosted air.

Another Indian policeman shot Catch-the-Bear.

Bile rose in the back of Shari's throat. The reverberation of the Indian policemen's gunfire deafened her. The camp people only had tomahawks, knives, and clubs, but they advanced.

The Indian policemen near the cabin grappled one another to get inside Sitting Bull's cabin. The policemen outside darted for refuge behind woodpiles. The policemen's horses panicked and charged into the encroaching crowd. A woman screamed as she fell beneath a mount.

Shari saw one of the Indian policemen galloping off across the prairie, knowing he rode for the cavalry. As recorded in the archives, Chief Sitting Bull's gray horse began dancing in front of the cabin, pitifully performing tricks it had been taught during the years the chief traveled with Buffalo Bill Cody's Wild West show.

Holding her breath, Shari watched for the seventeen-year-old boy she sought. Crow Foot stepped out of the cabin. She knew the worst was about to happen, and she didn't want to see it. But she had no choice.

Crow Foot ran from the cabin into the melee and several bullets struck him, making his body whirl around before he fell. Shari grimaced as Crow Foot landed on the ground near his father.

Gunfire continued to boom across the camp, from the corral to the cabins. Bloody bodies lay strewn about the encampment, and mourning wails quivered across the prairie.

Shari darted forward.

Reaching Crow Foot, she felt the boy's neck for a pulse. His pulse beat weakly, but he was alive. Slipping her arms under his, she pulled him away from his father. She continued moving backward, dragging Crow Foot around the corner of the cabin.

Behind the dwelling, Shari quickly took off her buffalo coat and threw it on the ground. She rolled Crow Foot into the garment, and then she towed the boy around the cabin toward the snowdrift and the hidden bag containing the simulative.

"Halt!"

Shari gulped air, but she didn't stop moving. Her desperation made her pull harder, clamber faster.

"Halt!"

Her buttocks bumped into a solid form. She glanced over her shoulder and saw the butt of a Winchester rifle come down.

John "White Wolf" McIntosh dropped his physician's satchel. "Damn it!" A woman lay face down on the snow behind the chief's cabin. Kneeling beside the woman, he gently rolled her over. She had a bloody gash on the side of her head, but her breath frosted the air, confirming she lived. Beneath the young woman lay a lumpy buffalo coat. John wondered why the woman wasn't wearing the coat. It was damn cold.

He felt the woman's neck for a pulse. Her heart beat strong and steady. She looked a little on the thin side, but she was pretty. Her sorrel-colored hair and azure eyes proved she was not Indian. He examined the bleeding knot beneath her hair, and he wondered why a white woman lay unconscious in the middle of this disaster.

John touched the buffalo coat and felt something firm. Curious, he lifted the lapel of the coat. Crow Foot! He quickly checked the boy's neck for a pulse. Crow Foot was dead.

"Damn, *ceska maza*!" John despised the Indian police. They were traitors.

"Who have you got there?" Captain Edmond Fechet demanded, striding toward John.

"A woman and Chief Sitting Bull's son," John snapped. "There is no excuse for this."

"I'll be the judge of that."

"No. God will." John gritted his teeth and clenched his fists because he felt livid and wanted to strike someone. Fechet would serve the purpose. The captain hadn't bothered to look at the boy or the woman.

"I'll get the boy's mother," the captain said, striding away.

John did not respond. The injustice of the deaths was despicable. Violence was not a solution to the multitude of problems the Lakota Nation on the Standing Rock Reservation faced. Picking up the injured woman, John carried her around the chief's cabin.

As he lay the young woman on the rear leather seat of his sleigh, he heard her mumble incoherently. "Shhh. It will be all right." He covered her with the quilts he carried in the event of an emergency.

Tucking the quilts around her, he noticed her clothing. Why would a white woman dress like an Indian? She could be a new teacher at the school, but still, teachers did not dress like natives. This woman was definitely in the wrong place at the wrong time. To help her, he first had to get her to safety.

John darted back around Sitting Bull's cabin and grabbed his physician's satchel, intending to bandage the young woman's head.

Before he could return to his sleigh, Four Robes, Crow Foot's mother, and Standing Holy, Crow Foot's sister, rounded the cabin corner and approached. John set his satchel down again and waited for Four Robes to see her son.

Four Robes dropped to her knees and bent over Crow Foot's body. She cried out and began to sob. Standing Holy knelt beside Four Robes and began to chant. John gave the women several moments to grieve. Then he gently disengaged mother from son and picked up Crow Foot's body. As he turned around, he noticed something haphazardly buried in a drift against the cabin.

He intended to uncover the buried object. Crow Foot's mother and sister continued their heart-wrenching mourning prayers, and their sorrow tore at John's heart.

John hated the Indian police for what they had done, and he hated even more the white officers who had given the order that caused this abomination. Mostly he hated being unable to stop the eminent war coming between his peoples. White versus red.

John left the Indian women and once more started walking around the cabin. He had to get back to his patient in the sleigh, but the object in the snow might be another wounded innocent. It could also be firewood or animal pelts, but he had to know for sure.

As John rounded the cabin corner, he noticed the compacted snow where Crow Foot's body had been dragged. He saw small footprints leading toward the haphazardly buried dark object, and he wondered why the white woman had dragged Crow Foot toward the object in the drift.

He bent and brushed snow off the object. It was a long black bag with unfamiliar napery. As John dug the bag out of the snow, he felt something inside. Something that felt like a body. He rolled the bag over and over again, but he couldn't find any ties or buckles.

"Shit!"

John pulled his white-handled knife from a sheath on his belt and poked at the bag. The point of the knife would not penetrate the bag. He jabbed harder. Still, he could not make a puncture. The strange fabric was soft, but it resisted the blade he kept as sharp as his scalpels. John panicked because whoever was inside could not breathe.

Stepping on one end of the bag and pulling the material taunt, John raised his arm and stabbed with all his might. His knifepoint entered the bag, and when it did, he heard a tinny sound. The sound reminded him of the noise a bullet made passing through a chuck wagon plate. He gritted his teeth, and exerting all his strength, he forced his skinning knife through the nearly indestructible fabric. As he sawed, he heard a high-pitched tearing sound. Even in the cold, John perspired from his effort.

Another inch and he stopped sawing to stare in disbelief. "Shit!" Inside the strange bag lay another corpse... Crow Foot. This was not possible.

John recalled he once heard Crow Foot had a twin brother, but that boy died long ago. However, now was not the time to ponder this quandary. He had a woman with a head injury.

John grabbed the buffalo coat off the ground. He wrapped the coat around the bag and the body concealed in it because he knew neither Chief Sitting Bull's family nor the Lakota Nation needed more trouble. John carried the mysterious second corpse to his sleigh. He placed the corpse on the floor between the seats. Checking on the young woman, he saw she still breathed and still lay unconscious.

"McIntosh!"

Craning his neck, John saw Captain Fechet heading his way. "What do you want, Fechet?" John kept his expression blank, not wanting to draw suspicion. He just wanted to get the hell away.

The captain strode to the side of the sleigh. "What have you got here?"

"A wounded woman and a buffalo coat. What does it look like?" He glared at the captain, but he held his breath. John's doubts and concerns grew per second because this second corpse could trigger a religious rebellion among the Lakota. The cavalry had already outlawed the Sioux sacred Ghost Dance.

Fechet cleared his throat. He looked annoyed. He pointed at the young woman on the back seat of the sleigh. "Where are you taking her?"

"Home with me. She has a head injury, and I need to tend to her. Unless you want to be responsible for her?"

"Of course not."

"I've dug out bullets, set and splinted bones, cleaned and dressed wounds. Now my son needs me." John climbed into the sleigh and sat on the front seat. "Is there anything else?"

"No. But I didn't say you could leave."

"Let me remind you, my services are volunteered."

Fechet glowered at John, making John want to smile. Out of his peripheral vision, he saw two Indian policemen lifting Sitting Bull's body into the back of a wagon. "Where are they taking the chief's body?"

"To the agency."

"Why can't his family have his body?"

"That is none of your business!"

"Whose decision is that, McLaughlin's?"

The captain did not answer.

John shook his head. He had never trusted the Standing Rock Indian Agent, James McLaughlin. Now his lack of trust burrowed bone deep. Where were they really taking the chief's corpse?

Snapping the horse team's reins, John drove the sleigh away from Chief Sitting Bull's cabin. Dire apprehension tightened John's gut. Did McLaughlin order Sitting Bull killed? If he had, John knew there would be more deaths to follow.

Because now he had a second body of a slain boy.

CHAPTER 2

SHE HEARD SOUND. She drifted toward light and tried to open her eyes but couldn't, and when she attempted to turn her head, sharp pain shot across her forehead. Breathing slowly and deeply, she waited for the crushing grip on her skull to ease.

Although she felt terrified of what she would see, consciousness tempted her, and she strained toward it. Each heartbeat made her head throb, but she had to follow the light. She had to awaken, not just to survive but because there was something she knew she had to do. Whatever she had to do, it was something important.

But no matter how hard she tried, she couldn't grasp the recollection of what her responsibility was. But she knew it was her duty.

"She moved," a raspy female voice said.

She moved her head and flinched.

"She moved again."

"Good. Grandmother, will you warm some of that beef stew?" a baritone voice asked.

Concentrating on the sound of the male voice, she struggled harder to rouse. She liked the voice. Its timber and cadence drew her. Who was this man?

A cool hand touched her forehead, and it felt gentle, comforting. She attempted to speak, to make a sound, and she heard herself squeak.

"Come on, wake up. You can do it," the male voice coaxed.

A finger pushed up her right eyelid, making blinding light pierce her eye. She jerked her head to the side and grimaced. Drawing strength from deep inside, she croaked, "Don't."

"Sorry. I need to see if your pupils are still dilated."

She slowly pried her eyes open and met an ebony gaze.

"Hello." The man leaned forward and looked deeply into her eyes.

He smelled nice. "Whhhooo…are you?" She closed her eyes because the man leaned too close, and it hurt her eyes to look at him. She heard him back away and opened her eyes again. He stood by her, watching her.

"Who am I? That depends on which side of the family you ask. I am John McIntosh, physician and rancher, or White Wolf, medicine man and mediator between the Lakota and the cavalry."

The man was tall and raven haired. His hair hung to his broad shoulders, and he had a straight, narrow nose and a square jaw. The mix of Native American and Caucasian complemented him.

She noticed the white handle of something sticking out of a sheath on his lean hip. Was that a knife? Her heart started pounding, and it made her head hurt worse. She slowly lifted her hand and pointed. "What's that?"

He looked down. "My knife."

"Do physicians use knives like that?"

"No. Ranchers do. If it makes you feel secure, you keep it." He pulled the knife from its sheath and laid it beside her on the bed.

She picked it up. The knife handle was white agate with his name engraved on it. "It's beautiful." She saw John smile, and her mouth went dry. She swallowed and licked her lips. "Where am I?"

"In my home. On my ranch."

Putting the knife down beside her, she laid her palm on it. As she rolled her gaze around the room, the log walls spun. Her head felt as if it were expanding and contracting, and bile rose in her throat. She pressed her hand over her mouth and rolled on her side.

John reacted instantly. He grabbed something from the floor with one hand and slipped his other hand beneath her shoulders. "Breathe deeply."

She did.

"Better?"

"Yes. No."

She vomited into a metal bucket John held.

When she was through, he eased her down. "It will pass." John pulled a red bandana from the pocket of his denim jeans and handed it to her. "It is clean. Wipe your mouth."

She did. "I'm…all right now."

"I doubt it." John took the bucket from her and set it beside the bed. He reached down again and lifted a small black satchel from the floor, and he set it on the bed. "I need to check your heart and pulse."

She stared up at him as she wrapped her fingers around the knife handle. She knew he saw her, but she remembered rule number one: trust no one. Whose rule was it?

"Do you feel any better now?" John asked.

She recalled he'd said he was a physician. "A little." She didn't nod because she feared moving her head.

"Good." John pulled a three-ended devise out of his satchel. Placing two ends into his ears, he leaned forward and placed the third end, a bell-shaped metal object, just beneath the top of the bedgown she wore.

The metal was cold, and it made her shiver.

"Sorry. I know it is cold. My satchel was in the sleigh." He looked straight into her eyes. "I just need to listen."

His dark gaze calmed her. She closed her eyes and relaxed. If he meant to harm her, it would already be done.

John listened through the three-ended object. He nodded. Taking her hand, he pulled a round pocket watch on a chain from his trousers, placed his fingers on her wrist, and then he waited as he looked at his silver watch.

She wondered at his actions but knew he'd done nothing untoward, and she did feel a little better.

"Would you like some water?" He smiled as he put the watch back into his pocket.

"Yes." She liked his smile. He had even white teeth and laugh lines crinkled the corners of his obsidian-colored eyes. He was handsome, especially when he smiled.

"Your necklace is in the top drawer with your clothing." John pointed toward a chest of drawers.

"What necklace?"

"The one you were wearing." He turned and strode to a pitcher and a glass on top of the four-drawer chest of drawers. He spoke over his shoulder as he poured. "I know you feel bad now, but you will feel better soon." He returned to the side of the bed and offered her the glass.

She took the glass of water and saw her hand tremble, nearly spilling the refreshment she craved. "Oh no."

"Let me help you."

Water had never tasted so good. While John held her in a semi-sitting position, she inhaled his scent again. He smelled like soap and fresh air. She inhaled sunshine lingering on his body.

As he lay her back on the pillow, she sighed. "Thank you, Doctor." Their gazes met and held, and she saw his dark eyes widen as if he felt surprised. He pulled his arm from beneath her and stood.

Squaring his shoulders, he cleared his throat. "Call me John."

She wondered if she had offended him. Of course, her breath? Her breath must smell terrible. "Sorry."

"You have done nothing wrong."

John's gaze darted away from her as if he felt embarrassed, and then he turned around and walked back to the chest of drawers to set the empty glass down. Several moments passed before he faced her once more. "You have a head injury. Actually, you are lucky to be alive. The *ceska maza* almost cracked open your skull."

"*Ces*…who?"

"Traitors." John opened the top drawer of the chest and reached inside. He stepped back to her bedside and extended his hand, palm open.

She saw a rectangular gold pendant. It had red and blue stone stripes with a cluster of white diamonds in a corner. Her heart fluttered. The necklace was exquisite, but John looked uncomfortable. He dropped the necklace on her lap. Was the necklace really hers? She wondered why John hadn't handed her the necklace. Her breath again. She smiled wanly.

John stepped away from the bed and leaned against the chest of drawers. "A *ceska maza* is an Indian policeman. He struck you with the butt of his rifle." John simply watched her for several moments. "What is your name?"

She touched the diamonds on the pendant and opened her mouth to answer, but words failed her. Now she felt uncomfortable. She closed her eyes and tried to think. She concentrated, trying hard to remember. Her mind remained blank. Fear gripped her. "I don't know."

She looked at John, and tears blurred her vision. Squeezing her eyes shut, she tried to stop the tears, but they seeped beneath her eyelids and slid down her cheeks. Then she remembered rule number two: show no weakness. But whose rule?

"Ma'am… Miss?" John stepped to the edge of the bed again. He sat and patted her hand. "Do not fret."

She sniffled, fighting a wave of insecurity and guilt. Whatever she couldn't recall she needed to do, she wouldn't be doing it now. And she felt panic.

John's jet eyes filled with compassion. "It is your head injury that is causing your loss of memory. Your memory will come back." He placed a callused thumb on her cheek and wiped away a tear. "Until your memory comes back, we will need to call you something." His gaze roamed her face and hair. "How about Sorrel?"

"Sorrel? Why?" She raised her brows, and the gesture painfully pulled the skin on the side of her head.

"Because of your hair color."

She self-consciously reached up, touched a braid, and looked. "Oh."

"What you need is food and a hot bath. Then you will feel much better." John rose. "Grandmother is heating food and water, and I will get the tub."

"John?"

"Yes."

"Here's your knife." She handed it, handle out, to John. "Sorry."

"There is nothing to be sorry for. You are hurt and frightened. I assure you, Sorrel, no one here will hurt you."

"I know that now."

"Good." John sheathed his knife.

She blinked at his red flannel-covered back when he turned around. Heating water? Get the tub? His statements made no sense to her. She heard his boots jingle and glanced down at his heels as he left the room. She saw spiked metal wheels on his boots. Spurs? She thought that's what they were called.

Why did she know that but not her name?

She raised her hand and touched the side of her head, where her pain radiated. Her fingers encountered sticky hair and a large egg-sized lump. She felt stitches.

Whatever her past might be, she was now Sorrel.

"Is she lost?" Grandmother asked, glancing over her shoulder. Grandmother stood at the kitchen sink, pumping water over dirty dishes.

"Her memory is lost. It is called amnesia. She needs help finding herself. I named her Sorrel," John replied. He wondered where his pretty patient called home. Her speech was slightly accented. Her flag necklace was very expensive, meaning she came from wealth. But none of that explained the second corpse.

Grandmother turned around and placed her arms akimbo. "You choose name for her?"

"We have to call her something. I named her Sorrel because of her hair."

Grandmother snorted and turned back around. Scrubbing at a plate, she replied, "You name her or not, she only one who can find herself. Like our people. Lost. Same. Same."

John's chest constricted. "Our people know who they are."

"*Hiya*. We are lost. The prediction come, and our people rule prairie again."

"Grandmother, listen to me." John walked over to his maternal grandmother and laid his hands on her shoulders. "To find our way, we must change. Adjust. The miracle is not going to happen."

"The Ghost Dance make it happen."

Shit! "They are still dancing?" John felt his grandmother stiffen beneath his hand. "The Ghost Dancing has been prohibited, and all the Lakota know it."

14

Grandmother shook off John's hand and walked to the wood-burning stove. She lifted the lid on a cast-iron kettle and stirred the stew bubbling inside. "Blue Coats not make us stop."

John sighed. "Yes, they can, Grandmother."

She whirled around and glared at him. "We dance more and make miracle happen."

"It will only antagonize the cavalrymen."

"They murder us now." Grandmother referred to Sitting Bull's death. "What white woman doing in chief's camp?"

"I do not know. I would like an answer to that myself."

More importantly, John knew it was urgent he solve the mystery of the second body hidden in his sod hut. He needed time to examine the cadaver. The cadaver was a catalyst for disaster. There had to be a logical explanation. At least Sitting Bull's family had Crow Foot's body to perform proper funeral rites.

The cavalrymen had denied the family the chief's body. John pondered the military reason for that. It made no more sense than the second corpse.

"Papa! Papa! Up."

John bent and whisked his two-year-old son into his embrace. "Good morning, Danny. How is my boy?" The foul odor of a full diaper assaulted John's nose.

"Who? Who?" Danny asked, pointing toward the spare bedroom where John's mysterious patient lay.

"Later, son, right now you need your britches changed." Striding across the cabin, John carried Danny down the hall and into the bedroom he shared with his son. He swung Danny playfully, making the little boy giggle with joy. "I am sorry we did not play last night. It was past your bedtime when I brought our guest home."

John squatted and laid Danny on a hairy bear hide that covered the polished plank floor in front of his iron-framed bed. He quickly unpinned the diaper and removed the offensive garment. "Arms up," he said, tickling his son as he pulled the flannel nightgown over Danny's head. "Lay still." John stood and poured water from a pitcher into a basin on his nightstand.

Dipping a washcloth into the water, John turned, intending to clean Danny's bottom. But his son was gone. "Danny!"

Sorrel heard a child giggle. A child? As she slowly rolled onto her side, she heard the mattress crackle beneath her. It was probably corn husks. How did she know that?

A naked child, barely older than a toddler, stood in the doorway. The child's raven hair looked mussed from slumber. The cherub stood with the thumb of one hand in his mouth and the fingers of his other hand holding his penis. His big ebony eyes stared at her.

"Hello," she whispered. The little boy was adorable.

The toddler released his penis and pointed at her. Then he pulled his thumb out of his mouth and smiled impishly, making his dark eyes sparkle. "Pretty lady." Whirling around, he darted away.

Sorrel gaped at the empty doorway. The toddler's buttocks had been smeared with something brown. Was that feces?

"Danny! Get back here."

Heavy footfalls sounded, and then Sorrel heard giggling again. She smiled at the happy sound. Sunlight shimmered into her room through sparkling clean glass. Pretty yellow-and-green flowered curtains decorated the window, and outside she saw snow falling on flat, winter-covered terrain. It all looked wonderful. She liked what she saw. She liked what she heard. Did she have a family somewhere?

A few minutes later, Sorrel heard the jingle of spurs approaching the bedroom door. She adjusted the colorful quilt over her nightgown. Whose nightgown did she have on? And who had put the gown on her? For the first time, she wondered where Danny's mother, John's wife, was.

Although John was a physician, the intimate thought of his hands dressing her radiated heat up Sorrel's neck and into her face. She pulled the quilt to her chin.

John entered the bedroom carrying a large metal tub, and the adorable toddler followed him. Danny was now clothed in a blue blouse waist frock. His stocking-clad feet padded along beneath the gown's hem. The cherub once again stared at her over the top of his thumb. Sorrel smiled at him, making Danny duck behind John's denim-clad legs.

"I hope you are hungry, Sorrel," he said as he set the tub down.

"A little." She sat up as her gaze traveled up John's long legs, his trim torso, and over his broad chest. He definitely represented a prime male. Without thought, her scrutiny dropped to his crotch. Heat engulfed her whole body.

The room spun, making her grimace.

"Move slower," John advised. He stepped toward the bed and gave her a quick smile.

Sorrel stopped breathing. John's smile discomposed her. She flinched when he reached out and touched her shoulder, causing her to sharply inhale. She instantly saw concern on his face. He was trying to help her, and her reaction to him felt improper. She gulped air.

"Do you need to vomit again?"

"No. I…uh…whose nightgown do I have on?"

"My wife's."

"Oh." A mixture of relief and jealousy washed over Sorrel. "Ah… I'd like to thank her for its use."

"That will not be necessary. Grandmother is bringing some beef stew for you. Do you feel well enough to eat?"

"I think so." Physically she did feel much better, but emotionally she was more confused than when she awoke, and now she felt strangely disappointed. Sorrel chided herself for her foolishness. She would meet John's wife, Danny's mother, soon, and she looked forward to that meeting.

John left the room once more, and a few minutes later, a gray-haired, rotund Indian woman entered the bedroom. Sorrel watched her. The woman's gray hair brought a fleeting memory, and then it was gone.

The elderly woman approached the bed. She carried a tray and set the tray on Sorrel's lap. Sorrel smelled aromatic food, making her stomach rumble and her mouth water. "Oh, thank you. I'm so hungry."

The woman bobbed her head. "You skinny as iron horse rail. John heating water," the woman explained. Danny crawled up on the bed and sat, staring at Sorrel. "Danny, be good," Grandmother briskly told the child.

Sorrel's stomach growled again as Danny crawled toward her, making the rope bed wiggle.

"Danny, be still," Grandmother ordered. The toddler froze in motion and then sat, still staring at Sorrel.

Sorrel lifted a cloth napkin covering the tray, sending delicious-smelling steam to her nose. She saw thick brown broth and chunks of vegetables in the gravy. Bread. Butter. A glass of milk. Her stomach cramped. She would have no trouble devouring this meal. It had been a long time since she'd had real food. Why did she think that? She didn't know. She didn't care. She just ate.

Danny watched her eat. His mouth opened and closed at her every bite. Sorrel laid her spoon down and broke off a piece of bread. She buttered it and handed it to the little boy.

"Tank hoo." Danny stuffed the bread into his mouth.

"Danny." Grandmother shook her finger. "No more. You eat before."

Danny grinned. Chewing open-mouthed, he slipped off the bed and scampered across the room. Then he darted through the doorway, calling, "Papa! Papa!"

Grandmother looked at Sorrel. "Eat more," she commanded before she turned and followed Danny.

A few minutes later, Sorrel heard John's spurs again. He entered the room, gripping buckets of steaming water with each fist. As he dumped the buckets into the tub, she watched his back muscles bulge and flex beneath his shirt. She felt an unexpected impulse to run her hands over his back and feel his body move.

Her breathing hitched. She looked down at her lap so John couldn't see her face. What was wrong with her?

"Are you all right, Sorrel?" John walked toward the bed. "You look flushed."

Keeping her gaze downcast, Sorrel answered, "I'm fine."

"Does your head still hurt?"

Sorrel shook her head. Then she closed her eyes because the room spun in front of her. John approached the bed and extended his long-fingered hand toward her face. She breathed in his now familiar scent.

John touched her chin and raised her face with his fingertips. She stared into his ebony eyes, feeling mesmerized.

John placed his callused palm on her cheek. His eyes searched hers. "You do not have to be so brave. I am your physician. You are supposed to complain to me."

"I do still hurt," Sorrel admitted. She wished she could hide beneath the bed. Her physical awareness of John was a disturbing experience, and she had no idea how to handle it.

"I thought so." John released her chin. He backed up a step and said, "I will fetch more water."

In a short time, he returned with two more buckets of hot water. He set them down and asked, "Do you feel up to a bath?"

Sorrel hesitated. If she got out of bed, he'd see her in the nightgown. But he was her physician! Still, it mattered to her. Her emotions were out of control. John's wife probably put her into the garment. She wished his wife would make her presence known.

"Well?" John stepped closer to the tub. "I want to clean your head wound. I have some scented soap for your hair, and then you can bathe. You will feel refreshed," he coaxed.

Slipping from the bed, Sorrel set her feet on the plank floor. She rose slowly and took a step. Then she ventured another. As she approached the tub, she thought of John touching her, helping her bathe. Her nipples tingled. Then her breasts hardened. She hunched her shoulders, trying to conceal the evidence of her thoughts.

John waited beside the tub, standing with his hand extended. "Sit on the floor and rest your head on the tub rim."

Sorrel stepped forward and caught a glance of her reflection in a mirror behind the dresser, and she cringed. Her braided hair escaped its confines in a tangled mess. Her forehead and right cheek bore large black-and-blue bruises. She looked even worse than she'd imagined. No wonder John was being solicitous.

John extended his hand further, and only because Sorrel felt weak, she took his hand and let him help her carefully sink to the floor. She pulled the nightgown taunt over her knees, tenting her body from view. As she leaned her head back against the metal tub, John slid a drawer open and withdrew a metal tin. When he faced her again, he pried the top off the tin, filling the room with a sweet aroma.

"What's that?"

"Chamomile and soapwort." John knelt beside her.

His body radiated heat along Sorrel's side. She closed her eyes. Where was his wife? Sorrel knew she had no right to enjoy John's ministrations. He was married, and for all she knew, so was she. Someone somewhere had to be waiting for her.

John undid her braids and then poured warm water over her head. Sorrel sighed.

John's fingers began working the chamomile and soapwort mixture into her hair. As the soap lathered, he said, "Besides the goose egg on the side of your head, you have a small lump on the back of your skull."

His touch was gentle, thorough. Lovely. "I don't know. I think I've always had it."

"It is probably a cyst. I can remove it for you."

"Maybe." Sorrel sighed again. John's scalp massage was pure rapture. Nothing had ever felt so wonderful. She bit the inside of her lip to keep from moaning in pleasure.

"I had to put three stitches in your wound. Your hair will cover the scar." John moved away from the tub, and when he came back, he poured more warm water over Sorrel's head, rinsing her hair with care. "Here."

She opened her eyes. John stood over her, offering her a white towel and his free hand.

"Wrap your hair."

"Oh. Of course." She stood with John's help and took the towel before she turned her back. Her face burned. She shuddered as she wrapped her hair in the towel, missing his touch, wishing for more, and completely discomfited by her reaction.

"John?"

Sorrel whirled around to see Grandmother standing in the doorway, watching them. The elderly woman held several fluffy towels. Sorrel saw Grandmother narrow her eyes.

"What is it, Grandmother?" John asked when the old woman stood stiff backed, angrily watching them.

"Injured from Chief Sitting Bull's camp are here. They wait in barn."

"How many are there?"

"Many." Grandmother hand gestured twenty. "They could not flee with others. Will you help them?"

"Certainly." John inclined his dark head. "They are my people."

"It is good you help them, White Wolf. But I fear. If McLaughlin learn you help them…"

"I am not afraid of McLaughlin."

"You should be."

CHAPTER 3

LATER THAT DAY, Sorrel felt like getting out of bed. She pulled the quilt off the bed and wrapped it around herself, and then she slowly walked down the hall and found the main room. She also found John and Grandmother.

John stood at a black cast-iron stove, heating buckets of water, and Grandmother sat at a huge table folding what looked like bandages.

"Can I help?" Sorrel asked.

Both John and Grandmother turned toward her.

Grandmother's white eyebrows drew together. "Why you do that?"

"I don't know. I just want to." Idleness didn't appeal to Sorrel, and because these people helped her, she wanted to reciprocate.

While she waited for John's answer, he looked at her strangely, hesitating as if he didn't know if he should trust her. Maybe she shouldn't have offered. "John?"

"You can listen for Danny. He is down for a nap. Then Grandmother can continue to aid me," he said. "I am almost ready to go back out."

Sorrel released the breath she hadn't realized she'd been holding. "How will I know when Danny wakes?"

Grandmother snorted.

John smiled. "You will know."

"What do I do after he wakes?"

Grandmother snorted again.

"Feed him," John answered.

"I can do that." This was good. She could do it.

John pulled out his pocket watch and checked it. "Let us go." He grabbed the handles of the two steaming buckets, off the stove, and strode to the door.

Grandmother picked up the folded bandages and stuffed them into a pillow case. As she threw a cloak over her round shoulders, she looked at Sorrel and said, "Clean clothes in chest of drawers. Be quick, like a rabbit. Cookies in jar for Danny." Then she waddled to the door and followed John outside.

Sorrel walked back to her bedroom and rummaged in the chest of drawers. She found white cotton undergarments, a gray wool skirt, a white linen blouse, and gray wool socks. She dressed and gingerly used a hairbrush she found in the chest of drawers. Feeling much better, she left the bedroom again.

At the end of the hallway, she stopped and took her time scanning the interior of the cabin. It was clean, homey. In the kitchen half she noted a square cast-iron stove, where John had heated water, and she felt heat still radiating from it. The stove's black pipe thrust through the puncheon ceiling, and Sorrel heard the wind striking the pipe outside. A stack of chopped wood lay in a corner near the stove.

In front of a glass window, she saw a sink that had a handle and spout mounted on it. The sink drained into a bucket. Cupboards stacked with glass plates and cups sat opposite the sink, against the back wall.

Before the front door, snow lay swirled on a round rag rug. The snow slowly melted on the rug after John's and Grandmother's departure. Across the room, she saw an overstuffed brown leather settee, a wingback chair, and a lovely polished rocking chair.

There was a fireplace on that end of the main room, and it also burned a stack of wood. She thought the parlor area invited gathering.

Between the two sections sat a beautiful, handcrafted, rectangular, dark wood table, where Grandmother had sat folding bandages. Six straight-back chairs accompanied the table, promising family meals.

Nice. Very nice.

Sorrel adjusted her skirt. It was too big, and she noted too short. "I hope John's wife doesn't mind my borrowing her clothes," she said to herself.

She pulled the rocking chair nearer the fireplace and sat. Her gaze drifted once more around the room. John must do well as a physician-rancher. As she rocked, her eyelids closed.

"Grumma! Grumma!" Cough. Cough. "Papa!"

Sorrel bolted upright.

"Papa!"

Danny! Sorrel jumped up and hurried down the hallway. She felt apprehension tug at her self-confidence. What was she afraid of? He was just a little boy.

She strode past two empty bedrooms, one she'd slept in, one she assumed to be Grandmother's, and the third bedroom she entered. It held two beds. One large. One small. The large bed was covered in hides. It was evidently John's and his wife's bed, and the realization made her feel like an intruder.

The small bed was a barred crib, and Danny stood in it. He held a green blanket with one chubby hand while he sucked the thumb on his other hand. Danny sucked so hard Sorrel heard him. As she approached, Danny hiccupped and watched her with watery, leery eyes.

"It's all right," Sorrel crooned as Danny wiped his nose on his blanket. She stepped up to the crib and held out her hands. "Let's go find something to eat."

Danny pulled his thumb out of his mouth and smiled a toothy grin. "Cookie." He raised his arms.

Sorrel picked him up. He was heavy, and he was wet. That had to be rectified. But a clothing change would have to wait. She didn't want to make Danny cry because she didn't know what she'd do if he did. John said to feed him, and that's what she'd do first.

As she turned around, she saw a stack of diapers on another chest of drawers. She grabbed two diapers and flopped one over her hip. With Danny's wet bottom settled on a dry diaper, Sorrel straddled his chubby legs over her hip and carried him to the main room.

"Cookie! Cookie!" Danny pointed toward the cupboard, where a white ceramic jar sat.

Sorrel lifted the lid on the jar, and a sweet cinnamon aroma wafted upward. Danny clapped his hands. She reached inside the glass jar and withdrew a golden confection. She gave it to Danny, and he greedily sank his teeth into it. "Let's sit in front of the heat source." Sorrel carried her gobbling burden to the rocking chair and sat with him on her lap. Danny munched as she rocked. "When you're done, we'll change your diaper."

Danny looked at her and smiled. Cookie crumbs littered his round face. "More." He pointed toward the jar. He was so delightful Sorrel's heart melted and she fetched him another cookie. He beamed at her as he devoured it. She mentally patted herself on the back. Child care was easy.

Danny belched and giggled. "More."

Sorrel wasn't sure about that. How many cookies could Danny's little tummy hold? "No. No more. Let's change your diaper."

A petulant pout scrunched Danny's face. His bottom lip trembled, and moisture gathered in his eyes. "More."

Maybe Danny was still hungry? Sorrel wanted to make sure he was content. She certainly didn't want him to cry. So she gave him another cookie. He ate that one too, and then one more. Danny burped heartily and squirmed, trying to get off her lap.

"Down. Down!"

Sorrel laughed. "Danny, you have as much cookie on your face and hands as you do in your tummy."

"Down!"

"All right. But I have to change your diaper and clean you up." Water. Where was the water? Sorrel saw a strange looking contraption standing against the opposite wall. The contraption bore a metal spout over a small metal tub, and it had a handle on the end of its wood platform. With Danny squirming his wet bottom on her hip, Sorrel pressed the metal spout. Nothing happened. She lifted the handle. Nothing happened. She touched the contraption all over. Nothing. No water. It must not be the aqua source. "Let's go back into the bedroom. I think the tub is the only answer for you."

Danny burped again as she carried him down the hall. In the bedroom, she quickly undressed him and dropped his sodden diaper on top of his cookie-smeared smock. She touched the water and found it cool. Still, she had to get Danny cleansed.

She lifted him into the tub. "Stand, Danny." He stood, but he pouted again.

Sorrel eyed him quizzically. He didn't look happy anymore. Maybe he didn't like baths. She patted the water. "Splash, Danny." He stomped and giggled. That was better.

Glancing around, Sorrel saw towels she hadn't used on the chest of drawers, a washcloth she hadn't used, and also the hairbrush she had used. Before lifting Danny into the tub, she grabbed the needed items.

Danny sat in the tub, on his own accord. Sorrel didn't think that was a good idea. She'd be quick with his cleansing. In the tub, he splashed.

Sorrel handed Danny the hairbrush to play with and dipped the washcloth in the water. Danny slapped the brush in the water, sending spray into the air and over the rim and over Sorrel. Danny laughed. That had to be good.

"Uh-oh," she said, reaching for a towel to wipe the floor. It didn't matter about herself because Danny was content.

"Uh-oh," Danny mimicked. He belched again, swallowed, and then he wrinkled his nose in distaste.

The toddler's breath smelled sour. Sorrel suspected the cookies didn't agree with his digestion. Danny dropped the brush into the water and whimpered. "It's all right." As the brush floated away, Sorrel coaxed, "Get it, Danny."

He leaned forward, stretching for the brush, compressing his bulging tummy. His brown eyes crinkled in his cherubic face, and then he vomited into the tub.

"Oh my stars!"

Danny let out an ear-piercing wail.

"I'm so sorry, Danny." Sorrel wanted to cry herself. She wiped his mouth and pulled him out of the tub, quickly wrapping him in a towel.

He cried, "Grumma! Papa!"

"What going on here?"

Sorrel whirled around to see Grandmother standing in the bedroom doorway. Grandmother's hands were planted firmly on her ample hips, and a scowl marred her face. "What you do to Danny?"

"I fed him. Like John said. Danny got messy…and I couldn't find any water. So I brought him in here to cleanse him…and he got sick." Sorrel knew she sounded incompetent. She felt incompetent.

Grandmother charged into the bedroom and snatched Danny out of Sorrel's arms. She glanced down at the cookie-smeared garment on the floor and the vomit floating in the tub. "What you feed him?" Grandmother demanded.

"Cookies." Sorrel felt awful because she knew she was responsible for Danny's illness. And she knew Grandmother knew it too.

"How many cookies you feed him?" Grandmother demanded. Danny rested his head on Grandmother's shoulder and sniffled.

Sorrel held up her fingers. "Ah, four."

"Four!" Grandmother glared at her in disbelief. "*Wacinhnuni.* She bent to touch the water in the tub. When she stood, she struck her forehead with the butt of her palm. "*Iapi ta'ku sni.* Why you bathe him in cold water?"

"I couldn't find any hot water." Sorrel felt like an imbecile. She suspected she'd been insulted, but she didn't respond to the defamation. She deserved it. These people had helped her, and she'd failed them. Worse, she'd made their child ill. Guilt heated Sorrel's face.

"Hot water in stove," Grandmother snapped. "What you need, flying *tatanka* show you?" Grandmother spun around and marched out of the bedroom.

Sorrel stood baffled. In the stove? How was that possible?

Even though she knew she wasn't wanted, Sorrel followed Grandmother.

Grandmother took Danny to the main room, and with her grandson balanced on her hip, she vigorously pumped the handle of the strange-looking metal contraption. Water gushed out of the spout into the small tub. It was a sink. Sorrel wondered why she didn't know that.

Sorrel saw Grandmother lift a metal plate, a cover on the top of the stove, and she saw steam rise. She was amazed. And she felt mortified. Grandmother used a dipper to withdraw hot water and pour it into the sink.

Danny squirmed as Grandmother pumped cooling water into the tub. Then she washed her grandson. "Grumma. Down."

"Shhh." The elderly woman grabbed a tin cup from the cupboard above the sink, pumped the metal handle again, and filled the cup. Danny drank greedily. "Easy, *on' sika*," she crooned.

"I'm sorry," Sorrel said.

Grandmother ignored her.

Danny rested his head on his grandmother's shoulder as she strode past Sorrel on her way to Danny's bedroom.

Sorrel sank onto the rocking chair. What was the matter with her? Why was she so inept?

*****

Several hours later, after attending the Lakota refugees, John entered the cabin to find his mysterious patient sitting near the stove. The expression on her face reminded him of a lost child. She looked harmless, but then he thought of the strange body that lay in his sod hut. The body was not rigor-mortising. It was not natural, and he did not know what to do about it or what to do with it. He could not give the body to the refugees spending the night in his barn. The Lakota people would interpret the body as a sign of evil, and he could not give it to the cavalry. The body was big trouble.

Still, he nodded to Sorrel before he hung his coat on an antler rack mounted behind his front door. When he turned toward Sorrel again, she stood. She looked like she was ready to cry.

John's gaze roamed over her shapely form, and he remembered undressing her and putting the nightgown on her. His groin tightened. It was a natural reaction, just his male needs. Still, he cursed himself for his lack of professionalism. "What is wrong?"

Sorrel blinked rapidly. "I made Danny sick. I'm sorry. So sorry."

John darted down the hall. What was he thinking, leaving Danny in the care of a stranger. A stranger involved with a nonde-composing body.

He bolted into the second bedroom, and he saw Grandmother seated on the bed she used when she stayed the night. She spoke to Danny in the Lakota tongue, complaining as she soothed her grandson.

"Papa!" Danny beamed his toothy smile.

John reached out and lifted his son. He cradled Danny close as he stroked his child's dark hair. A warm rush of paternal loved washed over John. He felt relieved but foolish because for a moment he had panicked.

There was a logical explanation for the second body and the indestructible bag. He just had to discover it.

"Can I come in?"

John turned around. Sorrel stood in the doorway. She chewed her bottom lip as she clasped her hands so firmly her knuckles turned white. Sorrel had not harmed Danny. The boy was fine.

Danny extended his arm and pointed. "Pretty lady. Pretty lady."

"Come in," John invited.

Sorrel stepped into the room. "I'm sorry, John. If I had known the cookies would make Danny sick, I wouldn't have given them to him."

"Cookies?" John looked from Danny to Sorrel. "Did he keep begging for more?"

Sorrel nodded.

John shook his head. He knew Sorrel had done nothing wrong. She had been conned by a two-year-old. Danny wiggled and stretched out his arms toward Sorrel. "I think you are forgiven." John did not hesitate before he handed Danny to Sorrel.

When he saw her press a kiss to the top of Danny's head, John felt like a mule kicked him in the gut. He wished he could… He suppressed the thought.

Grandmother abruptly stood. Her heavyset body jiggled from her repressed fury. "*Wacinhnuni. Iapi ta' ku sni,*" she said before she stomped past Sorrel and left the bedroom.

Sorrel looked wryly at John. "What did she say?"

"It is not important."

"I know when I'm insulted. I would like to know the words."

"She said, 'You are crazy, but it is no excuse.'" John swallowed. "You have to understand, Grandmother is very protective of Danny. He is her only surviving great-grandchild. There are not many of our race left. Danny is the only promise of the continuation of our line."

"I would never do anything to harm Danny. He wanted the cookies, so I gave them to him. I...should have known four were too many."

John's black brows arched. "Four? Grandmother makes big cookies."

Sorrel nodded.

John grinned and reached out to rub Danny's tummy. "You little glutton."

Danny giggled and squirmed. "Down. Down!"

Sorrel set him on his chubby legs, and Danny raced away. "John? What's a *tatanka*?"

"A buffalo."

"Oh."

"Did Grandmother say something about a flying *tatanka*?"

"Yes."

"It is one of *Onchi's*, Grandmother's, favorite sarcasms."

Sorrel laughed.

The sound was like music to John's ears. "You are not angry?"

"No. It's funny."

"Grandmother has her moments." John smiled into Sorrel's eyes. "Do not let Grandmother upset you. She only reacts out of her love for us."

"I understand."

John gently touched Sorrel's arm. He felt her body heat through the blouse she wore. His wife's favorite blouse. He pulled his hand back. "I have to feed the stock. Excuse me."

He did not know what was wrong with him. He had wanted to embrace Sorrel. He had treated attractive women before and not had a physical reaction. John also had no idea why he intuitively trusted

Sorrel. He had no logical reason for the trust, yet he would bet his ranch on the fact that Sorrel would not hurt anyone, especially a child.

However, he instinctively knew he was in danger of making a mistake with her. He had been without a woman for a long time. Sorrel was beautiful, and she appealed to him as no other woman had for a long time. Of course, she would appeal to any healthy man, and again, his physician's mind nagged at him because his attraction to her was out of line.

Late that night, beneath the glow of an oil lamp, John bent over the mysterious second body of Crow Foot. He glanced at the scalpel lying on the edge of the table within easy reach of his fingertips, and he felt his stomach knot. He hated to autopsy. But he had to know the truth. The existence of this body was beyond explanation.

John stared at the gunshot wounds in the abdomen. The reason for death was obvious, and this death was a crime. Still, he felt like Dr. Frankenstein, operating on a devastated body.

Although the weather outside the sod hut was cold and windy, the silence within the thick walls of the earth dwelling amplified the sound of John's heartbeat in his ears, and the sighing exhalation of each breath he took. With conflicting emotions, John picked up the scalpel.

His educated Caucasian mind compelled him to examine the corpse, but his Native American heritage urged him to believe in the magic properties of nature and just accept the mystery. John's medical training moved his hand.

He slid the scalpel down the corpse sternum and opened the chest cavity. Laying the scalpel down, he slipped his fingers into the thorax, pulling open the incision. As John's gaze scanned the cavity, a chill darted down his spine. He spread the rib cage wider and gaped at what he saw. The corpse had no lungs. The thing on his table was not human.

This was impossible!

CHAPTER 4

SORREL AWOKE. SHE lay listening to the sounds of the night. The fire crackled in the fireplace, the wind whistled and howled outside, and Danny coughed. She sat up and waited, expecting John or Grandmother to tend to the little boy, but Danny continued to hack.

Throwing back the bedcovers, she rose and padded across the floor to the bedroom doorway. She concentrated as she listened and heard Danny whimper. Grabbing the quilt off her bed, she tossed it over her shoulders and hurried down the hall.

John's bedroom door stood open, so she glanced inside the room. The moonlight allowed her to see John's bed was empty. *Where is he?*

As Sorrel entered Danny's room, she saw Grandmother's bed lay empty too. *That's strange.* She turned toward Danny's crib, where he lay tangled in his blankets, whimpering and coughing.

"Papa? Grumma?"

"I don't know where they are, Danny." She touched his skin as she untangled his damp coverings. Danny's body felt hot and sweaty, and she heard him wheeze as he struggled to breathe. "Oh, you poor boy."

Sorrel picked Danny up and wrapped him inside the quilt with her. Then she carried him down the hall and into the main room, where she settled on the rocking chair and cuddled with him. "Where are John and Grandmother?" she said to herself.

As she rocked Danny, he continued coughing. She attempted to comfort him, but he just cried, "Grumma? Papa?"

"I wish I knew, Danny. I wish I knew." She rose and propped Danny on her hip so she could walk to the cupboard. Pumping water, she filled a glass and offered Danny a drink. He shook his head. "Please drink, Danny."

The toddler tried to sip but couldn't because he couldn't breathe through his nose. He cried, and Sorrel wanted to panic. Instead, she stroked Danny's head and back, crooning to him in singsong words. He rested his head against her shoulder and finally quieted.

Sorrel wanted to scream for John but knew that would only frighten Danny, so she headed back toward the rocking chair. As she rocked the toddler, heat radiated off his body, and her fear made her perspire. Please come back, John.

As if in answer to her plea, the front door opened, and John strode into the cabin, bringing snow and frigid air with him. He saw her and stopped short, strangely staring at Danny in her arms.

"Danny has a fever, and he's congested," Sorrel said. "And Grandmother isn't here. I don't know what to do."

John bounded across the room. "Give me my son!" he said, pulling Danny out of her arms.

Danny let out a startled wail.

"You're cold, John, and you're scaring him."

Danny extended his arms toward Sorrel and whimpered. John glowered at her. "Pretty lady," Danny blubbered. John blinked and shook his head as if clearing his mind.

"Pretty lady!" Danny insisted. Then he coughed until his little body sagged against John.

"Where is Grandmother?" Sorrel asked as she stood. She felt extremely uncomfortable. John was acting as if he didn't trust her. But why should he? She'd made Danny sick, and now she had no idea what to do to help him. She wanted to cry herself. "Where is Grandmother?" she repeated.

"With our people." John walked away from the rocker as he tried to calm his son.

"What can I do?"

"Do?"

John seemed confused, like he'd never seen her before, and he still clutched Danny as if he feared her.

"What can I do to help Danny?" Sorrel stressed. John's behavior frightened her. Something was wrong. Something very bad must have happened outside. Should she ask him? No. Not now. Danny came first.

"Pretty lady," Danny whimpered, reaching for Sorrel once more.

"John, you're cold. Please give Danny to me."

John took several deep breathes. Slowly, hesitantly, he walked to her and handed his son back into her arms. Danny snuggled against her bosom. "Just sit with him," John said as he took off his coat and hung it on the antler rank.

Sorrel nodded and lowered herself into the rocking chair. What had happened? As she rocked Danny, he quieted, and she watched John stoke the stove. He kept glancing at her as if he feared to take his eyes off her.

He got a lamp from the kitchen cupboard and lit it. Then he dug around in the cupboard and withdrew several glass jars. Sorrel watched him read the labels, put some jars back, and withdraw others. Finally, he made a selection and measured spoons full from the contents of the chosen jars. Putting the ingredients into a pot of water, he set the pot on the stove.

"What are you making?"

John glanced speculatively at her. "I'm boiling herbs to ease Danny's fever and congestion." Stepping away from the stove, he strode back to Sorrel and rubbed his hand down his son's back. With glassy eyes, Danny looked up at his father.

John knelt beside the rocking chair. "Sorrel?" His voice was monotone. His gaze searched hers. "You would never hurt Danny, would you?"

Sorrel felt her mouth fall open. She took a deep breath. "No." Then she realized, John did feel exactly as she suspected. "No. Never."

John rose and walked back to the stove. He slowly turned his back to her and stirred the contents in the pot. Sorrel felt silence frost the air thicker than the ice on the windows. She didn't utter a sound. She just rocked Danny. He struggled to suck his thumb, but he couldn't because of his congestion. When he whimpered, she stroked his head.

As the contents in the pot boiled, steam filled the air, and a sweet aroma wafted beneath Sorrel's nose. "That smells good," she said, trying to make conversation.

John didn't reply.

"Is it expensive?" She didn't know what else to say.

John shook his head as he spooned some of the hot concoction onto a saucer and stirred it with a spoon. "Why do you think it is expensive?"

"Where I come from…" She didn't know how to finish her sentence. The memory felt so near. Yet she couldn't grasp it.

"Do you remember something?" John walked over to the rocker.

"No. I wish I could."

"So do I." John spooned some of the mint-smelling concoction into Danny's mouth. Then he took his son from her. "You should go back to bed, Sorrel."

*****

The next morning, when Sorrel awoke, she heard the wind pummeling snow against the window so hard it rattled the glass. She rose and wrapped the quilt tightly around herself before padding out of her room. Peering into the gloom, she saw Grandmother rocking Danny. John bent over the stove, stirring something in another pot, obviously making more medicine.

The sound of Danny's wheezing filled the large room. Sorrel took a step forward, desperate to do something, anything to help or at least apologize again. The floor creaked beneath her bare feet.

John turned around, and Grandmother craned her neck to look at her. "What you want?" Grandmother demanded.

"Just to help."

Grandmother snorted.

"There's nothing you can do, Sorrel." John's expression was stoic. "You should go back to bed and rest."

Sorrel felt like she'd been struck in the face. That was the second time John had ordered her from his company. She knew Grandmother hated her and blamed her for Danny's illness. Obviously, so did John.

John cleared his throat. "Sorrel, wait."

She slowly turned to face him.

"Danny needs to eat. We all do. Can you cook?"

"I don't think so."

Grandmother snorted, and her eyes narrowed. "You will learn." Grandmother pointed at Sorrel. "Go to root cellar. Get eggs. Bacon."

Sorrel nodded. "Of course. Where is the root cellar?" Eggs? Bacon? She didn't ask. But she wondered why she didn't know what the requested items looked like raw. She watched John take Danny from Grandmother, she assumed, to give his son more of the medicine.

Grandmother rose and waddled to the middle of the main room. She leaned over, grabbed the corner of a colorful, braided rug, and flipped the rug back.

Sorrel saw a trap door in the floor. She saw Grandmother point her gnarled finger at a pocket-like metal handle on the floor door. Sorrel walked to the floor door and bent to open it. It was heavy. Her effort pulled her shoulders and back muscles. Cold air drifted up as she looked down into a black hole.

Grandmother shoved a white apron at her. "Get onions and potatoes."

"Ah, all right." As Sorrel stared into the hole, she had no idea how she was going to see to do what she was instructed. Besides she had no idea what raw food looked like. What was wrong with her?

She hesitated and glanced back at Grandmother. The old woman now stood facing the cupboards. Sorrel heard a scratching sound just before she smelled sulfur. When Grandmother faced her again, she held a burning lamp and a long knife. The lamp solved Sorrel's first concern. The knife caused a new, bigger concern. Feeling like an idiot, she took the lamp and knife and stepped up to the dark hole. She saw a ladder, which she gingerly descended.

The dark hole was huge. It had dirt walls coated with frost. In the root cellar, Sorrel saw slabs of hanging, dried meat and barrels of produce. She walked around. The root cellar amazed her. Still, what did an onion look like?

Sorrel walked back to the ladder. "Grandmother! Which barrel are the onions in?" She heard Grandmother curse in her native tongue, and then heavy footfalls stomped over Sorrel's head.

Grandmother's angry face appeared above her. "Onions and potatoes near back wall. Onions yellow. Potatoes red."

Sorrel cringed from Grandmother's sarcasm. She walked toward the back wall and found the produce barrels. "How do I bring them up?"

Grandmother cursed again. "Use apron like sack!"

The condescension stung. "Uh…the eggs?"

"In straw. Eggs break easy!"

Sorrel knew she could learn. She would learn. The eggs she found in a crate filled with straw, like Grandmother had said, but when Sorrel stepped toward the frosted meat, her stomach curdled. Still, she grabbed a chunk of meat and cut it. The knife was dangerously sharp.

She swallowed bile as she walked to the ladder, and then she heard Grandmother and John talking.

Grandmother said, "I had dream. In dream, I see her fly into sun. I not know what means. I not know if she good or bad. I think she has powerful magic she not remember, and that I fear."

"Grandmother, she did not make Danny sick."

"Maybe. Do you not think she strange? She not know how pump water? Not know hot water in stove? She white woman. She not need know how clean buffalo bladder to bring water from creek. All she need know is how lift, handle, and pump. You say she might be teacher. She not know children."

"You are being too hard on her."

"I think she has spell on you."

"No, Grandmother. She does not." John paused. "But I agree, she is strange."

Sorrel clenched her teeth to keep her eyes from filling with tears. As she ascended the ladder, she wondered where she did belong. And she pondered how long John would let her stay.

The next few days, a winter storm raged across the prairie. John and Grandmother divided their time nursing Danny and tending the ill Lakota people hiding in John's barn. Not once did they leave Sorrel alone in the cabin. When John spoke to her, his aloofness chilled her to the bone. Grandmother refused to speak to her unless it was to give an order, and Grandmother's dark eyes condemned Sorrel when they were in the same room.

Sorrel's lack of confidence frustrated her. She didn't remember how to do anything, and no matter how hard she tried to please, she felt John's ambiguity toward her and Grandmother's abhorrence of her. Normally, usually, she believed she was a useful, productive person.

When Danny got better, Sorrel silently rejoiced. John relaxed, and Grandmother's stinging rebukes lessened. As Danny recouped, he pestered the adults to play with him, and when he insisted Sorrel play, John allowed it. Grandmother silently watched every move Sorrel made. Danny's acceptance soothed Sorrel's self-doubt.

Because Danny's mother never appeared, Sorrel suspected the woman had left John. Why would a woman ever leave John?

By the time the storm broke, Danny was himself. Adorable and mischievous. The first cloudless morning, they all sat in the kitchen. Danny gobbled down his breakfast, and Grandmother fussed over him. "Chew or you choke."

Grandmother smiled as Danny stuffed his mouth with oatmeal and blueberry jelly-slathered bread. She glanced at John. "Your medicine had much power."

"The cough syrup is a simple recipe, Grandmother. Peppermint, licorice, and ginger root."

The intimate familial scene plucked at Sorrel's heartstrings. Was anyone looking for her? Did anyone miss her? She picked at the food on her plate, fresh eggs and bacon and warm bread, which she had helped bake. She knew she should relish the meal, but she couldn't summon hunger. The return of this household's normalcy triggered urgency within her, and as it grew, it nagged at her. She sensed she had something important to do. But what?

"How are the people this morning?" John asked Grandmother.

"Sad in heart. They leave today. They go surrender at Fort Yates. They not survive winter without help. They have no choice."

"Grandmother, I would let them stay if I could, but I cannot."

"They will be punished."

"Grumma. More!" Danny banged his spoon.

Grandmother scooped more oatmeal into Danny's bowl.

Homeless, injured people punished, why? Sorrel wondered what reasoning lay behind Grandmother's and John's conversation. Curiosity prodded her. "Excuse me, why can't the people stay? And why will they be punished?"

"If they stay, I can be arrested for harboring criminals. Perhaps shot or hung. They will be punished because they attacked the Indian police when they came for Chief Sitting Bull."

Sorrel shook her head. "No. The native people didn't attack. Sitting Bull wasn't resisting arrest. The soldiers attacked out of fear, and the people only defended themselves."

John's dark eyebrows rose. "You saw this?"

Sorrel nodded.

Grandmother looked directly at Sorrel. "You not lie?"

"No. Why would I lie?"

"Shi—" John stopped speaking before he cursed.

Grandmother turned to John. "White Wolf, what you think?"

"The Indian Bureau would like nothing better than to accuse me of interfering in government affairs. But Sorrel witnessed what happened, and she is white." John offered Danny bites of bacon, but the toddler shook his head and sat, rubbing his eyes.

"It is time for a nap." John rose from the table and fetched a damp cloth.

"Doesn't the Indian Bureau know these people are helpless?" Sorrel asked.

Grandmother snorted.

"Probably," John answered as he wiped Danny's sticky hands.

"Can't you fight the bureau?"

"I have tried, and they have threatened to arrest me, and I ceased because I have a son to raise. However, with your help…maybe." John poured Danny's medicine into a spoon. "Open wide."

Danny swallowed the herbal concoction without complaint. "Mmmm."

"It is amazing what a little mint will do." John changed the subject when his gaze settled on Sorrel's plate. "You have not eaten much. I think you are losing weight."

Sorrel smiled wanly. She sensed John's reserve melting like icicles hanging in sunshine. A reprieve? Her spirits floated out from behind her cloud of apprehension. Still she cautioned herself. She shouldn't feel so elated, but she had no idea why.

"Not eating is not going to bring back your memory." John rubbed his clean-shaven jaw in thought. "Tomorrow morning, I will go to the fort with the people. I must try to make sure the people are treated fairly. Sorrel, will you accompany us and tell the bureau what you saw?"

"Yes. I will."

"Good." John's gaze captured Sorrel's and held as he smiled at her for the first time in days, and her heart basked in his smile's radiance.

Grandmother nodded her approval.

"Besides, Sorrel, we need to find your family." John's gaze dropped, and he didn't look up again as he finished eating.

Sorrel felt the emotional lift of her reprieve pop like a bubble. Yes. The fort was the place to start looking for her past. She realized John was taking her to the fort to leave her there. To her surprise, she wished she could stay. But wife or no wife, that was impossible.

Before dawn the next morning, Sorrel awoke at the creaking noise of her bedroom door. She lay still as a stone and kept her eyes shut, inhaling slowly as if she slept. She smelled leather and cold air, and she knew John stood near. He stayed at the foot of her bed for several moments. Sorrel felt him lay something on the foot of her bed just before she heard him leave.

Conflicting emotions roiled through her. Hope and despair. She wanted to find her family, but she didn't want to leave John's. Stop it! It was time to go back. But back to where? Back to whom?

Sorrel sat up and touched the bundle of clothing John had set down. Lifting the clothing to her face, she smelled fresh air and sunshine on the garments. So simple a pleasure. She wished there could be more.

After a quick morning ablution and a piece of buttered bread, Sorrel hurried out of the cabin. The sun peeked over the rolling prairie horizon, casting a pink illumination on the snow-covered ground. Her breath frosted in the crystallized air, and despite her uncertain situation, she gloried at the beauty of the sunrise and the smell of winter. She felt the morning sun kiss her nose and cheeks. This place…this time with John and his family had felt like a dream. But all dreams ended.

Beneath her buffalo coat, she wore John's clothing, a pair of his flannel underwear, bibbed denim overalls, and one of his wool shirts. The garments hung comically large on her small body, but she reveled in them because they were John's. She felt safe and comfortable wearing his clothing.

Sorrel chided herself for her nonsensical sentiment. It was definitely time to leave.

Reaching into the left pocket of her buffalo coat to retrieve a mitten, she touched a smooth round object and withdrew it. It reflected the morning light. It was pretty, but she had no idea what it was.

Sorrel heard animals snorting and looked toward the barn. John approached, leading a big black mount and a smaller brown horse with a red mane and tail. He walked straight-backed and square-shouldered. The sight of his raven hair blowing in the wind stopped her breath. Dressed in denim and furs, his rugged handsomeness made her wish for more.

John's physician's satchel hung tied behind his saddle, and the silver handles of a pistol, in his hip holster, gleamed in the sunlight. He was a tempting enigma. Wherever his wife was, she was a fool for not being here with him. Guilt bit Sorrel's conscience. She had no right to judge another, no right to her feelings, and she knew she'd regret them.

The horses' tack jingled, and Sorrel stared at them. The mounts were huge. Apprehension tightened her throat, making her swallow. She should be used to animals. They appeared well trained. Why did she fear these steeds?

She touched the blue disk in her pocket again before she slipped both mittens on her chilled hands. When John halted the mounts in front of the cabin, she smiled at him.

He greeted her with a nod. "Did you eat?" He snapped the lid of his pocket watch open and checked the time.

"Yes." Sorrel saw John's gesture with his watch, and she recognized his eagerness to be rid of her.

"Good." He cleared his throat. "I am glad you are wearing the clothing I left. The clothing will be warm and convenient for riding."

"Thank you." Sorrel's gaze darted away from John's face. She felt like a romantic fool. A memory of someone chiding her for her overreactive emotions flitted across her mind but evaporated like smoke. Maybe she really didn't want to remember.

"Let us go. We need to wear out shoe iron today."

"What?" Sorrel glanced back at John. Sometimes she didn't understand him.

John's gaze briefly returned to her as he dropped his watch back into his pocket. "It is a full day's ride, and it gets dark early. There will be no stopping because it is too cold. We will push all the way."

Sorrel understood. "All right."

"I am sorry to make you journey so close to Christmas," John said.

"Christmas?"

"Christmas. You know…"

No. She didn't know. "It's all right."

John's brows drew together. "You do not know what Christmas is?"

Sorrel shook her head.

"Your memory loss is worse than I thought. Do you need help mounting?"

Sorrel shook her head again.

"Suit yourself." John swung up into the saddle of the big black horse.

Sorrel descended the porch steps. She walked swiftly as she approached the brown mount's right side. Lifting her right leg, she reached up and grabbed the horn of the saddle, just as John had done. This was easy.

As she set her weight in the stirrup, the horse shied and side-stepped. Sorrel leaped back. "Holy Jupiter!"

"What are you doing?"

"Trying to get on the horse."

"You are mounting on the wrong side."

"Oh?"

John leaned over and crossed his arms over the saddle horn of his saddle. "Have you ever ridden before?"

"I don't know."

John silently sat for a moment. "Mount on the horse's left side. Your right side. Most horses are trained that way."

Heat suffused Sorrel's face as she turned and stepped toward the rump of the horse.

"No! Come around the horse's head. My mounts are well broke, but you are green as spring grass and nervous. The horse can sense that. I do not want you to get kicked." Then John shook his head. "Wait." He threw his leg over his mount's rump and dropped to the ground.

Refusing to be helpless, Sorrel moved toward the brown horse's left side. She lifted her left leg, grabbed the saddle horn, and gingerly tried to set her foot in the stirrup. This time the horse didn't move, but she couldn't get her foot high enough to mount.

"Let me help you." John stepped up behind her and clasped her hips.

Even through the layers of clothing, Sorrel felt the length of John's body against hers, and she felt his breath tease the back of her neck. She felt his hands settle on her waist. With her leg raised, his touch felt so…intimate. As John lifted her, her buttocks brushed against his loins, and she heard his sharp inhalation. "John?"

He yanked her higher and tossed her on the horse.

She hastily grabbed the saddle horn to keep from toppling over. After she settled solidly on the hard saddle, embarrassment burned the back of her eyes.

"Let us go," he growled. He turned and strode around her horse to his big black. Bounding into the saddle, he grasped the black's reins and heeled his mount into motion.

Sorrel's horse followed John's. She bit the inside of her bottom lip as she bounced, but the pain reminded her to control her emotions. She had no reason to feel rejected. She clutched her horse's reins and the pommel of the saddle.

Riding wasn't so bad. She could do this. She drifted into thought, wondering what in the Milky Way had she done to upset John.

CHAPTER 5

SORREL AND JOHN rode north along the west bank of the Missouri River. The frozen expanse of water conjoined with the snow-covered bottom land and presented mile after mile of white tundra. Black trees along the river thrust barren branches into the frosted air. By early afternoon, a gray blanket shrouded the sun, preventing any warmth from penetrating the clouds.

She realized they rode or they died.

Hours later, after the weak light of day passed and evening darkness encompassed them, John led them up a precarious path to the top of the river escarpment. On the ridge of the prairie plateau, the wind struck full force, making Sorrel's eyes tear. The moisture in her nose and mouth froze. Her fingers felt so brittle she could hardly hold onto her mount's reins, and her legs were so stiff she could barely stay on her horse. She feared their mounts might fall and strand them. If that happened, they would die.

Then she smelled smoke. Blinking rapidly, she searched across the frozen landscape, and she saw light.

"Iiiis thaaat Ffortt Yaattes?" The wind blew her words away, and she didn't think John heard her. She didn't want to speak again. Her chattering teeth hurt her jaw.

"Yes." John halted his mount and looked back at her. Sorrel's horse stopped beside his.

The fort sat postured on the prairie, like an amber crown on a head of white hair. "I'mmmm glaad hhhere."

"A hot meal and soft bed will make you feel better."

"Wherrre weee stay…ing?" Sorrel tried to stop her body from shivering, but she couldn't.

"At the fort's medical infirmary. Come."

Their mounts picked up their hooves and moved faster. Obviously, the animals' survival instincts were strong, and Sorrel followed John into the fort past picket fences and driftwood corrals.

"Those buildings are the Indian agency, and over there's the infirmary." John pointed to a squat building across the parade ground as they rode toward the single-storied white structure.

He dropped to the snow-packed earth in front of the infirmary and threw his horse's reins on an iced-over hitching rail. Sorrel knew the horses were too tired to wander.

She saw light beckon through two large windows, behind which stood a pot-bellied stove and chairs. She wanted to cry with relief, but she had no strength to weep. John appeared at her side. He lifted his gloved hands toward her, and she leaned toward him. She practically fell into his arms, letting him pull her off her mount.

Sorrel whimpered when her feet hit the ground, and she felt blood shoot up the back of her stiff legs. John whisked her off her feet, like a child, and pressed her against his chest. Without thought, Sorrel rested her head on his shoulder. The hair on his buffalo coat tickled her nose.

"I know you hurt," he whispered. Striding up three steps, he kicked the door.

The door immediately opened.

"For the love of God, John!" a woman chided. "What are you doing out in this weather?"

John carried Sorrel into the area she'd seen through the window. The room was crowded with the stove and chairs. John set her on a chair next to the stove. Heat radiated off the blasting furnace, and Sorrel curled toward it.

"Who is this?" the woman asked.

"I call her Sorrel, but I don't really know her name."

"What?"

"She has amnesia."

"I see."

Sorrel didn't have enough energy to look up. Instead, she closed her eyes and hung her head. The woman's voice had sounded concerned, and she obviously knew John. Curiosity slowly tempted Sorrel to open her eyes and look up. The woman was much older than John.

"Whatever possessed you to venture out on a day like this?" the woman chided.

"I needed to check on the refugees from Sitting Bull's camp?"

"They're fine. Thanks to you," the woman answered.

"Thanks to me?"

"Don't play me for a fool, John. I know you hid them. Now let me get a look at this frozen young woman. Bring her to the end ward."

John scooped Sorrel up again, and she glanced around as they left the reception area. She counted seven doors on the long hallway as John carried her to the last door, and the woman opened the portal. There were no occupants in the room.

John laid her on a cot close to the door, and Sorrel looked up as the woman unfolded a blanket over her. She saw sympathy in the woman's round, matronly face. The gray-headed woman reminded her of someone, but she couldn't remember who.

Sorrel wondered who this woman was to John. "Who are you?"

"I'm Cynthia Pingree, young lady. I am a doctor. May I see your hands? I fear you might have frostbite"

Sorrel lifted her mitten-covered hands and extended them.

Dr. Pingree removed Sorrel's mittens and examined her fingers. "No frostbite, thank God. May I see your feet?"

Sorrel nodded.

As the doctor started to kneel on the painted wood floor, John said, "Let me do that."

The doctor's posture snapped erect, and she glared at John. "You're near-frozen yourself. I'm not so old I can't do my job. Sit!" The doctor pointed to a chair. "You know the rules, John. Take the pistol off."

John unbuckled his gun belt and sat, holding his Colt .45 on his lap. "Cynthia, I should take care of the horses."

"Stay put!"

He did. He removed his gloves and rubbed his hands together.

If Sorrel hadn't been so cold, she would have smiled at John's compliance with the older woman. Sorrel found herself liking the doctor.

As Dr. Pingree attempted to remove Sorrel's right boot, she struggled with the frozen, knotted laces. She called out, "Howling Coyote! I need you!"

"What is wrong, Cynthia?" John asked.

"The laces are frozen and knotted. I can't seem to untie them."

"Let me help," John said. He grabbed the white handle of his knife, sheathed on his belt. With a quick flip of his wrist, he sliced the laces.

Sorrel's shoe opened. She sighed in relief, making the doctor smile.

"Thank you, John," Dr. Pingree said.

While the doctor massaged Sorrel's foot, she heard rapid footfalls approaching. A tall, gangly adolescent Indian boy entered the room. "Go take care of their horses," Dr. Pingree told him. And the boy left.

Dr. Pingree released Sorrel's foot and quickly pulled off her left boot and sock, and then rubbed that foot. "Good. Good. No frostbite. Stay here and warm yourselves. I'll get food." The doctor covered Sorrel's feet with another blanket, tucking the blanket in place before rising. She grabbed John's pistol off his lap and took it with her when she left.

"I am sorry, Sorrel."

Sorrel's gaze darted to John's. "You have nothing to be sorry for."

"Yes, I do." He rose and crossed the room to sit beside her. His expression bore regret. "You have been ill. I never should have brought you here in this weather."

"You had no choice. You had to come here, and I need to find… answers." John's tender ebony gaze warmed Sorrel's heart. Maybe he wasn't all that eager to be rid of her?

He took her hands in his, and pressing his thumbs into her palms, he rubbed outward toward her fingers. "I agree, but not at the risk of your life. I should have waited."

Sorrel felt a rush of physical awareness shoot from her palms to her breasts. "I'm fine." She lowered her gaze and watched John rubbing her hands, making her want his touch more with each heartbeat. Warm pleasure spread down her body all the way to her toes.

She wasn't cold anymore. But she wanted... What she wanted surprised her, confused her. She wanted John to kiss her. Just one kiss before they parted.

"I need to ask you about something, Sorrel."

She lifted her gaze to John's again. "It is the reason I foolishly brought you here." His tone deepened. "I found this strange bag containing—"

"Well. The two of you look better already." Dr. Pingree strode back into the room. She carried a tray laden with a loaf of bread and steaming bowls. "Eat while it's hot."

As Dr. Pingree set the tray on a nearby cot, John stood and helped Sorrel with her coat before he took off his own. He laid their garments aside before sitting next to Sorrel.

Accepting the bowls from the doctor, John and Sorrel ate the aromatic beef stew as the doctor sat on another chair. Sorrel hadn't realized how hungry she was until she started eating. She sighed in satisfaction as the delicious stew settled in her stomach.

"Well, young lady, why are you here?"

"I've lost my memory."

"You can't remember anything?" the doctor asked.

Sorrel shook her head. "I'm afraid not."

"Oh my. What is the first thing you do remember?"

"Waking up in John's cabin."

John paused with his spoon halfway to his mouth. "I found Sorrel in Sitting Bull's camp after the chief's assassination."

"Assassination?" Dr. Pingree gaped at John. "Are you certain?"

John nodded. "Murder or assassination? No one should have died. Sorrel told me the chief tried to surrender peacefully. And why was Crow Foot shot? What could the boy have done?"

"Oh my." Dr. Pingree pinched the bridge of her nose. "This is going to become complicated."

John reached for the bread and tore off a hunk, handing it to Sorrel. "I know."

"What are you going to do?"

"I do not know."

While Sorrel and John ate, Dr. Pingree watched them. A few minutes later, as they finished their meal, a floorboard in the hall creaked, and Sorrel looked up to see an adolescent Indian girl enter the room. The girl had a cradleboard strapped to her back and more blankets in her arms. She approached Sorrel and John, and she set the blankets beside John.

"For you, White Wolf, and your woman," the girl said.

The girl kept her gaze downcast and spoke so softly Sorrel had to strain to hear her. But John must have heard her clearly, for he quickly replied, "She is not my woman."

Then Sorrel heard a mewling cry come from the cradleboard. A baby? "Is that a baby? May I see it?"

The Indian girl beamed a maternal smile before she nodded and slipped her arms through the straps of the cradleboard, turning the board around. Sorrel set her bowl aside. She leaned forward and gazed at a beautiful, dark-haired baby bundled in the cradleboard. "Oh, so precious. Is it a boy or a girl?"

"A girl. Morning Mist her name. You like hold her?"

"Ah…yes." Sorrel glanced at John and found him staring at her, his eyes wide. "John? Should I not?"

He didn't respond.

"Go ahead," Dr. Pingree encouraged.

"I would love to hold her."

As the Indian girl unlaced the cradleboard, Sorrel asked her," What's your name?"

"Strong Flower."

John stood so Strong Flower could sit beside Sorrel. Strong Flower gently took the baby from its nest. Extending her arms, Strong Flower offered Morning Mist to Sorrel.

Sorrel hesitated. The baby looked so fragile. She didn't think she'd ever seen anything so fragile, a newborn infant, and she wondered why.

"Just support the baby's head," Dr. Pingree instructed.

Sorrel gingerly accepted the swaddled infant. The baby smelled good. She knew without a doubt she'd never held another life so small, so soft. She glanced at John again.

He stared at the wall, ignoring her. He had an almost pained expression on his face. "John?"

He shook himself.

"Would you like to hold the baby?"

"No."

Sorrel slowly lifted the tiny human to her shoulder. She rubbed her cheek against the top of the baby's downy head. The baby curled against her. "This is wonderful. You're so lucky. I hope I have a baby someday."

Strong Flower radiated motherly pride as she nodded and smiled. "I get pillows. You hold her."

"I would love to."

Strong Flower hurried from the room.

"I think I'm getting the knack of this." Sorrel lowered the baby, cradling the infant against her breast. The infant wiggled, rooted around with an open mouth, and then sucked the front of Sorrel's shirt. "Oh no. Don't do that."

Sorrel moved the baby away from her breast. A wet spot remained on her shirt. The baby fussed and squirmed, attempting to turn toward Sorrel's breast. Sorrel tried to quiet the infant, but little Morning Mist let out a surprisingly loud howl. Sorrel's gaze flew to John once more. "What do I do?"

John glowered at her as if she had asked if she should smother the infant. But he didn't say a word.

Sorrel lifted the infant to her shoulder again, but Morning Mist wasn't pacified. Sorrel patted the infant's back and crooned. Still, the baby fussed. "Maybe you should take her?" Sorrel offered the baby to Dr. Pingree, who watched Sorrel's exchange with John.

"You're doing a fine job," the doctor said. "You'll make a wonderful mother someday."

John abruptly stood and set his bowl on the tray. "I am going to check on the horses." He yanked his coat off the cot and strode out of the room, pulling the door shut behind him.

Sorrel's mouth fell open. What had she done? She looked at Dr. Pingree. "I didn't mean to upset the baby. I know I didn't hurt her." She continued crooning to the infant. Morning Mist's complaining continued. "And I don't know why John is upset with me."

"You didn't do anything," Dr. Pingree said. "The baby just wants to suckle. It's a natural response. As for John? Well, he's a man with a problem. You're inexperienced with children, aren't you?"

"I must be." Sorrel rocked the baby to no avail.

Strong Flower hurried back into the room. She dumped pillows on the cot and settled down beside Sorrel.

Sorrel handed Morning Mist back to her mother. "I seem to be inexperienced about many things. But I had to have a life before I came here."

"Of course, you did. I'd like to help you find it," the doctor promised.

Sorrel's eyes widened when Strong Flower lifted her blouse. The young mother wore no undergarments, and she revealed a plump, copper-colored breast, which she offered to the infant. The baby latched onto Strong Flower's nipple and began to suckle. Sorrel's mouth fell open as she watched in amazement.

"Have you never seen a baby breastfeed before?" the doctor asked.

Sorrel shrugged. For some reason, she doubted she had. "I don't think so." She knew she had no right to know, but she couldn't stop herself from asking. "What is John's problem?"

"John's in mourning. I think the baby reminded him of his son's birth and his wife's death," Dr. Pingree answered.

"His wife's death?"

Sorrel sat riveted on the cot.

"Yes. She died giving birth to Danny. John's been without a woman for too long."

Sorrel's mouth fell open for the second time.

*****

"Achoo!" Straw dust tickled John's nose as he lay in hay in a stall in the stable. His horse nudged him, and he pushed his mount's head away. "Stop." John's breath frosted in the icy air as he burrowed deeper into his prickly bed and pulled his blanket over his head. Fatigue plagued him because he had not slept well. The night had been frigid, but that was not the reason he had not slept. He had struggled with sleep because each time he closed his eyes, the image of the baby trying to suckle Sorrel's breast popped into his mind.

Sorrel's breast. He felt his manhood swell again. "Son of a bitch!" He was a physician. What the hell was the matter with him?

John threw his blanket off and bounded to his feet. Rubbing his hands together, he stomped up and down the wide aisle separating the stable stalls, attempting to warm himself. It had been a damn cold night, but his temper had not cooled one degree. He could have gone to the barracks or even one of the officers' homes for shelter. Instead, furious at the world, with his life, with himself, he had slept in the barn with his horse.

His stomach growled loud enough to make his stallion, Midnight, look at him. Food would satisfy his stomach hunger, but not what he really hungered for, what he craved. A woman. He needed a woman and not just any woman, but a woman he could love with both body and mind. There were women willing to appease his lust, but that was not what he wanted. He yearned for what he had had with his wife, soul-deep love and earthshaking sex. Maybe he had just been lucky with Wind's Song.

John knew he could pay for a saloon girl's service in Pierre, and he probably should because he was losing control. The hell of it was he did not want that. He wanted more. Much more.

The night he had dressed Sorrel in Wind's Song's nightgown, he had been so aroused he had had to relieve himself. He had attributed his adolescent reaction to his pretty patient and to his nearly three years of sexual abstinence. Then yesterday morning, as he had helped

Sorrel mount, her buttocks had brushed his groin, and he had gotten as hard as a ponderosa pine in the Black Hills. Right now, his shaft chafed against his trousers.

Sorrel was a mystery, as was the corpse of Crow Foot that was not a body. John needed answers. Even with answers, Sorrel was not for him. So why did she affect him like she did?

He checked his pocket watch and snapped it shut. It was time. With long, determined strides, John headed for the Indian agency office. He wanted to take out his foul mood on someone. It might as well be the Indian agent or the whole damn United States Cavalry for all he cared. All he needed was an excuse.

Halfway across the parade ground, he saw several elderly Lakota chiefs standing outside the agency building. They huddled beneath their buffalo robes. Because it was not one of the semimonthly ration days, John wondered why they were gathered. The old warriors turned in unison to look at him.

"Grandfathers," John addressed them with the traditional title of respect he knew would please his grandmother.

"White Wolf," one of the chiefs returned the greeting.

John recognized Chief Eagle Eyes of the Sisseton. "Grandfather Eagle Eyes, why are you all here?"

"We wait to speak with the white chiefs," Eagle Eyes answered.

"What is so urgent it draws my grandfathers from their fires?"

"Dishonor. The same dishonor that has brought us here every morning since our great leader's death. Every day we wait, and every day we are refused council."

John knew Eagle Eyes spoke of Sitting Bull. He glanced at the wrinkled copper-colored faces of the men around him, and he saw stoic determination. Shit! "Tell me of this dishonor."

"The blue coats disgraced our holy man even after his death. They buried him without his last rights," Eagle Eyes explained.

"Damn them." John had his just reason, a religious insult. He strode to the door of the agency and knocked. He knocked again and waited. Then he knocked harder. He turned the doorknob and found the door locked. Stepping to the window, he peered in.

He saw Indian Agent James McLaughlin and Colonel William Drum seated inside. The agent was dressed in his usual black attire and the fort's commander in his blue uniform. Moving back to the door, John raised his booted foot and kicked the door with all his might.

The cracking wood reverberated like a gunshot, and the door swung open. Heat from the coal stove in the office drifted outside. "Grandfathers, come warm yourselves," John said over his shoulder before he strode into the office.

"What the hell is the meaning of this, McIntosh?" McLaughlin rose to his feet and slammed his fist down on his desk.

"I should place you under arrest," Colonel Drum threatened, rising from a curve-backed chair beside McLaughlin's desk.

Both men glared at John. He glared right back.

"Arrest me, why? I am a physician, concerned because two men inside this building do not respond to my attempts to enter or at least communicate. I thought something was wrong." John arched his dark brows in mock sincerity.

"You're trespassing," Colonel Drum countered.

"I am a native. Here on business."

"What business?" McLaughlin asked.

"I am here to collect my pay for assisting at the camp of Sitting Bull two weeks ago." John smiled humorlessly.

McLaughlin and Drum exchanged glances.

"Speaking of Sitting Bull, why was his body never given to his family?" John asked.

McLaughlin cleared his throat. "We deemed it necessary to dispose of the body as quickly as possible."

Doubt crawled up the back of John's neck. They were hiding something. "Why? It is twenty degrees below zero. Kept in the cold, the body would not have decomposed until spring."

"That's enough!" Colonel Drum ordered. He stepped forward and stood nose to nose with John. "Leave or I'll have you put in the guardhouse."

"This is not over." John whirled around and walked out of the agency office. "Grandfathers, show me where our holy man is buried."

Chief Eagle Eyes and the other elderly warriors escorted John across the parade ground and out onto the prairie. Up a hillock to the west of the fort, they led him to the fort's burial plot. They showed John a new grave just outside the cemetery. The ground was frozen, and the grave was back filled with crystallized chunks of earth. John bent, licked his fingers, and touched a white substance in the dirt.

He tasted. He spit.

Lye laced the earth. In the spring, the lye would make Sitting Bull's body decompose rapidly. Why was Sitting Bull buried in a lye grave?

"Did you see our holy man's body?" John asked Eagle Eyes. The old warrior shook his head. "Did any of you see his body?"

Heads shook around him.

John paced along the side of the grave. "Where was our holy man's body taken after it was brought to the fort?"

Eagle Eyes pointed back toward the fort. "In the dead house behind the medicine house," Eagle Eyes answered. "What can we do, White Wolf?"

"Grandfather Eagle Eyes, please come with me. My other grandfathers, go back to your fires and wait for us."

That same morning, needing a chamber pot, Sorrel set out to explore the infirmary. She left the ward, where she had slept, and found another ward where Dr. Pingree worked with a patient. One of the rooms on the west side of the infirmary was a dispensary, which held shelves of medical supplies, and another room was the bathing room with a metal tub and a chamber pot. Sorrel availed herself of the chamber pot before continuing on to find the kitchen.

On the north side of the building Sorrel found Dr. Pingree's office and a large storage closet. The gray-painted floors throughout the infirmary smelled freshly scrubbed, and Sorrel saw through the frosted windows that it still snowed, but the day looked calmer.

As she headed toward the back of the building, she smelled coffee, and she knew she neared the kitchen. Her stomach growled from her hunger, but before she pulled open the door, Sorrel heard voices. One voice was female, the other male.

"I cannot. He will not let me." The voice was Strong Flower's.

"I will kill him," the male voice replied.

"No!" Strong Flower protested. "He has many who will help him, and you are alone. You should not be here. If he catches you, he and the others will kill you."

"Strong Flower, come with me," the male voice pleaded.

"I cannot."

"You do not love me?"

"I do."

"Then come with me."

"I cannot."

Sorrel heard crying, and then she heard the sound of a door slamming. She felt embarrassed for eavesdropping, so she whirled around and hurried back down the hall. She walked into the reception area to see John and an elderly Indian man entering the infirmary. A blast of cold air followed them inside. As she watched them brush snow off themselves, she saw a young male native gallop a pinto past the front window.

Her pulse quickened when her eyes met John's gaze. What should she say to him? His narrowed eyes told her he was still angry with her. And just why was he angry anyway? He continued to scowl at her, and she lifted her chin in answer to his rudeness.

She felt hurt and disappointed, but she stubbornly pressed on, broaching her concern. "Who is that man?" She pointed out the window at the young man riding rapidly away.

"Black Hawk. Why?" John asked.

"He looks upset."

John looked at her, and she saw his brows pucker. Sorrel did not want to mention the conversation she'd just overheard, so she kept it to herself. The heartache she'd heard was sadly close to what she, at that moment, felt.

"Black Hawk got big trouble," the elderly warrior with John commented.

Trouble? Sorrel wondered what trouble. All the natives certainly did.

"Sit here, Grandfather Eagle Eyes. You will be warm," John suggested, gesturing toward a chair.

The outside door to the reception area opened, and an Indian boy and his mother walked in, bringing another blast of frigid air. They looked so cold. The boy was about six years old, and he coughed incessantly as he huddled by his mother.

"I'll get him a blanket," Sorrel said before she darted down the hall to where she'd seen blankets stacked. She rushed back and handed a blanket to the boy's mother. The mother nodded in appreciation, and then she wrapped up the boy before she seated him near the stove.

John stepped up to Sorrel. "Thank you."

She gazed up at him. "For what?"

"The blanket."

"I remembered how cold I was last night."

"My people do not forget kindness. Where is she?"

"She?" Sorrel felt flustered by John's praise and confused about who *she* was. "You mean Dr. Pingree?"

"Of course."

"She's in the second ward."

John spun on his boot heel and strode down the hall.

Well, John might be rude, but she wouldn't be. These people needed help. She'd do what she could. Sorrel turned back to the elderly native man. "Would you like a blanket?" He shook his head, but he stayed settled close to the stove.

"Please, all of you, stay here and warm yourselves," Sorrel suggested.

Hesitant because of John's bad attitude but still determined, Sorrel pursued him down the hall. "John, wait."

He didn't.

He strode into the end ward and walked straight toward Dr. Pingree, who was bent over a patient. Sorrel watched from the ward doorway. She wondered at John's impatience. There obviously was serious trouble.

Sorrel's pique at John evaporated. Whatever the trouble was, she wanted to help. She reasoned she owed John. He didn't have a wife to aid him, but she could.

She now knew John was an available man, but she remained encumbered with a past she didn't remember. She was just an ex-patient to him. But she was not an incompetent ex-patient. Depending on her past, before she left him, she intended to correct John's misconception of her.

She heard John say, "This is bad, Cynthia."

"Yes, John. It is. It's measles."

Sorrel slowly walked toward John and Dr. Pingree, who stood with a native mother and a coughing toddler.

"What is it, Sorrel?" Dr. Pingree asked.

"I was wondering what I can do to help. There's a sick boy in the reception area."

The doctor's mouth was a straight line of worry. "Hand out blankets. Food will help. Tell Strong Flower to make soup. Lots of it. There will be more patients coming."

"Yes. Of course." Sorrel wondered if this illness was the big trouble. She didn't think so. She suspected John and Eagle Eyes had been referring to something different.

John reached out and touched the toddler's forehead. "High fever."

Dr. Pingree nodded. "And body rash."

"What's measles?" Sorrel asked. John and Dr. Pingree both looked at her strangely.

The doctor stared into her eyes. "If you don't know, you haven't had it. But it's too late now. You've been exposed." Dr. Pingree turned to the toddler's mother. "Your son must stay here. His illness will make other children sick."

Panic filled the mother's eyes. She looked up at John. He stepped closer and spoke in the Lakota tongue, and the mother nodded several times.

"I told her she could stay with her baby," John told Dr. Pingree.

"All right," the doctor said. "She's already been exposed too."

Sorrel suddenly realized measles was contagious. Measles could be catastrophic in this time. This time? Why did she think that? She watched the mother rock the toddler from side to side, and she heard the mother sing to her child as he coughed.

Dr. Pingree turned to John. "When you came in, what did you need?"

John looked into the doctor's worried face. "Did you see Sitting Bull's body?"

Dr. Pingree's gaze held John's. She did not answer for so long Sorrel thought she would not. Sorrel wondered why.

Finally, Dr. Pingree answered, "Yes."

"Do you know why McLaughlin and Drum would not release Sitting Bull's body to his family? And why he is buried in a lye grave?"

Dr. Pingree wrung her hands. "It's privileged information, John. Although I'm not military personnel, I did take an oath, and I fear telling you because of consequences."

John's back stiffened, and his nostrils flared. "Trust me, Cynthia."

"I do. But please don't involve me in this. I'm needed here, especially now." A tear rolled down Dr. Pingree's cheek. "John, they mutilated Sitting Bull's face."

"Shit!" John clenched his fists so hard his knuckles turned white. "Cynthia, I will help with the measles outbreak, but then I must settle this burial insult with the cavalry. I will get my satchel," John said.

Sorrel blinked rapidly as a chill overwhelmed her, making her tremble. Chief Sitting Bull's face had been mutilated. She realized she knew that. But how? She felt light-headed. Her vision blurred, and the walls spun.

Then Shari remembered everything just before the room went black.

CHAPTER 6

"SORREL! SORREL! WAKE up!"

Shari felt a slap on her wrist. She opened her eyes and stared into John's worried face. He sat beside her on a cot.

Relief flooded his features. "Sorrel, are you all right? You fainted."

"My name is Shari," she whispered. Her recollection was crystal clear, and she knew her mission had failed. But that wasn't her main concern. She had to go back, and she couldn't explain herself to John.

John lifted her hand and rubbed her knuckles as he leaned closer. "I am sorry about last night. I never should have…" He suddenly sat up, straight-backed, and stared into her eyes. "Did you say your name was Shari?"

"Yes. I'm Shari." She was Shari 12101918. She had chosen the name Shari herself when she was four years old. It had been Helaine's mother's name, and Shari had chosen it to honor her mentor.

John glanced over his shoulder at Dr. Pingree. "Cynthia, may we have a moment?"

"Certainly. I'll check on the patients in the reception area."

After the doctor left the room, John asked, "Where are you from?"

"Far away."

"Are you married?"

Shari shook her head and saw John's shoulders relax.

"What is your last name?"

Surprised by his second question, Shari felt embarrassed. How could she tell him her last name was a number? She inhaled, prepared for John's skepticism.

"Do you remember your last name?"

"Yes. No." She had to be cautious. It was best to play along. She'd thought when her memory came back all would be well. It wasn't. Not only had her mission failed, but she also feared a paradox. A paradox would affect millions of lives over centuries.

Shari watched emotions flit across John's face. Concern. Puzzlement. Disbelief. When she saw concern return to John's ebony gaze, the back of her throat closed. Her mouth felt as dry as Mars.

"Do not worry about your last name," John said.

Swallowing, she said, "John, tell me. Has anything strange happened lately? Anything unexplainable? Here or anywhere?"

John blinked at her several times. He inhaled slowly. "I found something of yours. Tell me, Sor... Shari, what else do you remember?"

"I had a large black bag." Shari held her breath. She saw John nod. So far so good. No paradox. But a paradox could still occur if John saw the simulative of Crow Foot. What else could she... Should she explain? "Where is the bag?"

"At my ranch."

Shari let out a sigh of relief. She wiped the back of her hand across her eyes. "I must leave. Where is my coat?"

John's eyes widened, and then his gaze narrowed as he abruptly stood and glared down at her. "You cannot go anywhere. You just fainted, and I want answers about that bag and the fake body inside it."

He knew. Shari closed her eyes and braced herself for the time-altering paradox wave. It didn't happen. She opened her eyes. "You saw the simulative, and nothing happened?"

John's dark eyebrows rose in perplexity as if he'd seen her mutate in front of him. She knew he was judging her. That hurt.

"I autopsied that thing." His voice was a whisper, but it reverberated with anger. "It looks like a corpse, but it is not. Why do you need a fake body?"

"Please, John. Where's my coat?" She had to get the return disk out of her pocket. Her only safe course of action was to return to her own time. But first, she had to jump back to John's ranch to get the simulative. It must not be discovered by anyone else. She would hide at the ranch until she could teleport back to Helaine.

"You are not getting your coat, Sor... Shari, because you are not going anywhere."

"Fine." She feigned acquiescence, but she felt panicked. She had to get her hands on her return disk before someone else found it. Body heat could activate the disk. It was a fail-safe in case of injury. As soon as she was alone, she'd be gone in a flash of light. She had to get back to her own time to make sure she hadn't inadvertently caused a future paradox. That was her duty.

"You are staying here, and you are going to answer my questions." John's black brows puckered, and he pointed his finger at her. "Stay put."

Shari nodded. She did not like John's male-dominating attitude. She had read about such male behavior in the archives. It was appropriate for his time. However, it would be a hot day on Venus before she submitted to it. "Where are you going?"

"To help."

Shari nodded. She again feigned obedience. But her heart thumped with desperation. The longer she stayed, the greater the possibility of a future paradox.

Still, she regretted not being able to tell John goodbye.

After John walked out of the room, Shari rose, determined to find her coat. Her duty now was to escape. Her coat wasn't anywhere near, so she headed for the front entrance.

As she strode out of the ward, Dr. Pingree walked in carrying a fussing baby. A Native mother and three children followed. All were covered with red spots.

"Good, you're up. Give me a hand, please."

The desperation in Dr. Pingree's voice and the near panic expression on her face stopped Shari's flight. How could she abandon them? There had been no paradox.

Although Shari knew she was breaking time-travel edicts, she decided she wanted to stay and help. Besides, the sky was laden with snow clouds. The disk needed bright sunlight to work safely. Right now, what she saw in this inadequate medical sanatorium frightened her more than a time wave. These people had no defense against this illness.

Mid-afternoon, snow still fell heavily, and both wards were filled with ill children and adults. Shari sponged foreheads, fetched blankets and pillows, and dumped vomit buckets. She offered food. But no one ate.

After sunset, so many ill crowded the wards they lay on the floor and suffered. Shari sat rocking a baby when John strode into the second ward. He came toward her, and his appreciative gaze warmed her blood.

"Thank you for helping," he said.

"I need no thanks, John. Have the sick stopped coming?"

"Until tomorrow. The weather has worsened. The sick cannot venture out. They will die in their homes."

Shari nodded, expressing her sympathy with her eyes and wishing she could touch John. Then she noticed he wore his Colt, and she remembered his earlier conversation with Dr. Pingree. Why did Dr. Pingree not object to John's revolver now? What was he going to do?

As John stood before her, Shari saw a myriad of emotions flit across his handsome countenance. Bafflement. Frustration. Sorrow. She sensed his pain and ached to comfort him. But she just kept rocking the sleeping infant cuddled in her arms.

"I have to leave," he said.

"Must you?" Shari suspected he was going to seek justice for his fallen medicine man, Chief Sitting Bull.

"Yes." John spun around on a booted heal and strode out of the ward.

A piece of her heart went with him. From the front door, she felt frigid air blow in, drifting all the way to the second ward. She thought she heard the frozen front door's iron latch click.

She rose and settled the sleeping infant in a crib, and then she darted out of the ward. She hurried to Dr. Pingree's office where earlier that day she's found her buffalo coat hanging on a wall peg.

Slipping into her coat, she retrieved her mittens from the pockets. She felt the disk still in the left pocket.

She couldn't transport until morning. She had the night to go after John. But she was going to help him, whether he wanted her help or not. Whatever he intended, she had no doubt it was dangerous.

Since Shari hadn't researched John's life, she had no idea if he succeeded in what he planned to do or if he died. Her chest constricted at the thought of his passing. She was determined he wouldn't die this night. Even at the risk of her own life, she couldn't just do nothing.

Shari knew she was again breaking time-travel edicts, but she still stepped out of the infirmary into the frigid night. Never before had she endangered herself or the future. But she couldn't stop herself. Her heart told her to follow John.

Beneath wane moonlight, she caught glimpses of John as he darted from building to building, heading west, and she followed him. Peeking around a corner, Shari saw him meet several dark, buffalo hide-covered men. They carried no lanterns. Instead, they toted picks and shovels. She saw John dip his hand into what she assumed was a jar, and then she watched him smear something on his face before the group moved on in eerie silent harmony.

Beneath the illusive moon, the stripes of war paint on the other men's foreheads and cheeks looked silver. Shari realized she'd seen John paint his face too.

A sense of excitement helped warm her as she pursued John and the warriors. They went to the graveyard. Hiding behind a snow-covered bush, Shari watched John pickax open a grave. It had to be Chief Sitting Bull's grave.

She watched as two elderly warriors stepped forward and threw away the clods of frozen dirt John dislodged. With their backs bent in labor, their frosted breaths clouded around them as they dug.

Shari kept her mitten-covered hand over her nose and mouth to hide her frozen breath and her position.

Woof! Woof! Woof!

She spun around and saw a large dog of nondiscernable color charging toward her. In her time, dogs were extinct, as were many other animals. She stopped breathing because of fear. This dog was huge!

Bolting out from behind the bush, she bounded after John. Her feet barely touched the snow-covered earth as her legs carried her toward the graveyard.

Woof! Woof! Woof!

The dog pounced on top of her. Shari covered her face with her mitten-covered hands. A wet nose attempted to shove her hands away and almost managed. She feared she was going to be eaten alive. What an awful death!

"*Hiya!*" a male voice hissed.

The dog's nose poked at Shari's temple. Sniff. She kept her face hidden.

Woof! Woof! Woof!

"Shut that dog up," John ordered.

Shari turned her head and peeked out between her mittens. The dog's nose was insistently in her face again, and she got a hot, wet lick.

Woof! Woof!

Eagle Eyes and John rushed toward her and tried to catch the dog. But the beast evaded capture.

Woof! Woof! Woof!

Shari felt a hand grab the back of her coat and yank her to her feet. She was spun around to stare up into John's angry face. His war paint was white, not silver. He lifted her higher by the front of her coat, making her feet dangle. His eyes were narrowed to angry slits.

She swallowed. "I'm sorry."

Woof! Woof!

"I will kill that dog." John dropped Shari on her feet and pulled his knife from a sheath on his belt. As he lifted his arm to throw the blade, the sound of a cavalry bugle filled the night air.

Shari whirled around to see the fort behind her. A group of mounted soldiers as black as wraiths charged toward the graveyard on horses that looked like smoke-breathing monsters.

"Shit!" John cursed. He grabbed Shari again, this time by her coat sleeve, and he pulled her toward the open grave. He knew she had no idea of the danger she was in.

Eagle Eyes stepped forward. "The dog is bad medicine."

John shook his head. "The dog just followed her." He inclined his head toward Shari. "She did not know better. Grandfather Eagle Eyes, when the blue coats get here, let me do the talking. All of you, just surrender."

"No, White Wolf," Eagle Eyes protested. "We want this as you do. We not surrender."

Shots filled the air, and a bullet struck the dirt beside Shari's foot. John shoved her to the ground.

"Stay down!" He put his foot on her back. Bullets whizzed over his head. He would not cower.

The cavalrymen rode into the graveyard and surrounded the Lakota. John heard thuds and grunts of pain, and he knew the soldiers were gun-butting the elderly chiefs. He closed his eyes and hoped no one had been shot.

When the sounds of attack ended, Shari whispered again, "John, I'm sorry."

"Shhh." Shari's safety and the survival of the elders came first. He helped her stand. Justice must wait.

"Don't touch that Colt, or you're dead."

Sergeant Raymond Walker dismounted and strode toward John. The tall, barrel-chested cavalryman grabbed John by his coat label and yanked him forward to press the blade of a Bowie knife to John's throat. Nose to nose John stared into Walker's gray eyes. Another time, another place, John would teach the son of a bitch how the Lakota used a knife. John would skin Walker alive. The bastard deserved it.

"Arms up, breed. Search him. Bind them all!" Walker pushed John backward and punched him in the ribs.

Pain exploded in John's chest as he gulped air. He watched Walker slide his black-handled Bowie knife into the sheath on his belt.

Pain stabbed John's side when two cavalrymen bound his arms. He figured his rib was broken.

"Well, well, a squaw," Walker said.

John intended to skin Walker very slowly. A trooper took his revolver, and another searched him. A trooper pulled John's knife from the sheath on his belt, and then the trooper tossed the white-handled blade to Walker. Walker dropped John's knife into his saddlebag. John felt a trickle of blood ooze down his neck from the nick Walker had cut.

"Aren't you a pretty one," Walker said as he stepped forward and grabbed Shari's chin, forcing her to look up at him. "You ain't Injun. You're white. I'll be damned."

"Let her go!" John demanded.

Sergeant Walker whirled around and drove his fists repeatedly into John's stomach. The air in John's lungs whooshed out, making him double over in agony. Oh yes, his rib was broken.

"I'll do what I want!" Walker roared.

John saw Walker leer at Shari, and he promised himself skinning would be the last of many tortures he would inflict on the sergeant.

Walker remounted. "Move out!"

Cavalrymen, astride their brown Morgan mounts, surrounded the warriors, pressing everyone together. Shari slid her arm around John's waist to support him. He sucked in air through his teeth as they walked toward the fort.

They were herded back to the fort, where they were driven into a single-window, two-cell guardhouse. There was a heating stove, a desk, and two chairs in the office. The cells smelled of body odor and urine. A cavalryman locked the cell of the warriors. John saw Shari cover her nose with her hand when she was pushed into the other cell.

"What's the matter? You don't like our accommodations?" Walker taunted as he sauntered into her cell. He strode up to Shari and grabbed her, pulling her against his chest.

"Don't touch me!" Shari struck Walker repeatedly. Her facial expression twisted with loathing.

Walker laughed.

"Leave her alone, Walker," John threatened.

Through the bars, a trooper bashed John in his stomach with the butt of a rifle, sending John to his knees.

"Stop! Stop!" Shari struggled against Walker, but the sergeant held her firmly.

John craned his neck, only to see Walker fondle Shari's breast. "I'll see you later," Walker promised.

John vowed Walker would suffer for days before he killed him.

Shari lifted her chin and glowered at the ruddy-faced sergeant after he locked her in her cell. Pride swelled John's heart. She had courage.

The troopers filed out, leaving Walker to hang a lit lantern on a hook by the cell area entrance. He chuckled as he walked out, flipping John's knife in the air and catching the white handle.

Shari whirled toward the other cell. "John?" The warriors moved out of her line of sight.

Eagle Eyes settled John on the plank floor against the cell bars. Shari leaped toward him and knelt. Then she reached through the bars and touched his forehead as if checking for fever. "Are you all right? I'm so sorry."

"Did he hurt you?" John asked as his gaze swept over her.

She grasped his hand. "No."

John saw determination on her face, not fear. What a brave woman!

"Are you cold?" she asked.

"I am too angry to be cold." But in fact, he was freezing, and he felt his rib scream with pain.

Shari unbuttoned the buffalo coat she wore. "Here, take my coat. I don't think we'll get blankets."

John refused her offering. However, through the bars, he touched her cheek. She had come to mean so much to him. Too much. Way too much.

His heart ached with his newfound knowledge. He could love again even though he did not want to because it hurt. How had she gotten through the wall he had built around his heart? Was it her pretty smile, her caring warmth, or her exciting touch? Oh yes. All of those. But more. He felt a lot more than he was ready to face. He had lost a wife, and now Shari's life was in danger because of him. He had no right to the yearning gnawing at his insides. She was not meant for him.

Then he heard Shari's teeth chatter.

"Better put your coat back on," he said. In the dim cell, he saw her moving. "Better?"

Shari nodded. "Yes."

After several minutes of silence, the warriors started to chant and sway in unison. "What are they doing?" Shari asked.

"Praying and moving to stay warm. You should move too. It will help you keep warm. We will be here all night." John gingerly rose, struggling against his pain.

"Where are you going?" Shari remained huddled beneath her coat.

John nodded at the Lakota warriors, who kept their gazes forward. "I need to check their wounds."

"Oh, of course."

John looked into her trusting eyes. He saw her soul-deep goodness. How could he have ever doubted her? "Walk around to stay warm."

"I'm sorry I caused this."

"You did not cause this. Hatred caused this."

While Shari walked back and forth in her cell, John examined the elderly warriors he thought of as fathers. He also thought of Shari. She had cured his loneliness. He could feel with his heart again. And his loins.

He knew to save Shari and the Lakota people, he had to think through his pain. He had to reason with his educated mind and control the hatred in his heart. First, he had to keep them all from freezing. John looked at the lantern near the door and saw it flicker. The light would not last long.

John finished his examinations and approached the front of the cell. "We need heat back here! Someone open the door and stoke the stove! Freezing us to death will not look good on McLaughlin's report!"

A few minutes later, the door to the cell area opened. John saw a trooper stoke the stove and soon felt heat radiate down the aisle and into the cells. John returned to Shari and stood next to the cell bars beside her.

"Do you think they'll keep the stove burning?" she asked.

"No. Try not to fall asleep." He leaned against the bars for support. His rib burned like the fires of hell, and his stomach ached.

Shari reached through the bars and touched John's arm. "Are any of them seriously hurt?"

"No. Just bumps and bruises."

"Shouldn't they get medication for pain? Certainly you should."

John snorted. "We are lucky we are not dead. Those troopers could have shot us."

"Why? You were only... What were you doing?"

"Digging up the body of Chief Sitting Bull so he can have a proper Lakota funeral."

"Still, that's nothing to shoot you for."

"The cavalry think it is."

"Why?"

"We are Lakota."

"John, I need to tell you something important."

"Shh, not now. Just try to rest. It will be a long night."

"But I need to explain some things."

"Later." John listened to the elderly warriors chant. He had never been prouder of his Lakota blood. He would die for his people.

The lantern flickered and blinked out.

CHAPTER 7

THE SOUND OF cold, creaking metal woke Shari as she lay cuddled against the cell bars and John's side. She felt John's body tense and knew he was also awake. The door from the guardhouse office stood open, and morning light filled the doorway. However, the cell area was still dark and frigid. The troopers had indeed let the stove go out.

Shari watched four cavalrymen enter the cell area.

One of them was Walker. "Come here, pretty girl."

"What do you want with her?" John demanded.

Walker yanked John's knife from the sheath on his belt and pointed it at John. "I'm fetchin' your squaw for Colonel Drum. Mind your own business."

"She is my business." John gingerly stood and helped Shari rise. "Stay back," he told Shari. As he approached the front of the cell, the elderly chiefs stood.

"Just what are you going to do to stop me?" Walker antagonized.

Shari swallowed. Her throat felt as parched as the surface of Mars. Whether she thirsted from dehydration or fear, she didn't know.

"Do not take her, Walker," John said.

Walker laughed. "Why all the fuss over a pretty piece of tail?"

"I am warning you, Walker. Do not take her."

"Men!" Walker commanded.

Three troopers stepped toward the cell area, and the sound of cocking Spencer rifles filled the guardhouse. Shari cringed at the ominous sound the Spencer guns made, and she saw all rifles pointed at the defenseless warriors who only wanted to protect her.

"Is she worth it?" Walker taunted John.

"Stop! I'll come!" Shari called out.

"That's a good girl," Walker crooned as he sheathed the knife.

Shari stepped to the front of her cell. She saw a hand reach through the bars, and she turned. Eagle Eyes held out his hand to her. His dark eyes were filled with sadness.

"Walker is a bad man," Eagle Eyes whispered.

"I know. But I can't let you all die for me."

"Do not let him get you alone," Eagle Eyes whispered again. "He will hurt you."

Eagle Eyes moved away, but John remained in the front of their cell, watching her. Her gaze locked with John's. Was it love she saw looking back at her?

"Be careful," John said.

"I will. Don't worry." The presidents' council of Shari's time had made sure she and all time-travel agents were trained in the art of self-defense. She remembered her instructions, and she felt confidence surge through her. She could and would take care of herself. John didn't know. It was one of many things she wanted to tell him.

As Walker unlocked the cell, John said, "If you hurt her, I will kill you."

Walker snorted. "You can try. Then I'll have the pleasure of hanging you." Walker grabbed Shari by the arm. "Come along, sweet meat."

Shari ignored Sergeant Walker's sexual comments as they walked across the icy parade ground. She wondered what the fort commander wanted with her.

As she walked up the steps to the commander's office, Sergeant Walker patted her buttocks. Shari whirled around. "Touch me again and you'll regret it."

Walker guffawed.

Shari thought he sounded like a lunar-crazed idiot. She knew some men of this time, and other times, didn't treat women respectfully. Walker was an example of that barbaric mentality. The idea of showing the male supremacist how to behave tempted her.

Then she chided herself because she knew she shouldn't break another time-travel rule. At least not yet.

Shari opened the door to the command post and stepped inside, quickly pulling the door closed behind her and cutting off Sergeant Walker's entrance. The commander sat behind a scarred wood desk. Colonel Drum stood when Shari entered. He was a distinguished man who wore his blue uniform well.

"Ma'am."

"Colonel. You wanted to see me."

"I want to help you." The colonel remained standing. "Please, sit." He gestured to one of two straight-back chairs near a pot-bellied stove.

Shari arched her brows. "I prefer to stand."

The colonel looked surprised. "Suit yourself. I really do want to help you."

For some reason, Shari doubted the colonel's word. Her reaction might have been biased by what she'd read in the historical archives. However, the archives clearly attested the government of this time did little to help the Natives or approved of those who chose to help the Natives.

"Help me how? And why?" she asked.

"Why? Because you're a white woman in the wrong place at the wrong time."

"Again, how? Just what do you think you can do for me, Colonel?"

"I can help you get back to your family. Don't you want to return to them?"

Biting back a retort and hiding her mirth at the colonel's folly, Shari asked, "What do you want for your *help*?"

The colonel smiled. "I see we understand each other. Of course, you must help me too." The colonel again gestured toward one of the chairs. "Please, sit, Ms...."

Shari stiffened her back. "Smith," she lied. She knew it was coming. Coercion. The colonel wanted her to betray someone. It had to be John. She would never do that. "I said I'd rather stand. Just how do you think I can help you, Colonel?"

74

"I understand you were at Sitting Bull's camp when he refused to surrender," the colonel said, "and you have since been residing at the home of John McIntosh." Shari nodded. "You will verify John McIntosh's attempted sabotage at the capture of Sitting Bull and later McIntosh's aid and abetting of fugitives from Sitting Bull's camp."

Shari smiled at Colonel Drum. She cleared her dry throat. "No. I will not. First, Sitting Bull would have surrendered, but the Native police attacked on their own at Sitting Bull's camp, and secondly, John McIntosh is a physician. If he did any aiding and abetting, it was in his practice of medicine."

"That's how you see it?'

"It's the truth."

"I suggest you reconsider." The colonel squared his shoulders.

"Is that a threat, Colonel?"

"Of course not. I would never threaten a white woman."

Shari felt a rush of adrenaline and an urge to commit brutal violence. The colonel wanted to frame John. Shari's lips curled under as she said, "Do you need a flying *tatanka* to show you the truth?"

The colonel's head jerked back in surprise at Shari's imitation of John's grandmother, and Shari felt another rush, this of pure satisfaction. Sarcasm. It was an effective tool. She smiled.

"Sergeant Walker!" the colonel shouted.

The door burst open. "Sir?"

"Take her to the infirmary and keep her under guard." The colonel sat and glowered at Shari.

Shari strode out of the command post and back across the parade ground. How dare the colonel threaten her! Poor John. He was in a lot of trouble.

"Move it along, pretty girl," Sergeant Walker antagonized her.

Thwack! Shari jumped forward when Walker swatted her buttocks. She stopped short and spun around. Although she hadn't actually felt the man's touch through her heavy clothing, the insult was no less. "Touch me again and I will hurt you."

Walker laughed so hard tears rolled down his fat cheeks.

After he sobered, Walker said, "You know you like it." He extended his hand toward Shari's breasts, which heaved beneath her buffalo coat. "After that half-breed, I figure you're hungry for a white man again."

Walker's remark was all the incentive Shari needed. She grabbed his forearm and yanked him toward her. Walker fell forward. As his barrel chest lowered, she leaped at him and drove her knee into his stomach. The air whooshed out of Walker's lungs. Landing solidly on both feet, Shari braced herself with a wide stance. Bending and charging with her shoulder, she rammed into Walker's midsection. Rising swiftly, she threw him over her back.

Walker landed face up on the frozen earth. Shari spun around and set her foot on his throat. His eyes widened in disbelief.

"You there!"

"You, stop!"

Shari heard the shouts. She glanced over her shoulder and saw two cavalrymen running toward her. She lifted her foot from Walker's throat.

"You bitch!" Walker cursed. He reached for John's knife, now hanging on his belt.

Shari stomped on Walker's arm. "A female dog? I don't think so. Don't ever touch me again."

"What's goin' on here?" the taller of the cavalrymen demanded as he halted beside Walker and offered a hand. Walker swatted the soldier's hand away and rose.

"What happened, Serg?" the other cavalryman asked.

"I'm going back to the infirmary," Shari said.

The two cavalrymen exchanged glances. Sergeant Walker brushed the snow off the cape of his blue uniform. "Take her there and keep her under house arrest. She can wash bedpans and clean up puke."

As Walker stomped away, Shari looked at the cavalrymen. "Gentlemen, shall we?" She turned and sauntered toward her destination.

*****

The next morning, out of patience and exhausted from lack of sleep, Shari rolled off a cot in the storage closet where she'd slept. It had been a night of crying sick children and her personal worry over John. The measles epidemic ran rampant, and John was still locked up. She had to do something.

She hurried with her morning ablution before reaching for her buffalo coat. "Take me to see Colonel Drum," Shari demanded of the heavyset young cavalryman standing guard in front of the infirmary.

"What?"

"You heard me."

"Ma'am, you can't just go over there."

"Yes, I can." Shari strode out of the infirmary and across the parade ground with the guard following at her heels, complaining all the way. She sprinted up the steps and onto the boardwalk in front of the colonel's office, only to stop short when the door opened.

A cavalryman carrying a bugle stepped outside and set the bugle to his lips. He trumpeted an alert before running off in pursuit of whatever order he'd been given.

Shari walked boldly into the colonel's office. A wall of blue-uniformed officers blocked her view of Colonel Drum. She pressed herself up against the log wall and listened.

"What does the wired message say?" The colonel's authoritative voice barked from the front of the room.

"It says, 'December 29, 1890. Hotchkiss cannons used. Hundreds of Indians dead at Wounded Knee Creek,'" an officer read.

"How many of our men went down?" the colonel asked.

"Twenty-five, sir."

"Evacuate the Natives from the fort and prepare for hell to break loose," the colonel ordered.

A flash of research information passed through Shari's mind, and she remembered the dire archives account of the date. She spun around, and then she bounded outside, pushing the young guard out of her way. She knew no reasoning or begging would help John now. However, perhaps she could help the Natives. She sprinted back across the parade ground.

"Halt!" a young guard called after her.

She kept running.

Shari bounded up the steps of the infirmary and burst into the waiting room, firmly slamming the door in the guard's face. The sound of suffering children carried from both wards. Determined, Shari kept going. She needed to find Strong Flower because the Natives had to be warned.

The sound of miserable children magnified as Shari neared the first ward. The ward was full of red-spotted children and mothers, but neither Wild Flower nor Dr. Pingree was there. Shari moved on and found the doctor in the second ward, which was as packed with the ill as the first ward. New arrivals found standing room only in the infirmary overflowing with sufferers of the measles epidemic.

Dr. Pingree worked frantically among the spot-covered children and mothers. Most of the young mothers also had the disease. A meteor storm couldn't have been a worse disaster.

Strong Flower wasn't in the second ward either.

Shari had no choice but to interrupt Dr. Pingree. "Do you know where Strong Flower is?" she asked.

"In the kitchen."

"I need her." Driven by her fear of the colonel making the sick Natives leave the infirmary, Shari bolted toward the kitchen.

Rushing into the kitchen, Shari found Strong Flower stoking the stove. Steam filled the kitchen as white bedding boiled in large black kettles. "Strong Flower, there's trouble."

"More trouble than the red spots sickness?" Wild Flower asked, adjusting the cradleboard on her back that held her sleeping infant.

"Yes. At Wounded Knee, many of your people have been killed."

Strong Flower blinked, and a single tear ran down her cheek. She wiped it away. "I feared trouble after our holy man's murder."

"I heard Colonel Drum order the fort evacuated."

"What is evacuated?"

"He's forcing your people out of the fort."

Strong Flower's dark eyes rounded. "What of White Wolf and others in guardhouse? All sick here in sick house?"

"I don't know."

"We need Black Hawk."

"Do you know where he is?"

Strong Flower nodded. Shari heard booted feet stomping into the infirmary. She heard Sergeant Walker bellow, ordering all Natives to assemble on the parade ground.

"I demand an audience with Colonel Drum!" Dr. Pingree's angry rebuttal lashed back at the sergeant.

"Tonight," Strong Flower whispered, "we return." She switched the cradleboard to her chest before she grabbed a buffalo robe off a peg by the kitchen door. Wrapping the robe around herself and the cradleboard, she fled.

Shari took over Wild Flower's laundry duty.

Shari didn't think the situation at the fort could get worse, but it did. A blizzard struck. By nightfall the fort was buried under several feet of fresh, ice-crusted snow. Shortly after midnight, Shari stepped out of the kitchen, and on aching feet, she walked to the infirmary reception area, where she dropped onto a chair. The raging wind pelted the snow against the windows. The glass was so encrusted Shari couldn't see outside. She closed her eyes and rested her head against the wall behind her as she listened to the wind howl.

Dr. Pingree soon joined her. "Thank you for helping, Shari." She sat next to Shari.

Throughout the long day and evening, Dr. Pingree had been incredible. The doctor had forced a meeting with Colonel Drum, and she made the colonel capitulate and let the sick children stay in the infirmary. However, all Native adults, except John and the old warriors in the guardhouse, were evicted.

"You're welcome. I wish I could do more. The children were terrified when the cavalrymen stomped in here and forced their mothers out."

Shari realized the colonel's edict actually held the Indian children hostage.

It had taken all day and well into the night to calm the children, but finally most of them slept. Whether they rested from illness or exhaustion from crying, Shari didn't know. But she was thankful for those that slept.

"I could not have controlled the situation without you," the doctor said.

Fatigue burned in Shari's arms and legs, and defeat weighed her heart down. She knew Strong Flower couldn't bring aid because of the raging blizzard glaciating the fort. She closed her eyes in exhaustion.

John. How's John?

Shari jumped when someone touched her hand. She had fallen asleep. Dr. Pingree was gone. Strong Flower and Black Hawk stood in front of her. The snow-covered buffalo robes over their heads and bodies made them look like snowmen. Shari saw weak dawn light diffused through the iced-over windows.

Black Hawk raised a finger to his lips as Strong Flower handed Shari her buffalo coat. How had they managed to make it past the guards and back into the infirmary? How had Strong Flower survived the frigid weather to find Black Hawk and make it back to the fort at all? Relief overwhelmed Shari. She rose and slipped into her coat before following the couple. Wild Flower's infant was not with them.

Huddled together, the three of them struggled against the wind as they crossed the fort compound.

The eastern horizon lightened to a clear sky as the trio reached the stables and slipped inside the barn. The night guard lay gagged and tied in an empty stall. The night guard was surrounded by twenty strong young warriors. Shari read anger on their faces. Maybe there was a chance.

Shari turned to Black Hawk. "What's your plan?"

Black Hawk gestured to the young warriors. "They make much noise. You and I get White Wolf and chiefs."

"A distraction is a good idea."

"It old Indian trick." Black Hawk smiled. "I hear what you do to Walker. Good idea."

"That was an old woman's trick."

Black Hawk nodded his approval before he and the young warriors set to work. Several warriors grabbed bags of feed and carried them outside. Others carried barrels and still others straw. Shari watched as they built a mound at the rear of the corral.

The frigid morning air burned exposed skin, but the wind was peaceful. Black Hawk and his friends moved silently. "What exactly are they doing?" Shari quietly asked Strong Flower.

"Make big boom."

"What?"

"Come. You see." Strong Flower walked out of the stable and hurried toward a hay pile beside the barn. She scooped her arms full of dried grass and strode toward the corral gate.

Shari scooped up hay and followed Strong Flower. She feared they were all in over their heads, but she didn't care. John was worth it. The frozen grass scratched Shari's chin as she carried it.

They carried their burdens to an empty barrel. "Help fill," Strong Flower instructed.

As Shari dumped her hay into the barrel, Black Hawk approached. He pulled a tubular brown object about a foot long from beneath his buffalo robe.

"What's that?" Shari softly asked.

"Dynamite," Black Hawk answered.

Shari swallowed. She suspected the risks in this escape attempt were many, and now she knew the degree of danger in the risks. Although she was willing to take those risks, caution had to be exercised to lessen the danger to innocents. "This is dangerous."

"Not unless we caught," Black Hawk said with a smile. "This make noise. Bullets follow."

Shari nodded. Desperation offered them no choices.

"Follow me," Black Hawk said. He hesitated only a moment to speak quickly to Strong Flower, and then he gave her the dynamite.

Shari put her hand over her mouth in surprise. Strong Flower's bravery impressed Shari. Black Hawk gestured to Shari, and she followed him out of the corral. She noticed he left the corral gate open.

Outside the guardhouse, Shari and Black Hawk pressed themselves against the back wall of the jail. And they waited.

Boom!

Hay and debris flew into the air just before the corral burst into flames. The horses in the corral screamed and charged out of the open corral, galloping across the parade ground and out onto the prairie.

Cavalrymen dressed in disarray poured out of the fort's barracks and raced toward the fire.

Cautiously, behind the cavalrymen's backs, Shari and Black Hawk crept into the guardhouse. Once inside, Black Hawk grabbed a ring of keys from a peg on the wall and gestured for Shari to follow.

Shari followed Black Hawk into the cell area. Thick frost covered the cell bars, and Shari knew there had been no heat all night. The only light to guide them came from a few embers glowing through the stove's open door. Shari heard the clink of the key in the cell lock, and then the shuffle of the warriors in the cell. As the cell door swung open, Shari jumped forward into John's arms.

"No time," Black Hawk said.

"Later," John whispered before he drew away from Shari.

Black Hawk shoved John's Colt into his hand, and then he and John helped the elderly warriors flee.

As Shari and John ran out of the guardhouse, she saw confusion governed the fort. A few remaining horses darted back and forth across the parade ground as half-dressed cavalrymen tried to capture the hysterical mounts.

Meanwhile, other men fought the fire with buckets of water from the pump house. A few cavalrymen ran in and out of the stable, leading burned mounts. John held Shari's hand as they followed Black Hawk and led the escapees away from the guardhouse. Then mounted young warriors charged out of the smoke, yelling war cries. More melee ensued.

Outside the fort, other warriors awaited the escapees and led mounts to the old warriors. The agility of the elderly chieftains amazed Shari. Without a verbal exchange, Shari and John and Eagle Eyes followed Black Hawk as he ran toward the infirmary.

As the foursome rounded the back of the infirmary, they saw Strong Flower waiting, holding the reins of four horses. Buffalo robes lay on each mount. When the back door of the infirmary opened, John pushed Shari behind him.

Dr. Pingree stepped outside, carrying hide bundles. "Take these. Hurry."

Shari stepped from behind John as the doctor passed out the bundles, and she saw Black Hawk approach Strong Flower. The pain on Strong Flower's face foretold the immediate future.

"Come with me," Black Hawk pleaded.

Strong Flower shook her head. "I cannot. I cannot leave my baby. We would slow you. If I go, he will know you did this."

"I do not care," Black Hawk vowed.

"I do. He will kill you," Strong Flower said.

Shari saw Black Hawk pull Strong Flower into his arms.

Shari's heart ached for the young couple. Who was the man the couple spoke about? She touched John's arm. He glanced at her, and his eyes looked sad. Did John know?

"Someone should kill him," Eagle Eyes said.

Shari looked at the elderly warrior. "Who are you talking about?"

"Walker," Eagle Eyes said, and then he spit on the ice-encrusted ground.

"What did he do?" Shari asked.

"Raped Strong Flower," John answered.

Shari's stomach soured at the thought. Now she understood.

"We will kill him soon, Grandfather Eagle Eyes. We must live to fight another day. Now we seek safety." John led Shari toward a mount.

Black Hawk, Eagle Eyes, John, and Shari mounted before they threw their buffalo robes over their shoulders and galloped north into the glacial night.

The fugitives trekked well into the morning to make their escape and to keep from freezing. The afternoon found them riding single file. Black Hawk, Eagle Eyes, John, and Shari trudged through a ravine filled with horse-belly-deep snow. Suddenly, a trilling bird call broke the ominous silence. Black Hawk answered with a warble.

A fur-covered, mounted visage crested the butte above the ravine, and a rider descended. Four horses on a rope line followed the rider. He led fresh mounts to aid the escapees.

Shari huddled inside her buffalo coat. Even under the buffalo robe Dr. Pingree had given her, she still felt frozen, wishing they could stop. But they couldn't. She told herself she actually appreciated the cold because, without its numbing effect, she would scream in pain.

"Hurry! Walker follows!" the Native rider called as he neared them. The rider pointed behind the group. "I saw blue coats from the crest."

"We must split up," Black Hawk stated.

John jumped from his heaving horse and darted to Shari. She slid into his arms and, without hesitation, he lifted her onto the back of the nearest fresh horse. "Hold on!" He grabbed her mount's halter rope and pulled the animal forward to another horse, which he mounted.

"Stay low and hold tightly. We must ride swiftly."

Shari wondered how much faster a horse could run. After all were mounted, John led Shari west. Black Hawk and Eagle Eyes rode east, along with the warrior who'd delivered the fresh mounts. They left their exhausted horses in the ravine.

Shari huddled low on her mount's back. The deep snow impeded them. The best their mounts could do was a chest-deep, plowing gait.

As John and Shari came out of the ravine, a bullet whizzed past Shari's shoulder. She hugged her horse's neck. A second shot struck Shari's mount in the left flank. The animal toppled sideways, almost falling against John's mount. Shari flew into the air. She landed on her back several feet from her thrashing horse. She gulped air, realizing she wasn't hurt. The snow had cushioned her fall.

She heard a third shot splinter bark off a tree, and she lifted her head to see mounted soldiers closing in on them. It was Sergeant Walker with four cavalrymen. The snow she and the others had broken through had opened a path for Walker and his men. Walker had his rifle aimed at John's back.

Shari heard Walker's rifle discharge, and she saw John topple face forward off his horse. She screamed when John landed. His body smeared the white powder beneath him dark scarlet.

"You three, go after them!" Walker shouted, pointing his rifle in the direction Black Hawk and Eagle Eyes's road.

Shari watched Walker's horse high-step through the snow toward her. She saw the killing lust in Walker's twisted expression.

When Walker reached her, he threw his leg over his mount and dropped to the ground. He yanked Shari off the ground with one hand. He held her up by the lapels of her coat. He pointed his rifle at her head, ready for the kill.

"No!" Shari struck Walker's head, punched his nose, and tried to knee his groin. Walker cursed and threw her. Then he leaped forward and landed on her. Grabbing her face, he pushed her head deeper into the snow. Blood from Walker's nose dripped on Shari's face. She didn't fight him. She clung like a tick and bit Walker's leather-gloved hand until she tasted blood.

Walker cursed her again. He was bigger and stronger than her. Using his weight to hold her, he pressed his cold rifle barrel against her cheek. "I'm gonna rape ya, and then I'm gonna shoot ya."

When Walker knelt and fumbled with the opening of his trousers, Shari lifted her foot and kicked upward, hitting Walker in his shoulder. As Shari brought her leg down, she kicked Walker's fat belly and yanked him off-balance. He fell sideways into the snow. When Walker rolled over and sat up, he'd lost his rifle. He fumbled in the snow for the rifle but couldn't find it. He searched frantically.

Shari saw her chance. Her one and only desperate chance. She tugged off her right mitten and dove into the snow. The snow burned her face and hand as she searched for Walker's weapon. Luckily, her fingers touched metal, and she twisted around, holding Walker's rifle just beneath the snow.

Walker lumbered toward her. Four feet away. Three feet. Shari lifted the weapon out of the snow and fired. She hit Walker in the leg. He screamed as he fell backward. He lay in the snow, holding his leg and crying like a baby.

"John!" Shari scrambled toward him. She pulled John tightly against her as she reached into the pocket of her buffalo coat, retrieving her return disk. She prayed to John's God as she pressed the center of the disk with her thumb. A blue light engulfed them.

CHAPTER 8

"SHARI? ARE YOU awake?"

She knew that voice. She felt her hand being held. Shari forced her eyes open. White walls, white bedding, she inhaled and smelled the lack of pleasant odors, just chemical sterility. Rolling her head to the side, she saw Helaine seated next to her bed in the sanatorium.

She was back. "Where's John?"

"Oh, thank the lucky stars!" Helaine leaned over and threw her arm over Shari, hugging her. "I was so worried."

Shari hugged Helaine in return and felt every bone in her body ache. She supposed that was natural from tumbling off a horse. When Helaine released her, Shari saw tears in her mentor's eyes. "I'm sorry I worried you."

Helaine sniffled. "You came back nearly frozen."

"I know. I'll explain. Helaine, where is the man I brought with me?"

Helaine straightened and dabbed at her eyes. "He's in the intensive care unit in a regeneration tube. He's not Sitting Bull's son. The archives say the chief's son was still a boy."

"Sitting Bull's son was still a boy."

"Was? What happened?"

"The worst happened. I failed my mission."

"So who is this man?"

"John McIntosh. He's a physician and rancher. He's the man who..." Shari's voice cracked as her throat clog with emotion. She recognized her emotion as fear. Fear for John's safety.

"Who?"

86

Moisture gathered in Shari's eyes. "Who saved me," she whispered.

"Oh, my dear." Helaine wrung her hands. "The presidents are very upset with you."

"I bet they are." Shari coughed and cleared her throat.

"Let me get you some water."

Shari blinked and cleared her throat again to unclog the terror she'd felt mere seconds before, or centuries ago, which constricted her breathing. She silently thanked whatever deity was listening for sparing her and John's lives. She glanced around while Helaine walked over to the nutrition module and held a glass beneath the serving spout.

Scanning the room, Shari saw no soothing color. She sniffed and smelled no sweet fresh air. She felt no comforting buffalo coat. This place offered her no respite. The presidents' council would know she'd returned. They knew everything.

Shari accepted the glass of chemically enhanced water from Helaine and drank. She grimaced. "Phew." It tasted bitter, artificially created. But then life here was artificial. For the first time in her life, Shari wondered why she ever accepted her dictated existence.

Helaine stood, watching Shari's every move. "Is something wrong?"

Shari didn't think there had been a future paradox. Still, anything was possible. "Has there been a time wave?"

Helaine's white brows lifted. "No." She stepped back and sat again on a chrome chair beside Shari's bed. She steepled her hands, and she looked at Shari over the tips of her fingers. "What happened?"

Shari reached out and Helaine took her hand. "I need your help. Please. Trust me and get me out of here."

Helaine's white brows lifted. "Of course."

Within the hour, Shari was seated in Helaine's quarters. Helaine's residence wasn't far from the medical complex and even closer to the launch facility. Her home was a regulation dwelling for one person. It had a single room and a private bath. It had a window through which imitation trees and shrubs stood to trick human eyes. Government regulations forbade live foliage within the city.

Shari sat on Helaine's sleeper, missing 1890. Mostly she yearned for John. Helaine silently worked at her desk, busily searching for information from her computer. Shari knew Helaine concentrated as she attempted to help, but Shari also knew her mentor was upset. "I'm sorry, Helaine."

"I know." Helaine reached into her white pants pocket and retrieved a round object on a chain, which she handed to Shari. "The man's watch."

Shari clutched John's silver watch. "Thank you."

"The robots would have destroyed it. I hope your John McIntosh's life has not affected yours by association with him. You must stop time traveling."

"I will."

"Good. You're needed here. There is so much I need to tell you."

"I want to know. I want to help you, but first I must help John."

Helaine started working again. Shari heard the computer voice modulator hum. She rose and stepped behind Helaine.

The male-sounding voice of the computer stated, "1891, John White Wolf McIntosh, charged with a cavalryman's murder. Sergeant Ezra Walker died of gangrene from a leg wound inflicted by McIntosh. McIntosh was convicted and hanged on March 2, 1891."

Shari hung her head. The archives report was worse than she expected, and it was her fault.

In the early hours of the next morning, Shari followed Helaine down a hall in the sanatorium. Helaine attracted the attention of the nursing robots away from the intensive care unit as Shari rushed into John's room.

John lay on his side, beneath a glass dome. A green light beamed down on him. His skin was paler than she'd expected. He had lost so much blood. Shari ached to touch him. She could see the wound in his chest where the bullet had exited his body. Although John's chest still appeared a ravaging red color, the wound was closing rapidly via the medical marvel that buzzed as it healed him.

Shari rested her forehead against the glass. This was an impossible situation. Their lives were separated by centuries. She knew better than to let emotions influence her mission, but she had. At least she knew what love felt like, and she'd cherish it until the end of her days.

A tear slid down her cheek as Shari heard Helaine enter John's room. She wiped the tear away.

"You care for him," Helaine stated as she placed her hand on Shari's shoulder.

"More than I should."

"Are you sure you don't just feel gratitude for what he did for you?"

"I do. But this is different."

"I see." Helaine rubbed Shari's back. "So what are you going to do about your feelings?"

"Nothing. He has a son to return to. His love for his son is so strong he won't stay here, no matter the danger to himself."

"That's admirable." Helaine wrapped her arm around Shari's waist and whispered, "And it's a good thing because the presidents, especially Artemis, will never let him stay."

"John is admirable, and that's why I must go back and try to correct his future to prevent his death. He didn't kill Walker. I did."

Helaine sighed and lifted her arm from Shari's waist. "You'll have to get permission from the presidents."

Shari gently laid her hand on the warm surface of the restorative dome, wishing she could caress John's face. "I know." She looked directly into Helaine's eyes. Conscious of the invisible cameras that always watched, Shari put her arms around Helaine and hugged her, whispering into Helaine's ear, "I need to take John back as soon as possible because I fear the presidents will kill him."

Helaine nodded against Shari's shoulder, whispering back, "So you realize that?"

"Yes." Shari patted Helaine's dainty shoulder. "I don't know the whole truth. I just know the presidents' truth is not reality."

"Shari, it's Artemis." Helaine kept their backs to the camera, and her voice was barely audible even at a whisper. "There is much you need to know. This isn't the time or place I'd have chosen, but the circumstances force me to tell you about the revo—"

"Visitors must leave." Shari and Helaine stepped apart when a nursing robot entered John's room.

Shari and Helaine stood casually, wiping at their faces as they looked at the robot.

The robot approached John and scanned his body with a beeping medical instrument, and then the robot turned toward Shari. Its red glass eyes flashed as it scanned Shari. "You are Shari 12101918. You are to report to the capitol."

"I will do so immediately." Shari gritted her teeth. She watched the nursing robot walk out of John's room. "This is not good."

"I know." Helaine's gaze held Shari's. "Would you like me to leave you alone with John for a few moments?"

"No. I must report. But before I do…" Shari reached inside the collar of her silver jumpsuit and retrieved the diamond flag necklace Helaine had given her. She offered it to Helaine. "Thank you. It did bring me luck. I'm still alive."

Shari turned and strode out.

Shari followed an armed robot into the pyramid-shaped glass and gold capitol building. The guard led her down an inner glass hallway to a triangular room where the leaders of her civilization sat around a crystal dais. The twelve presidents, seven men and five women, stared at her. A portion of the dais opened, allowing Shari to stride to the center of the circle. She held her head high, but she was sweating beneath her synthetic uniform. She feared the presidents' anger.

They could order her death for failing her mission and for endangering the current world with a paradox. They could kill her for bringing John back. She could die for involving Helaine. She had broken many rules.

Shari silently waited. She stared back at the presidents, refusing to acknowledge their intimidation. She didn't believe her society's philosophical doctrines.

However, she was more than ready to beg for John's life.

Finally, Artemis, the senior president, rose. He was a tall, lean man with graying dark hair. Artemis vainly adjusted the front of his white gown. "We have made a decision," he said. "You will take the man back to his own time. Then you will return to do your duty."

"Yes, sir. I will do my duty. I am compelled to ask the presidents' council, may I temporarily stay in the past to help the man I brought back? I have checked the archives. I know he will be convicted of murder, and I know he did not commit that murder."

"We will check the archives," President Artemis said, raising his gavel. Then he paused. "Do you know who did?"

"I did."

President Artemis stiffened. "You failed your mission and endangered your own time and your peoples' lives through threat of a paradox." Shari flinched. "Let me remind you that because of your ability to procreate, you have had the best of everything our society has to offer. Now it is time for you to repay your fellow man."

"Yes, sir. I appreciate all that's been done for me. I just want to try to help John McIntosh survive. I can speak on his behalf, of his innocence, in their court system."

Shari knew the presidents of the council of power also had been chosen. The people voted for the presidents. The presidents were able to have children, and they had experienced all the best of their society too.

Artemis turned toward the president seated on his right. He whispered to the man. That president softly spoke to the woman next to him. She spoke to the next man, and the next president spoke to the next. Soon all the presidents seated at the circular table were debating in whispered tones.

The striking of Artemis's gavel caused Shari to flinch. Her future, her life, was about to be decided.

"Let us vote," Artemis declared. "All in favor raise your right hand." Unanimously all twelve presidents lifted their hands.

Shari's stomach knotted. She felt like she might vomit. The presidents had voted in favor of what? She felt herself perspiring again. Dear John and little Danny. Dear Helaine. What were their fates to be?

Artemis stood. "Because of your excellent military record, you are granted an indulgence. But John McIntosh will face his own fate. We will not allow you to further endanger yourself or your people. You will take McIntosh back. Then you will directly report to perform your duty. If you do not report, you will be terminated." Artemis slammed his gavel down.

Anger boiled inside Shari's veins as she marched out of the capitol building, escorted by armed robot guards.

*****

John awoke in degrees. First, he became aware of warmth, and he felt the heavy buffalo robe covering him. Next, he heard sound and knew he lay near a crackling fire. Then he smelled peyote, and he remembered.

He had been shot. John opened his eyes and saw he lay in a dark lodge. Gritting his teeth, he braced for pain. Great pain. But he felt none. What the hell?

John touched his chest. He had no wound. Throwing off the heavy buffalo robe, he sat up and looked. The meager firelight showed him his chest was slightly red, but any wound he had was healed. He should have a hole in his back and a huge exit wound in his chest. Impossible!

Where was Shari?

His gaze darted around the hide and brush *wikiup*. It was hot as hell inside the sweat lodge. Soft furs covered the ground, keeping out the cold and damp. He saw a pipe hanging on a pole. The medicine lodge was sparsely furnished but filled with healing steam and peyote smoke.

"Shari?" he croaked.

"Not here," Eagle Eyes answered.

John whipped his head around to see Eagle Eyes sitting behind him in the dark. Eagle Eyes's white hair hung damply over his shoulders and down his bareback. The old warrior was naked. John realized he, too, was naked. All the better because he dripped sweat.

"Where is she?" John asked.

"Gone."

"What do you mean gone?"

Eagle Eyes crawled around the fire pit and knelt beside him. "I not know. She disappear. You disappear. You come back. She not."

"Bullshit. She was with me and..." John touched his healed chest again. "I should be dead."

Eagle Eyes nodded.

"How?" John asked.

Eagle Eyes stared into John's eyes. "I not know."

"You were there. You have to know."

"I do not."

"Shari? She..."

"I not know, White Wolf."

"You had to see where she went. There had to be tracks."

Eagle Eyes shook his head. "I ride away. Escape Walker. Other blue coats come. I come back. You gone. She gone. Walker and blue coats ride away. You come back."

"Bullshit!" John knew Eagle Eyes had smoked too much peyote. He shook his head as he started to stand. Eagle Eyes pushed him back down and offered John the peyote pipe. John angrily pushed the pipe away.

"White Wolf, Great Spirit make big medicine."

"No!"

The old warrior ignored John's outburst. "Walker, take your knife."

John sat totally befuddled. Disbelieving. Eagle Eyes pulled John's pocket watch from the trouser pocket of John's pants, which lay beside him.

John took the watch. "It was my father's." John rubbed his chest again, again expecting pain. And again he felt nothing.

In fact, he felt refreshed as if he had slept for a long time, and he also felt completely confused. His patience snapped.

"Shari!" he yelled.

He closed his eyes. Wherever she was, it was not good.

Eagle Eyes offered John the peyote pipe.

John shook his head, checking his watch for no reason other than it was a rational, normal behavior. His watch lay heavily in his palm. He heard it ticking. "Is it day or night?"

"Night."

"How many?"

"Three."

John felt his reality, his beliefs, his self-confidence shake like the ground under a cannon volley. He reached for the peyote pipe and inhaled.

CHAPTER 9

EARLY THE NEXT morning, John awoke, and he was alone. He was glad because he wanted to grieve Shari's loss. But he had no time. He needed to go home to Danny as soon as possible. Grandmother was going to skin his ass for being gone so long. John had no idea what to say to Grandmother. Although if anyone could, Grandmother would believe the truth. The cavalry officers never would.

The truth could put him in a mental sanitarium. More likely he would end up on the end of a hangman's noose.

He rose and pulled his trousers on, buttoning the top button.

"Easy. Easy."

John heard Shari's voice.

He charged out of the sweat lodge only to stop short. Shari stood just outside the lodge, petting a horse Eagle Eyes left. John grabbed Shari by her hand and pulled her into the sweat lodge. He led her to the fur hide on the floor of the lodge and not too gently pushed her down. Then he dropped sitting with his legs akimbo in front of her.

He put his hands on her shoulders as he stared into her eyes, willing a common-sense explanation from her lips. Lips he desperately wanted to kiss. But first, he braced himself and demanded, "What happened?"

"I teleported."

Shari's expression implored him to believe her and begged for his trust. She sighed. "Time travel. My time AD 2751." She lifted her hands, palms up. "Poof... 1890... Your time."

John released her and ran his hands over his healed chest. Then he pushed his fingers through his hair so hard he pulled his hair free of the queue on the back of his head. "How is this possible?"

"Technology," Shari answered. "The speed of light, eradication of gravity, and then cell degeneration and reanimation."

John stared at her.

"I don't understand it myself. I just do it."

He could be dreaming. Hell, he could be insane, but he knew he was not. He looked up at the dome ceiling of the sweat lodge, shaking his head. Maybe he was crazy because he believed Shari. However, that belief did not take away his sense of bewilderment.

John inhaled deeply, calming himself before he looked at Shari again. "What is that thing I found that looks like Crow Foot?"

"It's a simulative."

Breathing deeply again, John asked, "What's a simulative?"

"A fake body."

"I learned that much when I did an autopsy. What was it for?"

"To replace Crow Foot."

"Shit."

"It's all right, John."

"I burned it. But when I tried to burn the bag it was in, it would not burn. I buried the bag."

"That's all right too."

John's head ached so he rubbed his temples. "Eagle Eyes and Black Hawk must be alive or the food would not be here."

"I don't know. Our archives have no information on them."

John continued breathing deeply, slowly as he looked at Shari, trying to read her face for emotion. The situation was surreal. "Where are we?"

"In an abandoned Mandan village along the Knife River. Near Bismarck."

"I know of it. Why did you come to the past? Why take Crow Foot?"

"I came to retrieve Crow Foot before he died, and then return him to my time, where he'll be healed, as you were. In my time, Crow Foot will grow up and reproduce."

TIME QUEST

"I was in your time?" John asked. Shari nodded. "That explains my wounds healing so fast. What do you mean Crow Foot will reproduce?" John reached out and cupped Shari's cheek. "Are you saying people in your time cannot have children?"

"Most can't." Shari reached forward and placed her hand on John's chest over his heart. "That's why there's a need for missions like mine."

"Have you done this before?"

Shari nodded again.

John groaned and lowered his hand from Shari's cheek to place his hand over hers, which still lay on his chest. "I understand now."

"There's more." Shari's gazed implored John to trust her. "In the next two centuries, mankind makes many grievous mistakes. There will be wars."

Shit! This was tragic. Her words were so horrible he did not want to believe her, but he did. God have mercy! A thought occurred to John, and he looked Shari up and down. "Are you human?"

Shari yanked her hand from beneath John's. Tears formed in her eyes, and John watched her blink them away. "Yes."

John reached out and took her hand. "I am sorry. That was stupid of me." In a society as advanced as Shari's, infertility seemed improbable. "Can nothing be done?"

"No." Tears seeped from Shari's eyes.

He wiped her tears away with the pad of his thumb. "Thank you for whatever you did to save my life." John reached up and cupped the back of Shari's neck, slowly drawing her forward. He had to kiss her.

She closed her eyes, and John realized she wanted him as much as he wanted her. Shit! He should not do this because he knew he would never heal.

Shari's skin felt so soft. Her sweet smell intoxicated him. His groin hardened, and it felt so good. After everything she had told him, he still felt a driving need to make love to her.

But he stopped just before their lips met. He was still haunted with the pain of losing his wife. He could not lose another woman he loved. Yes. He loved her.

97

Shari opened her eyes and gazed at him with longing in her expression. "You can kiss me, John."

"No." His voice reverberated with his carnal starvation.

"Why not?"

"I just cannot."

"Why?"

"Shari, nothing can come of us."

Sadness, emptiness, regret hung between them as they stared at each other. Bullshit! Why was God, the Great Spirit, putting him through this?

Shari moved away from John and knelt at the fire, where plates and utensils lay. She looked at John. "I thought I smelled cooking food."

"Eagle Eyes," John replied as an explanation.

"Yes. He would help you." Shari scooped food onto plates from an iron kettle on the coals. "Please eat, John."

John took a tin plate and a spoon. "There is a water pouch hanging on the pole." Shari nodded but did not look at him.

He sniffed. The food was venison stew. He would thank Eagle Eyes and offer him a gift. A bag of grain or a foal in the spring. John watched Shari.

Her actions were so domestic. So normal. So much like the woman he wanted. A mate. Like hell! He struggled for words to describe this situation. Farcical torture. And the joke was on him. John took the coward's way. He remained silent and ate.

One kiss. Just one. He feared if he kissed her, he would not be able to stop.

"It's good meat," Shari said.

Of course, it was. John asked, "What do you eat? Where you are from?"

Shari shrugged. "Seaweed."

"What?"

"When we imitate something, we do it well. You know that stew Grandmother served me when I first awoke in your home?" John nodded as he chewed. "That was the first real meat I'd eaten in a long time."

"How is seaweed food?"

"Seaweed is very nutritious."

"Is that all you eat?" John wanted to keep Shari talking. Mostly so his cock would shrink back to normal. His trousers were still open. One wrong move and his cock would poke out of his trousers. He wanted Shari so damn bad.

"No. We eat nourishment capsules. They're synthetic vitamins and minerals, protein too. Once a year, when the crops under the dome are harvested, we have a feast. But the real food doesn't last long."

No wonder she was so skinny. She fell silent and stared at her hands. John suspected she was remembering the desire she had just felt. He would never forget. "You should eat, Shari."

"I'm not hungry."

"Please, eat." He desperately wanted more human exchange between them. At least there would be some normalcy in eating together. Eating and talking would keep his mind off his still hard cock.

Shari helped herself to food, but she just picked at it.

John lost his appetite. He knew he had offended her. His heart ached because their time together had come to an end, and he could not delay her departure. He gestured with his empty spoon, drawing a circle in the air, and said the first thing that entered his mind. "This village has been abandoned for years. But this sweat lodge is recent. Someone must still come here to worship."

"Your people are religious, aren't they?"

"Yes." John chewed another mouthful. Then he asked, "Why did your people send you here? To this village?"

Shari's gaze snapped to his. He saw fear in her eyes. "Because this is where the cavalrymen will capture you."

John set his plate aside. "You are not supposed to tell me that, are you?"

"No. I risk the future. A paradox."

"When will I be captured?"

"In the morning."

99

In the morning, he had so little time alone with Shari. John could not resist. He reached out and touched her cheek. He would miss her so much. He gazed into her eyes, knowing he should not be touching her. "My capture, is it because of the jailbreak?"

"No. It's because the cavalry thinks you killed Sergeant Walker."

"Why would they think that?"

"Because you were with me when I shot him."

"Shit!" He never imagined that. He knew he should leave. He should run for his life. But he could not. He yearned to hold her, to tell her how he felt, but he now feared her paradox. Still, he feared life without her more. "It is a coal-black night, and it is freezing outside."

"I know, but running is your only chance."

John suspected running would be useless. The cavalry would find him. Most importantly, he had to arrange a future for his son before he was captured. "Your leaders could have sent us somewhere else. Then I might have had a chance."

"But that would alter the future."

John nodded. "Perhaps."

He felt cheated. He knew his carnal desire made him selfish. But he did not care. "Let us spend this night together." His gaze searched hers. "Tell me more about where…when you are from."

"We live under a glass dome because war and pollution destroyed our environment. It's a highly advanced lifestyle. But it's sad."

"Because you cannot have children?" He saw Shari nod. He could not resist. He reached for her hands, circling her palms with his thumbs, rubbing to soothe her, and wishing for the night to never end.

"Yes," she answered. "And we have no choices. We are born in a hierarchy. The more privileged, the better our lives. The less privileged, the worse are conditions."

John's shoulders stiffened. "Like slavery?"

"Much like it." Shari's face reddened. "I am of the upper hierarchy. I know the system is wrong. You're all so different here. You have real freedom. We don't. You have personal names. My name is Shari 12101918." Shari sighed and relaxed.

John knew his hand massage affected her. He knew he should release her. Instead, he rose and moved around behind Shari and began to massage her shoulders. "Who named you, Shari? Your mother?"

"No. I never knew my mother. I was told she died giving birth to me. Shari is the name of a very dear friend, Helaine, gave me. She's like a mother to me."

"So some people can have children?" John asked as he manipulated Shari's neck. She rolled her head against his hands.

"Yes. But few. I am one of them. I was born to be a breeder. I should be honored."

"But you are not?"

"No." Shari trembled.

John knew he should stop, but he did not. He could not. He told himself he needed to hear more about her life to remember her better. That was a lie. He just wanted to have his hands on her a little longer.

"The thing I desire most is freedom to choose the mate I want. Freedom to have children, raise those children, and grow old with the mate I want."

John stared at the back of Shari's head in disbelief. This beautiful woman, the woman he wanted, would be forced to accept a man she did not want. Rage flowed through his veins.

Shari jerked. "Ouch."

"Sorry." John gentled his touch. He saw Shari relax again and lean against his hands as he continued rubbing her neck.

"I am to mate with Thorne 06031913. But I don't want him," Shari confessed. Then she trembled.

"Are you cold?" John asked.

"A little."

"Sit closer to me." John knew he was out of his mind as he slipped a hand around her waist and pulled her backward. "Closer," he whispered.

Her butt bumped against his cock. Shari startled. "Is that your penis?"

"Yes." He waited. This was her opportunity to deny him. She just had to say one word. Yes or no. "You probably should move away from me." He waited again. She smelled musky warm. Sexy.

John knew he should push her away. This was wrong. This was dangerous. In a few hours, she would leave him forever, and he had no right to act on his desire. No right to take her innocence or teach her to experience carnal fire.

"John?"

"Yes, Shari."

"You're the man I want. Will you make love to me?"

He cleared his throat. "You do not know what you are asking. Making love is a commitment. A lifetime commitment. Especially with a woman like you."

"A woman like me?"

"Yes. A woman like you." He breathed deeply, inhaling her scent. "Because you have never made love before."

"How do you know?"

"It is obvious." John's groin hardened to a full aching erection. The decision was not his. He had no right. No right. No right!

A decent man did not take advantage of an innocent woman. He pushed Shari away and stood up. John shoved his cock to the side, inside his trousers. He buttoned his denim trousers.

She stared up at him. "Is that your century's moral code or your personal choice?"

"It is my decision." He gazed down into her eyes. "You are going back to your time, and we will never meet again. I do not want to live with the memory of intimacy between us. I have that memory already, of my wife. I do not want that memory of you. But even more important is that you mean too much to me. I cannot bear it. If I could, I would not hesitate to make you my wife and love you forever."

Shari nodded. "I understand."

He saw her squeeze her eyes shut. "In my time, a man does not take advantage of a woman. Wrong is wrong."

She looked up at him. "I don't think it would be wrong." Shari bit her lip, and John knew she only pretended to understand to enable herself to hold on to her self-control. She was suffering from unquenched desire.

So was he. He had to get away from her before he could not. She had taught him to love again. Why did his broken heart mend for a futuristic beauty? "I have given what you said more thought, and I have decided to leave now. I have Danny to think about, and it is best for both of us." John grabbed a buffalo robe off the floor. He tossed the hairy garment over his shoulder. "I will never forget you."

Shari rose and stood proudly before him. "Goodbye, John."

John grabbed her, pulled her into his arms, and lowered his head. Just one kiss. One taste. He drove his tongue into her mouth and mated with hers. Then abruptly, he pushed her away. He was insane.

Two steps took him to the hide door flap. John shoved aside the flap to bend at his waist and crawl quickly through the small entrance.

The next morning, light beaming through the smoke hole awoke Shari. Her head ached, and her stomach churned, and her mouth felt as dry as Mars. And John was gone. She exhaled a shaky breath. Now she knew what a broken heart felt like. Love didn't just maim. It killed. She rolled onto her stomach and sobbed into the fur beneath her.

She cried herself back to sleep.

When she awoke again, the sun had moved past the smoke hole. Shari trembled from cold air in the little lodge. She knew it was time to go home. She had to face the presidents. She'd broken the rules, failed her mission, and been rejected by love. It was time to own up to it all.

She pulled her return disk from her pocket and pressed the center. Nothing happened. No blue light. No spinning.

Shari slipped into her buffalo coat and mittens and crawled outside. She stood in the frigid winter sunlight and tried the disk again. Printing appeared on the top of the disk. *Contaminated.*

"No!" She remembered the measles at the fort. She yanked off her mittens, letting the wind chafe her exposed skin. Red spots. She pushed up the sleeve of her buffalo coat and looked at her arm. More red spots. She had measles.

She didn't know how long the disease was contagious, but until then, she wasn't going anywhere. She looked around at the abandoned Mandan village. Desperation, more than the temperature, would freeze her where she stood.

Oh, John. She wanted to scream out her need for him. But the act would be futile.

As the icy wind whipped her hair around her face and frosted her exposed flesh, Shari realized the presidents had to have known. From her medical examination, when she returned with John, they had to know that she was going to be ill. That was the reason they allowed her to accompany John back. Had they left her here to die?

Her anger fortified her survival instinct. She would survive until the presidents opened the time portal, and when she returned, the leaders of her time were in for a surprise.

She would not obey their dictate. She would never mate with the man chosen for her. Never! She thought of her last conversation with Helaine. Shari believed she understood now what Helaine was hinting at. There were others who felt the same way she did about the presidents' rulings. She'd seek them out. United with others of like opinion, they would take a stand.

But first, she had to survive.

Shari grabbed chopped wood from beside the small lodge and stacked it in her arms. "Thank you, Eagle Eyes."

Then she heard something. She heard the tinkle of tack and the snort of horses. Shari turned and saw two burly cowhands riding toward her. Was this when she would die? "Damn you, Artemis."

Artemis had told her the cavalry found John. The president had set her up to die or be raped or both. The cowhands halted their mounts a few feet from her.

"You alone here?" one of the men asked.

Shari stood her ground. "No. My husband is inside."

The first man snorted. "Sure he is."

"Jesus Christ!" the second cowhand exclaimed. He reined his mount back. "Look at her face. She's got measles."

"I know," Shari said, pressing her hand to her forehead. "My family brought us here. They're afraid for the others."

"They got reason," the second cowhand said. "I ain't searching for strays around here no more." He glanced at the first cowhand before he whirled his horse around and galloped away.

"Well, I had me the measles. And you ain't got no husband inside." The cowhand's gaze slid up and down Shari's body. "What say you and me get to know each other a little better?" He threw his leg over his horse and dropped to the ground.

"Stay away from me," Shari warned, blinking against the wind.

The cowhand sauntered forward, holding his hat on his head.

Shari dropped the wood and whirled to flee, but the cowhand pounced and knocked her to the frozen earth. She fought like a wild animal, clawing and biting. But her efforts did no good. The cowhand laughed as he pinned her arms above her head.

As he lowered his head, she grimaced. When the cowhand's cold, whiskered face touched hers, she bit his chin.

She saw the man raise his arm to strike her, and she closed her eyes. She knew his angry punch would hurt.

"Whaaa...," the cowhand gargled.

Shari popped her eyes open.

John stood over them, and he had his leather belt around the cowhand's throat. Shari saw the cowhand's eyes bulge as John pulled backward. She watched the cowhand's face turn white and then blue. John was killing for her.

"John! Don't!"

John let the cowhand sink to the ground. The cowhand was breathing, but unconscious. John reached for her hand. "We must get out of here."

Shari and John trudged north along the river. She cursed the leaders of her time. How could such a highly developed civilization be so vile? She felt betrayed, like a gullible fool, and she longed for comfort and warmth in John's arms. However, that did not happen. He didn't touch her. He didn't even really look at her.

He remained stoically silent as they walked. He strode ahead of her, solemnly breaking the snow, making it easier for her to pass, and

105

he avoided looking back at her. Shari wondered what he was thinking. As glad as she was he'd come back, she pondered why he'd come back, and how he'd managed to show up at the exact right moment. He had to have been watching her. That meant he wasn't indifferent to her. Not at all. He could have run. Should have run. But he didn't. The thought filled her with hope.

As the sun set, she saw the roof of a building ahead of them. "What's that?"

"I think it is the Bismarck brewery. You stay here and I will see if it is safe."

Shivering in her buffalo coat, Shari huddled in the trees. She waited. It grew dark and colder before she heard footsteps. She didn't move. Shari held her breath so it wouldn't frost the air just in case it wasn't John.

"Shari, come to me."

Shari hurried toward John's voice and gray shadow. She followed him to the brick building, and then she stood back as he kicked the door open. They stepped into an office area and were engulfed in warmth and the yeasty smell of beer.

John shut the door, and they were instantly enveloped in darkness. "Do not move," he whispered.

She didn't.

A few moments later, a match flared, and the smell of sulfur tickled her nose. John stood a few feet away, holding a kerosene lamp. The lamp's sharp smell soon burned Shari's nostrils and made tears gather in her eyes, but she'd never been so glad for light and warmth. When John set the lamp on a desk, she took off her buffalo coat and stepped forward. "I'm sorry, so sorry, John."

"It is not your fault. Nothing has been your fault." He reached out and pulled her close.

He held her so tightly Shari thought her ribs would crack, but she didn't mind one bit. John could never hold her too tightly. She hugged him back just as fiercely.

"I saw the cowpokes approaching this morning, and I hid. When only one rode away, I knew you were in trouble. The cavalry did not come for me."

"Artemis lied, John."

"Artemis?"

"Our ruling president."

"Why would he do that?"

"I'm not sure. To punish me. Or to make sure you were captured or killed."

"Why would Artemis want to kill me?"

"I don't know. Maybe just to remind me he rules." Shari pushed away from John and looked up into his dark gaze. "Why did you come back?"

"I could not leave. I made it to the trees and spent the night freezing my ass. I had to make sure you were all right. When I saw the cowpokes, I panicked." He pulled her close again and nuzzled her cheek as he ran his hands up and down her back.

He felt wonderful. Shari sighed when his lips descended and lingered on her throat, only to suddenly stop. John stepped back.

"Shari, you have a rash."

"I have measles." The loss of his body heat chilled her, and her teeth chattered.

"How do you feel?"

"I felt ill. But I think that was just from your leaving. I feel much better now." She didn't want him to stop kissing her. She wanted more. More! He'd already touched her, so if he was going to be contaminated, it had happened.

"Let me see." He pulled at the collar of her blouse. "I can't see a damn thing. I need more light." John fetched the lamp off the desk and lifted it over Shari's head.

He nodded as he examined her skin. "It is the measles. Is that what made the one cowpoke hightail it out of there?"

"Yes." She grinned up at him.

"But not the other one?" John asked.

Her smile vanished. "No. He said he'd had the measles."

John searched her gaze. "Are you sure you feel all right?"

"Fine. I hope I haven't contaminated you." She touched his cheek.

"You have not. I had measles as a child."

"Good. John…"

"Yes."

"I felt better when you were kissing me."

"If I start kissing you again, I will not be able to stop."

"I don't want you to."

"Remember what I said about making love being a commitment?"

"Of course. I agree. I don't want to go back, John. I want to stay here with you and Danny."

John groaned as he pulled her against him. "I want the same thing. I have wanted to make love to you since you awoke in my cabin."

"Nothing is stopping you now. Nothing past, present, or future."

A woman's first time was a precious gift. John's gaze never left Shari's face as he bent and grabbed her buffalo coat off the floor. He spread her coat between two desks on the brewery office floor. Then he took her hand and pulled her down onto the coat with him. His heart beat so hard he felt it to the tip of his manhood. It had been a long time since he had had a woman, but he knew he had to rein himself back to make Shari's first time special for her.

As they sat facing each other, he lowered his head and kissed her. Open-mouthed, he teased her tongue with his until her breathing became irregular, and she weakly leaned against him. Gently he lowered Shari onto the soft, hairy coat.

He knelt before her as he undid the buttons on her cotton blouse, bending to kiss the satin skin of her neck and upper chest between each button. He lifted his gaze to search her eyes as he untied her chemise and spread it open, revealing her breasts. "I have never seen anyone more beautiful," he whispered.

"I'm sorry I'm covered with measles."

"You could not be lovelier." She had gained a few pounds since he had found her behind Sitting Bull's cabin. She truly could not have been lovelier. He leaned forward and sucked one of her pert nipples into his mouth.

Shari gasped and arched her back. Giving her pleasure shot pure lust through John's veins. He felt like a giant.

As he suckled one breast and then the other, he undid her skirt and pushed it down over her hips. Her petticoat went with her skirt. When she lay before him in her drawers and socks and shoes, John stopped worshipping her breasts to sit up and quickly shuck his buckskin shirt and trousers. He left on his flannel underwear to retain himself and because he suspected she was not quite ready to see his erection hard as stone. After he pulled off his boots, he took off her shoes. Finally, he stretched out beside her.

John reminded himself to go slowly. He had been blessed, and he wanted to savor her gift of virtue. It had been a long carnal famine for him. He ran his hand over Shari's breasts, down her stomach, and into her drawers, where he cupped her womanhood. As he massaged her, he listened to Shari's ragged exhalations.

"Part your legs, Shari," he whispered. "I will make it even better."

She did, and he slipped his finger into her core. She felt wet. He closed his eyes and swallowed a shout of joy.

"Ah," she moaned.

He felt her velvety flesh squeeze his finger as he rubbed her vagina, thumbing her nub of desire. John felt his manhood move against his underwear. He gritted his teeth and breathed through his mouth, trying to cool his lust. His need for release was almost unbearable. He slowly pulled his finger from her core and sat up. This first time he was her teacher. He must give her pleasure first.

"Don't stop," Shari whimpered.

John gazed into her entreating eyes. "I am not going to. I just want to take my time. There is much to enjoy. Shari, I am honored to be your first. I love you, Shari."

"I love you too, John. You are my first and my last," she promised.

Now it was time to show her his love. He untied her drawers and pulled them off. Then he leaned forward and opened her nether lips. Placing his mouth on her, he licked the center of her core.

Shari gasped and arched against his mouth. "Oh, John, don't stop. Please don't stop."

Carnal power filled him as he watched desire overwhelm her. Her need, her words, filled the void in his life. A void that had lain empty within him for a long time. He felt lust burning through his veins, but first he would satisfy his woman.

Someone banged on the door. "Who's in there?" a male voice demanded from outside.

"Shit!" John rolled away from Shari and grabbed his trousers.

CHAPTER 10

SHARI ENTERED BISMARCK riding a dapple gray mare, seated behind a blue-uniformed policeman. John walked between her and another mounted policeman. John's hands were bound. He'd been captured because he'd stayed with her. She would have cried if she hadn't been so angry.

Liars! Her presidents were all liars.

She rode down the dirt street named Main Avenue and cursed Artemis with every breath she took. Her mind whirled as she passed boardwalk fronted businesses. There had to be a way to escape. There had to be a way to save John. There had to be a way to save the life she craved with him.

When they reached the center of Bismarck, Shari noted numerous brick buildings. The police station was one of those buildings. She and John were taken directly to a small holding area in the station office and ordered to sit on a bench.

"What are they going to do with us?" Shari whispered.

"Nothing good," John replied.

"Silence!" a policeman ordered.

Shari and John sat for several hours. She hadn't slept a wink, and she knew she should be exhausted, but she still felt far too upset to be tired.

Then her stomach growled so loudly John turned his head and looked at her. "They should bring us food soon," he said.

His tender smile fed Shari's heart.

She thought about what she and John had been about to do when they were discovered. Her desire for John was an incredible thing. A magical thing.

"I crave more than food, John. We have been robbed," she whispered.

John lifted his bound hands and dropped his arms over her shoulders. He rested his chin on the top of her head, cuddling her. "I agree. The luckiest day of my life was the day fate brought you to me," he softly said.

"This wasn't fate. This was Artemis."

"Silence!" the policeman bellowed from across the office. The policeman looked at them before he stood. "Move away from her, McIntosh! Or I will make you sorry!"

John lifted his arms, and Shari sat up straight. She saw dust mites floating in the light through the window. The midday glow shone on John's ebony hair. His dark eyes met hers and held her gaze, offering her solace. She had never seen a more handsome man or a more doomed soul.

John must have sensed the turmoil she felt for he took her hand, and when the policeman glanced away, he brought her hand to his lips and kissed her fingers. Shari vowed she would not let Artemis win.

The door from an inner office opened and a big man with an impressive dark mustache and square goatee strode through the doorway. He stared at Shari and John.

"Come with me," the big man ordered.

Shari and John rose and followed the man into the inner office, and then the authoritative man reached behind them and shut the door.

"Sit," the man ordered before he rounded a desk and sat himself.

Shari and John took seats in two straight-back chairs in front of the man's desk.

"I'm M. L. Marsh, police chief of Bismarck." As he introduced himself, he raised his hand to shake a piece of paper. "This telegram says you, John McIntosh, are charged with the murder of Sergeant Raymond Walker from Fort Yates. Indian Agent McLaughlin wants you back there for trial." Police Chief Marsh puckered his dark brows and looked at John. "Why? You're not a military man. This should be civil. Just who are you, McIntosh?"

"I am a physician and rancher."

"Did you shoot Walker?"

"No."

"I did," Shari blurted, bounding to her feet.

The police chief's eyebrows rose. "The hell you say." He pointed to the chair. "Sit back down."

Shari sat, realizing this man could help them if he wished. "Really, it was me."

"She is upset and trying to protect me," John stated. "I shot Walker."

Shari jumped back up. "He did not! I did!"

"No. She did not," John countered.

"Enough!" the police chief roared. He ran his hand over his face in frustration. "Neither of you will be returned to Fort Yates. Agent McLaughlin can come here if he is so inclined. Right now, I need to think about this situation. Officers!"

The door flew open, and two burly policemen strode into the inner office. John's gaze flew to Shari. "Do nothing."

She tried to reach out for him, but the policemen blocked her and grabbed John, dragging him away and muscling him through the doorway.

"Her too." The police chief pointed at Shari. "McLaughlin says she helped bust McIntosh out of the Fort Yates guardhouse. Besides, she's got measles and needs to be quarantined."

Shari stood. "There's no need for force. He'll go, and I'll come willingly." She followed John and the policemen.

"See you do," the police chief said before he closed the door of his office.

Shari hurried after John. The policemen took John through another door and into the cell area, where she and John were put in separate cells. But this time there was a cell between them, and they couldn't touch. The cell doors clanked shut, and the scrape of keys in the locks was the loneliest sound Shari had ever heard. She looked at John and bit her bottom lip to keep from screaming.

"If I could come through these bars, I would," she told him.

John was silent for so long Shari thought he hadn't heard her. Finally, he said, "I did not think I could feel this way again. In fact, for a long time, I made sure I did not make it possible. But I feel it now. The pain of loving you and knowing I cannot save you is killing me. You must save yourself. Go home, Shari. Go back."

"I cannot." Shari's voice cracked.

John sank down on the bunk in his cell. He leaned his head against the brick wall behind him as he said, "I do not want you to see what will happen to me. Please honor my request. As soon as you can, go back to when you belong."

Shari stood and clutched the bars of her cell, letting tears of heartbreak slide down her cheeks.

John and Shari spent the next week in the Bismarck Jail. They were treated well but never allowed to touch. By the time the district judge came to town, Shari's measles were gone. And John felt desperate. He begged her every sunrise to save herself, but she would not leave. His anxiety grew with every sunset because he knew what was coming. His hanging.

Finally, one morning, he and Shari were taken to the Burleigh County Courthouse, a two-story brick building with a white belfry.

They were led inside a pine-smelling courtroom, and the first person John noticed was his grandmother. She sat stone-faced in the rear of the courtroom. Where was Danny? How was he? His poor beloved son. Danny had lost his mother, and now he would lose his father. If that happened, Danny would have one hell of a sad childhood. Thank God for Grandmother. At least, Danny would grow up under her devoted care.

A deputy unlocked Shari's handcuffs first, and then John's before pushing him onto a chair. Shari silently sat next to him. Beautiful, stubborn woman, she might hang too. Because of him. If she was lucky enough not to be charged, John knew he had to save her from herself. Emotional pain tightened his chest as he realized what he had to do.

A man in a gray suit sat down next to John. "I'm your attorney, Andrew Johnason." The man extended his hand to John and then Shari.

John felt Shari's eyes on him, but he kept his gaze on Johnason. "Do whatever it takes to save her," he said.

"No, John," Shari protested.

John's gaze stayed on the attorney.

"Whatever it takes?" Johnason asked. John nodded. "You're sure?"

"Yes." John felt relieved because he felt sure the attorney understood *whatever* meant letting him hang to save Shari. "Who hired you?" John asked Johnason.

"Your grandmother."

John's gaze darted to the back of the courtroom. He saw his grandmother staring at him. Proud. Defiant. He looked back at the attorney. "You are representing Shari too? Right?"

"Oh yes. Your grandmother insisted on it."

Turning back around, John silently mouthed to his grandmother, "Thank you." He had never loved his grandmother more. He felt Shari's gaze burning into the side of his face, knowing she wanted to see his eyes for the love he felt for her. But he stubbornly refused to look at her.

"All rise!"

Shari's arraignment passed quickly. There was no hard evidence, only circumstantial, that she had helped with the Fort Yates escape, and there was no witness to Sergeant Walker's shooting. The attorney's statement rationalized that Shari was a confused young woman who had lost her memory and felt indebted to the man who had saved her life. She was released into her own custody and recommended to the nuns of the Catholic church for guidance.

John breathed easily for the first time since he had been arrested.

He pleaded self-defense, but he was denied bail and ordered back to jail. His trial would be in one month when the judge returned to Bismarck. As John was led from the courtroom, Shari rushed after him, and he sensed she wanted to embrace him. But he could not allow it. He was not that strong. If he touched her, he did not think he could let her go. It was time to force her back to her own time and place. So he set up a ruckus, fighting the guards, so they dragged him away from Shari.

Shari stopped short and called out, "John! John!"

John jerked back on his cuffs one more time in order to glance toward his grandmother before he left the room, and he saw his grandmother walking toward Shari. To her credit, Grandmother did not cry.

He heard Shari call his name again. He did nothing. His head ached, and bile rolled in his stomach. John hated himself. He had never been a cruel man, but he had to make Shari return to safety in her own time.

If she hated him, so be it.

Outside the courthouse, Shari stood with Grandmother. "How did you get here?" Shari asked Grandmother.

The older woman's eyes widened when she looked up at Shari. Then Grandmother rolled her big brown eyes. "On a horse."

Shari gritted her teeth. "Where is Danny?"

"With my people."

"Good." Shari recalled reading in the archives that the Catholic church often gave aid to those in need. Grandmother needed a safe place to sleep in a white town. "Grandmother, I want you to find the Catholic church. They will give you shelter. I'm leaving."

"Where will you go?" Grandmother snapped.

"I'm going to use your horse to go back to Fort Yates. I need to talk to Dr. Pingree."

Grandmother snorted. "About time you do something."

CHAPTER 11

ONE MONTH LATER, early the morning of his trial, John sat polishing his boots when a policeman entered the cell area. John saw the policeman carried a bundle of clothing.

"A woman brought you these." The policeman handed the clothing through the bars to John.

"My grandmother?" John asked.

"No. A pretty auburn-haired gal."

John could have sworn his heart stopped. Shari was still here. He had asked Grandmother after his arraignment if Shari had left, and Grandmother had told him she was gone. He believed she had returned to her own time. Now he felt torn between sorrow and elation. Sorrow because Shari risked her life to stay, and it made him care all the more for her. Elation because he had thought he would never see her again.

"I'll bring hot water and soap," the policeman said.

"Thank you."

"Everybody gets their day in court."

John looked through the clothing. He saw his dark-brown suit and a white shirt. His church-going clothes. There was clean underwear and socks too. In the breast pocket of the suite, he found his black bow tie. He knew Shari had returned to the ranch to fetch the clothing. God, he missed her.

John turned his face to the sun as he walked from the jail to the courthouse, handcuffed and guarded by three policemen. He still enjoyed the sunshine. Melting snow and running water made the Bismarck main road a quagmire. He thought of home and the nourishing melt taking place on his land. It would have been nice to share spring with Shari.

He entered the courtroom with his head held high. He scanned the crowded room until his gaze found Shari. She sat in the back of the courtroom beside Grandmother. Shari was dressed in sky blue. She wore a belted shirtwaist dress with buttons all the way down the front. A dress she no doubt remade to fit her slender body. Her hair lay loosely down her back. She was so beautiful. Their gazes met as John passed her, and he saw love and longing in her expression. Although he felt exactly the same way, he looked away.

John had to make Shari leave him. After his hanging, the townspeople could turn on Shari and Grandmother. Bloodlust-crazed people. Grandmother would realize the danger but not Shari. Shari was love blind.

As he walked toward the front, John saw Indian Agent James McLaughlin, Colonel William Drum, several soldiers from Fort Yates, and Dr. Cynthia Pingree. John wondered why Cynthia was here. She nodded to him as he walked by her.

John glanced at the jury. He saw twelve men. Twelve white men. Bullshit. They might as well take him out back and hang him right now. He saw his attorney seated in the front. John stopped at the defense table, and Johnason stood while a policeman unlocked John's handcuffs.

"Are you ready?" Johnason asked, gesturing to the chair beside him.

John sat. "Never more so." He wholeheartedly meant his words, although he knew his chance of acquittal was nonexistent. Someone had to pay for Walker's death, and John knew he was the one. It was fate. He also knew Shari and his grandmother suffered. The sooner this farce was over, the better. Then the two women needed to seek safety.

He turned to Johnason. "I do not want my grandmother or Shari on the stand."

"Why not?"

"No."

"But..."

"All rise!"

John's trial began. Johnason and the prosecuting solicitor, Edward Olson, both blustered with righteous arrogance during their opening statements. They reminded John of the clowns in the circus he had seen a few years ago in Minneapolis. He could feel the rope around his neck tighten. He bit the inside of his cheek to keep from yelling in frustration.

Johnason's first witness was Bismarck Police Chief M. L. Marsh. "Did McIntosh resist arrest when he was captured?"

"No," Marsh answered.

"Did you find any weapons on McIntosh at the time of his arrest?"

"No."

"In your opinion, did McIntosh behave in the manner of a fleeing murderer?"

"I object!" Olson jumped to his feet. "Not only hearsay but leading the witness."

"Overruled!" The judged banged his gavel. "You know better, Mr. Johnason."

"Excuse me, Your Honor. I have no further questions for this witness at this time."

"Mr. Olson, would you like to cross-examine Mr. Marsh?" the judge asked.

"Not at this time, Your Honor." Olson sat down.

"You may call your first witness, Mr. Olson," the judge stated.

"The prosecution calls Colonel William Drum."

John looked at Solicitor Olson. Olson had short gray hair. He wore fancy city clothes. At least, he was not military.

"Colonel, what can you tell us about Sergeant Walker's mission to recapture John McIntosh?" Olson asked.

"I ordered it."

"Did you feel McIntosh was dangerous?"

"Yes, of course. He and others blew up the stable in which several men were wounded and livestock was lost."

"I object!" Johnason intervened. "It is not a proven fact that my defendant had anything to do with that explosion."

GERI HAWTHORNE

The judge leaned forward. "Overruled."

Solicitor Olson approached the witness stand. "Colonel, please explain why if you think the defendant is dangerous."

Colonel Drum cleared his throat.

"Go ahead, Colonel." Olson paced back and forth in front of the witness stand.

"Last summer, McIntosh assaulted Walker in a Fort Yates saloon."

"Were charges filed?"

"No."

Olson stopped before the stand. "Why was that?"

"It was a personal disagreement. Sergeant Walker refused to file civil charges."

"Why would Walker refuse to file charges against McIntosh if the man assaulted him?"

"I don't know. Only Walker could answer that."

The judge scowled. "Get to the point, Mr. Olson."

"Have there been any other altercations between McIntosh and Walker?"

"Yes."

"Tell us about it," Olson said.

"Last spring, McIntosh came to the fort claiming that Walker had raped an Indian woman."

"Go on."

"I questioned Walker, and he said the young woman had been willing and accepting of his advances."

"I see. And what did McIntosh do?"

"He threatened Walker's life," the colonel stated.

"No further questions."

John closed his eyes as Solicitor Johnason rose to cross-examine. He remembered last April, Strong Flower had not been willing or accepting. He recalled her tears and bruises and the sutures he had sewn on her knife wounds. Strong Flower loved Black Hawk then and still did now. John had no doubt Walker raped her.

"Colonel Drum. When McIntosh escaped from the guardhouse at Fort Yates and was fleeing capture, how do you explain McIntosh having a gun to shoot Walker?" Johnason asked.

"Objection," Olson said. "Colonel Drum would only be speculating. Hearsay and leading the witness."

"Overruled."

"Is it not true that Walker did not die from his gunshot wound but died later in the Fort Yates's infirmary?"

"Yes, that's true."

"No further questions."

"Mr. Olson, you may cross-examine the witness," the judge said.

"No questions, Your Honor."

John swallowed annoyance. This trial was a total farce. He wanted to get it over with now.

"Solicitor Olson, you may call your next witness," the judge said.

The cavalrymen who had ridden with Walker each took the stand. None of them had seen Walker shot. None of them knew how John had gotten Walker's gun. John gritted his teeth so hard his head ached. Worry over Olson calling Shari to the stand turned his stomach sour. If Shari testified, he feared she would admit she had shot Walker. Did she not realize he was doing this for her? Shit! If she wanted to stay in this time so badly, maybe she should. She could raise Danny. She would make a good mother, but she had to be free to do that.

John closed his eyes and imagined Shari back at his ranch, Danny in her arms, her belly protruding with his child.

After a short recess, the defense called the cavalrymen back to the stand, but nothing was resolved because they knew nothing. So the judge allowed prosecution to call their next witness.

"Dr. Cynthia Pingree," Olson said.

John watched Cynthia walk to the stand. Poor Cynthia. She would lose her beloved position if she helped him. That would be very bad because the Lakota people, his people, needed her and because Cynthia truly cared about her patients. John met Cynthia's gaze and saw her eyes fill with tears.

"Dr. Pingree, who found Sergeant Walker's body?" Olson asked.

"I did," Cynthia said.

"You pronounced him dead?"

"Yes."

"Where was his fatal wound?" the prosecuting solicitor asked.

"Objection! It has not been established that the wound was fatal," Johnason stated.

"Sustained."

"In your professional opinion, was Sergeant Walker's wound fatal?"

Cynthia hesitated. "Any gunshot wound can be fatal."

"Explain yourself," Olson pressed.

"If infection sets in, any wound can be fatal."

"Was Sergeant Walker's wound infected?"

"Uh…"

"Answer the question," the judge ordered Cynthia.

"No."

"So he probably would not have died from the wound?"

"I don't know."

"In your professional opinion, what are the chances he would have died?"

"I don't know."

"I object!" Johnason roared. "Bullying the witness."

John knew Cynthia was afraid. He did not blame her. He was a hung man anyway.

"Sustained," the judge ordered.

Grunts and whispers sounded from the crowd, followed by insulting, supportive prosecution comments that disrupted the courtroom. Courtroom viewers rose and raised their voices.

"Silence!" the judge yelled.

"No further questions." Olson sauntered back to his seat.

"You may cross-examine," the judge said to Johnason.

Johnason took his time walking to the stand. "In your professional opinion, what do you think was Sergeant Walker's prognosis?"

Cynthia looked at John as tears dripped from her eyes. "Full recovery."

"So what do you believe he died from?"

"Suffocation."

The crowd reacted again at Cynthia's statement. This time the crowd shouted with angry disbelief. They stood and raised their fists. Some people threatened John.

"Silence or I'll clear the room!" The judge banged his gavel.

"Explain your answer, please," Johnason said.

"Walker was smothered with a pillow. I know this because I found a piece of a goose feather in Walker's throat, and his pillow was on the floor," Cynthia testified. She stared at her hands, clenching and unclenching her fists.

"I see. Do you think Walker was recovering up to the night you found his body?"

"Yes. His wound was healing."

"So someone with superior strength smothered him?"

"Well, yes."

"I object!" Olson stood up. "This is assumption."

"Sustained. It's a reasonable assumption," the judge countered. "Go on."

"How many people, besides patients, are in the infirmary at night?" Johnason asked.

"Usually just one, it's myself or an aid. That evening I was there."

"Did you see or hear anything unusual that night?"

Cynthia wiped at her tears. "When I was in the kitchen, through the window, I saw someone behind the infirmary."

"Was that person Caucasian or Indian?"

"I didn't see their face."

"How was the person dressed?"

"The person was covered with a buffalo robe."

"So the person was probably another Indian?"

"I object! Fort Yates is a military fort with people moving about day and night," Olson quipped. "The defense is just trying to establish reasonable doubt."

"Overruled.

"Dr. Pingree, please name the people you told about the feather in Sergeant Walker's throat," Johnason said.

"Colonel Drum."

"Only the colonel?"

"Yes."

"Was there anything missing from Sergeant Walker's personal possessions?"

"Yes. A white-handled knife that was on Walker's person when he was brought in," Cynthia testified, her eyes meeting John's again, silently asking for forgiveness.

Olson strode to a table in front of the judge and picked up a white-handled knife lying there. "This knife?"

"Yes."

"Objection! Anyone could have stolen that knife at any time."

"Overruled."

John closed his eyes and shook his head. Johnason sounded desperate.

"No further questions." Olson returned to his seat.

Johnason stood and approached. "Did you tell anyone about the knife?"

"Only the colonel."

"What did the colonel do?"

"Nothing," Cynthia said. "The colonel just said, 'Anyone could have stolen it.'"

"No further questions," Johnason stated.

John knew Johnason looked pathetic. He just wanted this over! He had to stop his loved ones' suffering!

The prosecution called Agent MacLaughlin. John was surprised when the Indian agent gave an accurate review of John's services. John knew MacLaughlin hated him because he always argued for the Lakota. His people.

To all other questions, MacLaughlin answered, "I don't know. I wasn't there."

The court recessed for the noon meal. John was handcuffed and taken to a small room off the courtroom. He was given a beef sandwich and hot tea, but he could not eat. He was terrified. Would Olson call Shari next?

After the recess, the prosecution called Cynthia back to the stand.

"One more question, Dr. Pingree. Have you ever seen the white-handled knife in anyone else's possession?" Olson asked.

Cynthia froze on the stand, her gaze darting to John. "Yes."

"Whose?"

"In John McIntosh's possession."

The courtroom erupted! Threats and curses toward John sullied the air. Some man yelled, "Hang him now!"

Cynthia hung her head and sobbed.

The prosecution rested. As Olson swaggered back to his seat, John felt the weight of the world settle on his shoulders. He gave in to his desire and turned around to look at Shari. As he gazed at her, she tried to smile, but he saw her lips tremble. He felt his heart crack wide open.

The defense called several character witnesses, all local ranchers John knew. The men spoke of John's hard work and kindness. But John knew it was useless.

Final statements were given, and the jury rose and filed out. Ten minutes later, they returned. The verdict was guilty. "John McIntosh, in the morning, after sunrise, you will be hanged by the neck until dead." The judge banged his gavel.

CHAPTER 12

THE SUN SET as Shari and Grandmother followed John back to his jail cell. The police chief fetched two chairs, and the women sat outside John's cell. "Would you like to see a minister or a priest?" the police chief asked John.

"Would you let me see a Lakota holy man?"

"I can't do that."

John nodded and asked for a priest.

Shari took Grandmother outside into the office area while John and the priest spoke. When they returned to John's cell, they all prayed. Shari was surprised John and Grandmother knew the words to the priest's prayers, and she felt embarrassed because she didn't.

After the priest left, Grandmother began chanting in her Lakota tongue. Soon John bowed his head and chanted along. Shari listened, finding their form of prayer heartbreakingly beautiful. She then prayed to any deity that might listen to their desperate pleas.

When Grandmother ceased chanting, she whispered to John, "Go bravely."

John kissed his grandmother's forehead. "Raise Danny to be a good man."

"He will be a man of honor," Grandmother promised. "Now I go back to nuns." Then she turned away and called for the police chief.

"You've got to leave too," the police chief told Shari.

"Please, let me stay," Shari begged, wanting every minute, every last second she could have with John.

"Just a few more minutes." John's voice was barely a whisper, but it echoed inside Shari's heart.

The police chief shook his head, and then he surprised Shari. "All right. But you, miss, have to step outside the cell."

Shari walked out of John's cell to stand in the shadow of the kerosene lamp hanging on a peg near the door. She heard the police chief lock the door between the office and cell area. Shari was finally alone with John, and she didn't know what to say to him. The love she felt in her heart mixed with the agony in her soul and clogged her throat.

"Come here, Shari," John said. As she approached, he withdrew his pocket watch from his trouser pocket and handed it to her. "Give this to Danny."

She took the pocket watch through the cell bars while she gulped back tears. She would not waste a moment. She would not cry. Snaking her arms through the bars, she pressed herself against the metal and reached for John. His arms encircled her in return.

Awkwardly their lips met through the bars, and they kissed, noses bumping. But still, they continued their embrace, lips and tongues searching and finding.

Shari felt John's hand slid down over her hips and press her belly to his groin. She heard his breathing labor and increase, becoming a pant. Shari felt his engorged manhood against her. John groaned in frustration as he attempted to reposition his lower body.

Abruptly he pulled away. "Go. I cannot bear this. Please blow out the light."

Shari walked to the lamp. She turned the wick down, putting the lamp out and dropping the cell area into near darkness. The only light available peeked beneath the door. She strode back to John's cell.

"What are you doing?" John asked.

Shari slipped her arms through the bars once more. Her fingers touched John's shirt, and she pulled him to her. "I'm not leaving you. Hold me, John."

Shari felt his arms encircle her once more, and they desperately kissed, fumbling in the dark to make closer contact. Lowering her hands, Shari pushed them between herself and John, and she opened his belt.

"Do not," he spoke into her mouth.

"Yes." She never broke the kiss.

Without hesitation, she unbuttoned his trousers. She felt panic driven, afraid of being caught, but desperate to be as close to John as possible. She slid her tongue over his again and again. Then she reached inside his trousers, beneath his cotton underwear, and found his penis.

As she wrapped her fingers around John's bulging shaft, he groaned and pressed his hips against the bars. Shari felt him remove one of his hands from her back, and next, she felt his hand fondle her breast.

"Shari, I cannot stop now," John moaned.

He leaned his forehead against hers as she stroked his engorged flesh. Darkness surrounded them, covering them like a blanket, offering them privacy, security, and one last chance to express their love. Shari knew if someone unlocked the door from the office, she would hear it and know someone was about to enter. But she didn't care. She wanted to give pleasure to John, to the man she loved.

She felt John open the buttons on the front of her dress. His deft fingers lifted her breasts out of her chemise, and she leaned forward, pushing her breasts between the cell bars.

Shari bit her lip to keep from crying out when she felt John's warm, moist mouth latch onto one of her nipples. She awkwardly held his head to her breast. Her legs went weak as she felt the hot rush of her feminine moisture coat the inside of her vagina. She loved this man. Oh, she loved this man very much.

John suckled her other nipple, and her quivering legs gave out beneath her. She slipped to the floor.

John followed her down, kneeling in front of her on the other side of the bars. "Shari," he whispered. "Lift your skirt and lower your drawers."

She did, tying her skirt behind her back. Then she reached through the bars, finding John once more. And he found her again too. Her fingers encircled his penis, and his fingers found her wet core and he pushed inside her.

They strained against the bars, kissing and stroking each other. When she thought she could stand no more, Shari's body convulsed, and lights exploded behind her eyelids. Then she felt John's seed gush over her hand.

Together they slipped the rest of the way to the floor, both sitting on their shaking haunches. Their hands held each other's arms, and their foreheads still touched between the bars.

"I love you," John said.

"I love you too."

*****

At the first rays of dawn, John awoke to the sound of hammers. He heard the strikes again and again, and he knew they were building his gallows. Shari slept on the floor beside him. His arm was between the bars, still holding her. They had shared her buffalo coat through the bars of his cell.

He felt surprised and grateful the police chief had let her stay the night with him. He lay on the floor and listened to the sound of his death approaching.

At full light, he gently shook Shari. "Wake up, Shari."

She stirred and opened her eyes. The love in her gaze shined as clearly as the sun, melting John's last ounce of strength. Before he shamed himself with tears, he pulled away from her and rose.

"You must go now."

"No."

"You must. I need to sing my death song."

"John, please." She reached through the bars, grasping for him.

He stayed out of her reach. He suspected the noose just might not kill him because his heart would implode before he ever got that far. He had to end her suffering. And his.

"Guard!"

"Noooo!" she cried.

The door to the office opened, and a burly policeman entered.

"Take her," John said.

The policeman approached Shari, and she hit him in the face. "Pete!" the policeman bellowed.

Soon another policeman entered the cell area. Although both were big men, Shari fought like a wild cat, but soon they pinned her between them. John turned his back for he could not bear to watch her struggle. However, he still heard her crying as the policemen carried her out. When he could no longer hear her sobs, he began his death song.

Police Chief Marsh and two officers came for John shortly after full sunrise. He was ready, for he had purged his soul as a Christian and also in his people's way. He stood. He would not keep his maker waiting.

A policeman handcuffed him, and under guard, John walked outside. The sun beamed brightly. He saw the gallows in front of the courthouse. The counterweight of sandbags looked to be the right size. John knew his neck would snap, and he would feel no pain. He would be free. All in all, it was a good day to die.

However, his heart pounded with burden because he knew those who loved him would continue to suffer. He resolved, in his last moments, he would make them proud. John walked toward the scaffold with his head held high, not glancing at the crowd lining the muddy street. He heard members of the crowd mumble, and once a man called out a snide racial remark.

Grandmother and Shari stood near the steps of the gallows with two policemen posted next to them. Grandmother remained stone-faced, but as he neared her, he saw tears on her cheeks. Shari stood somber and tearless. He was so proud of her. Her courage, her respect honored him. Their gazes brushed before he took the first step past her.

"Guards!" the police chief ordered. The policemen closed in around the scaffold and blocked Grandmother, Shari, and the crowd from the gallows steps.

John climbed the stairs and stepped on the trap door. His heart beat so loudly he could no longer hear the ugly comments yelled at him. He had served the community well, but now he was hated.

"Any last request?" Police Chief Marsh asked.

John shook his head.

"Do you want a hood?"

John shook his head again, and he closed his eyes as he felt the rope settle around his neck.

Suddenly, a shallow thud sounded beside him and made him open his eyes. He saw an arrow quivering near his shoulder, in the right post of the gallows. John heard the crowd gasp. A second later, another arrow landed and stuck in the opposite post, making a woman in the crowd scream. The whole crowd whirled around, shouting and fleeing in panic.

"The roof! Across the street!" the police chief bellowed above the cries of the hysterical crowd.

John looked up. Eagle Eyes stood on the roof of the mercantile. The old warrior's face was painted for battle, and he wore his ceremonial bonnet and dyed hide shirt. What was the old warrior trying to do?

Shots rang out, and John saw Eagle Eyes collapse on the roof.

"Go get him!" the police chief ordered.

In minutes, two policemen dragged Eagle Eyes off the mercantile roof and brought him to lie on the dirt in front of the gallows. Eagle Eyes's colorful fringed shirt was covered with his blood, and he struggled to breathe. John heard the sucking sound of Eagle Eyes's chest wound.

"Let me see him," John begged the police chief. "I am a doctor."

"No. We have a physician here. The one meant to declare you dead," Police Chief Marsh said.

"It is my last request!"

The police chief lifted the rope from John's neck.

"Please. Release my hands," John implored.

"No."

John quickly stepped around the police chief, and then he jumped to the ground.

The doctor, who had been standing in the crowd, came forward and knelt beside Eagle Eyes. He lifted the old warrior's shirt, examining his wound. "It's fatal," he said.

"Let me help him." John dropped to his knees next to Eagle Eyes.

"You can't help him." The other doctor stood and glowered at John before he walked away. Several officers gathered around John and the police chief, who came down the gallows steps.

Eagle Eyes opened his eyes. His pain-glazed eyes met John's. "I could not let you die for me."

With his hands still bound behind him, John leaned forward. "Save your strength. Do not talk." John stared up at the police chief. "Release me. Let me help him!"

"White Wolf," Eagle Eyes whispered. "I…kill Walker…for rape… Strong Flower and others."

The police chief stepped closer and stared down at the old warrior.

"A false confession won't work," the police chief said. "McIntosh is going to hang."

"In…legging. Knife…" Blood gushed from Eagle Eyes's mouth, and his breath gurgled.

Police Chief Marsh searched Eagle Eyes and pulled a white-handled knife from the lining of his right legging. Stunned silence enveloped the policemen gathered near.

John heard Eagle Eyes draw his last breath.

"Let him go." The clink of a key in John's handcuffs echoed around the gallows. John's hands fell free, and he reached forward to close Eagle Eyes's eyes.

CHAPTER 13

AT SUNSET, ONE week later, Shari and John rode into the yard of John's ranch. She and John were man and wife. They'd married in Bismarck with Grandmother as a witness. Shari wondered what the old woman thought of their union, but Grandmother hadn't voiced her opinion, and that was a good sign.

Shari and John were alone because Grandmother and Danny were staying with Grandmother's people. Grandmother would bring Danny to the ranch in the morning. It was Shari and John's wedding night.

John dismounted and helped Shari to the ground. When their eyes met, John smiled tenderly, making butterflies tickle Shari's insides. She didn't know why she was nervous. She wanted what was to come and the future they would have. Her dream had come true. Still, her insides trembled with anticipation.

"Go inside. I will bed down the horses."

John's voice sounded normal, but his gaze stroked over her face, and Shari knew he was thinking the same thoughts she was. Soon. Very soon he would physically make her his wife.

When she walked into the cabin, Shari found the house welcoming. A lamp burned in the kitchen, and the cabin smelled wonderful. She inhaled the aroma of a delicious meal baking in the coal stove oven. Grandmother had told them Black Hawk, who had been pardoned, and Strong Flower had been tending to the cabin and ranch chores. By marrying John, she now had family and friends, and her heart swelled with gratitude. She looked forward to seeing their family and friends again and thanking them.

But not tonight. Tonight was all her and John's.

Shari looked around the cabin. Home. They were home. She hugged herself as she stood in front of the stove, relishing the warmth, savoring the food smell, and appreciating the security of her future life.

When John came in, they needed to eat. So she unbuttoned her coat and hung it behind the front door. Eager to please her new husband, she went to work, performing her first domestic chores as his wife. Shari fetched plates and utensils, and she set the table. She checked the food in the oven and stirred the rich, meaty stew.

She turned when she heard John open the front door. She watched him take off his coat and hang it on the peg next to hers. When he faced her, she saw the bulge in his trousers.

Shari slowly raised her gaze to John's. "I thought we'd eat." She spoke in a whisper and wondered why.

"Are you hungry?" John asked, speaking in an equally soft tone.

Shari shook her head because she knew she couldn't eat a bite. Her heart beat so rapidly she felt light-headed.

"Good." John strode toward her, picked her up, and carried her down the hall.

He set her on the edge of his bed and laid her back, following her down across the width of the mattress. Then open-mouthed, wet and eager, he kissed her. Shari returned John's kiss with all the passion she'd stored in her heart. They kissed again and again until both were gasping.

Slowly John slid to her side, and Shari watched his fingers work to open the buttons of her blouse and chemise. Heat uncurled in her stomach, spreading to her fingertips and toes. Her breathing hitched when he pealed her blouse and chemise open. The cool air on her nipples puckered them in invitation.

John lowered his head and sucked her right nipple into his mouth.

Shari closed her eyes and moaned. Arching her back, she pressed more of her flesh into his mouth. She felt his hand slip beneath her, and she lifted her buttocks, giving him access to the button on the back of her skirt. She helped John push her skirt and petticoat down and off, but the action separated his mouth from her breast. The loss was unacceptable.

"John?"

"Yes?"

"More."

John's warm, wet mouth latched onto her left breast, suckling her harder, driving her mad. Shari moaned again and lifted a hand to hold his head to her breast. She felt his engorged man organ press against her side, leaving her skin wet with his preparation to be inside her.

John massaged his hand down over her belly, under her bloomers, where he boldly cupped her aching vagina. She gasped as he slipped a finger into her core. "Oh, John."

He lifted his head and blew on her breast. He gently rolled one hard nipple, then the other, between his thumb and finger, making her tremble. "You are so beautiful, and I want you so badly."

"I want you too."

John rolled away and sat on the side of the bed, quickly pulling off his boots. Shari heard each boot hit the floor. She saw his shirt fly across the room. Then he stood and looked down at her as he unbuttoned his denim Levi's trousers, shoving them to the floor with his underwear.

Shari stared at John's penis. She'd seen pictures, but she never realized how large a fully engorged male organ really was. His penis hadn't felt that large in the guardhouse cell. It had been dark, but still… Maybe John was overly large. Would his size help her conceive?

John's gaze scorched her. His penis grew even more, and Shari saw a white drop of semen on the tip. His sperm-swollen cock stood ready to impregnate her. Oh, she liked that thought. But his size gave her pause.

Shari knew where his penis needed to go. She needed to be naked. She began to untie the string at the waist of her bloomers, and she felt her hands shake. John pushed her hands away and completed the task, taking her stockings and shoes along with her bloomers.

Shari smiled coyly, wanting to beckon him but cautious because of John's male volume. She reminded herself this was what she had dreamed about. The emotion of love is expressed in the act of conjugal joining, a sharing experience of passion. Exactly as it should be. Exactly as she'd dreamed.

She raised her upper body on her elbows and started to push herself up on the bed, making room for John's big body.

"No, not yet." John knelt on the floor beside the bed and clasped Shari's hips. He pulled her to the very edge of the bed. Leaning forward, using his fingertips, John opened the lips of her female center and pressed his mouth to her opening.

Shari cried out as he licked her, probing her with his tongue. She had never read about this act, could not have imagined its intensity. She arched her back, pressing her head into the mattress as she undulated against his mouth, squeezing his tongue each time he wiggled it into her. She squeezed her eyes shut as he drove her near madness with pleasure.

She felt so hot. She felt on fire. "Please, John. Please…" Her body tightened. Light exploded behind her eyelids as her body convulsed.

John rose and placed one knee on the edge of the bed. He gently cupped her thighs and spread her legs. "This is the beginning of together forever." Lowering his body, he thrust his penis into her.

Shari grunted at the stab of pain.

John lifted his torso with his bulging arms and shoulders and looked into her eyes. "The pain will ease."

"It's gone already."

"Good." He kissed her mouth tenderly. "Are you sure you are all right?" She nodded. And then he began to move inside her. Slow, short strokes.

Shari's pleasure flooded back. Her desire built once more. She squeezed the muscles of her vagina, and she felt moisture refresh her core. "Oh yes."

John's rhythm quickened. His strokes became faster. He pushed deeper.

Shari lifted her legs and wrapped them around John's waist. She slipped her hand around the back of John's head and whispered against his lips, "Kiss me. I want more."

John complied. The bed rocked as he pushed his tongue into her mouth and drove his engorged penis into her body. The faster and harder he stroked her, the tighter Shari squeezed him until her love for him exploded in her loins again. She screamed in her joy.

John drove into her one more time, pressing his weight against her, forcing his manhood into her as deeply as possible.

Shari felt his penis jerk as he shot his sperm up inside her.

Then John collapsed beside her, and she hugged him close.

Slowly her body began to cool. Sex. It was wonderful. Better than she had imagined. She was a woman now. A wife. Maybe, John's seed was even now taking root inside her.

Close to noon the next day, after a night of lovemaking, Shari and John sat cuddled on the settee in the main room. Suddenly, the front door burst open, and Danny charged in.

"Papa! Papa!" The toddler vaulted forward on his short, chubby legs straight into his father's arms.

"Hello, Danny." Father and son embraced. "How is my boy?"

"Hungy."

John laughed as he rubbed his son's back in a second hug.

Danny smiled. His angelic face beamed as he pointed at Shari. "Pretty lady." Then he reached out for her.

Shari took Danny in her arms and held him close. He smelled like home, like love. Her heart did a flip-flop because she loved Danny as much as his father. She blinked back tears that flooded her eyes when John gathered them both close, and all three of them embraced.

At the sound of the front door closing, Shari sat back and stood. "Hello, Grandmother."

"You got anything to eat?" the old woman asked.

"Yes. We do." Shari smiled. Now the family was complete, and this family was all hers.

A short time later, they all sat around the table, eating and drinking and even conversing. Danny dominated most of the conversation with his mouth full. But it was so pleasant to be together that no one corrected the toddler on his table manners.

Beep! Beep! Beep! Oh no. Shari's spine stiffened. She froze with her fork halfway to her mouth.

"What is that?" Grandmother asked.

How was Shari going to explain her teleport disk? She didn't wonder why the presidents were summoning her. She knew. "It's a machine, Grandmother. Just a machine." She looked directly at John.

Shari rose from her place at the table, never releasing John's gaze. He looked worried. She saw it in his eyes. "It'll be all right, John."

"We will make it all right."

"What will be all right?" Grandmother demanded.

Shari swallowed. "Grandmother, I need to explain some things, but first I better answer."

She walked over to her buffalo coat, hanging on a peg near the door, and reached into a pocket to retrieve her disk. She had thought, married to John, she'd never feel afraid again. She'd been wrong. She felt terrified.

The blue crystal glowed in her hand. *Beep! Beep! Beep!* She turned around and looked at the anxious faces watching her. The faces of those she loved. She was not leaving them. Ever! She extended her hand and pressed a button on the side of the disk. A beam of bright light shot out three feet in front of her, and a square blue communication screen appeared between her and her family.

Artemis's image formed on the screen. "12101918, where are you? What is the status of your mission? Respond!"

Shari heard a thud. She looked through the screen at her new family, and she saw Grandmother lying on the floor.

"More! More!" Danny clapped his hands in glee.

John knelt beside Grandmother, but he stared at Shari.

Shari turned the disk around and faced the tiny hole that emitted the image of Artemis. She pressed a button in the rear of the disk. "My mission is complete. However, I have decided not to return. I am staying in the past." She pressed the button on the side of the disk again, and the blue light disappeared. She slipped the disk into the pocket of her skirt and hurried to John and Grandmother. "Is she all right?"

"Yes. She just fainted." Shari helped John lift the old woman onto her chair.

*****

The next morning, while Shari stood pumping water in the kitchen, to prepare breakfast coffee, the disk summoned her again. She whirled around and saw John's apprehensive gaze meet hers as he settled Danny in his toddler's chair. Grandmother sat at the table, cutting fruit.

"The demon calls you again," Grandmother said.

"He's not a demon, Grandmother. Only an evil man." Shari realized Grandmother didn't understand the technology, but she did understand the relevance. Last night, Shari had explained her situation as best she could.

Shari pulled the disk from her apron pocket. She feared Artemis wouldn't leave her in peace. It was best to face him, so she answered his summons. Artemis's image displayed his angry countenance even before he spoke. "Return now, 12101918, or face court-martial. If you do not return of your own free will, we will come for you."

John stepped up to Shari's side and put his arm around her as she rotated the disk. John ground his teeth so hard Shari could hear him. "Why can't you leave me alone? You have nothing to gain if I return," she said. "I will not obey your dictates."

John took the disk from her hand. "If you come here, you will die." He dropped the blue crystal on the floor and smashed it with the heel of his boot.

"The demon will come," Grandmother predicted.

"I think Grandmother is right, John," Shari said.

"Then he will die." John pulled Shari against his chest, and they clung to each other.

"You must fight him, White Wolf." Grandmother calmly reached for a loaf of bread. "It is the way of our people." Then she stabbed the bread with a knife as if it were a demon.

*****

After sunrise, the following morning, Shari rose to use the chamber pot. She hadn't slept all night. Worry consumed her because she knew Artemis wasn't finished tormenting her. How far would he go?

Then she heard Danny whimper.

As Shari stepped into the hall, she saw Danny's bedroom door close of its own accord, and she saw blue light peek beneath the door. The strong light glowed on the floor planks.

She bolted to the door and shoved it open to see the room whirling in blue light. In the center of the light stood a robot, and in the robot's arms lay Danny.

"Noooo!"

CHAPTER 14

"THE ROBOT LEFT this for me." Shari held up the blue crystal disk she'd found in Danny's crib. "I must go back, John."

"That does not mean they will give Danny to you."

"It doesn't. But if I don't go, I know we won't get him back. At least, if I go, there is a chance of getting Danny."

"And there is a chance you will never return to me."

"Yes, there is that."

John ran his hand through his hair, pulling at his scalp. Then he sighed and said, "You are not going alone. I am going with you."

"You could be killed."

John pulled Shari into his arms and pressed her head against his chest. "I have no reason to live without you and Danny."

She breathed in John's beloved scent. She had no life without them either. It was time to fight. In her time, there wasn't any belief in deity. However, she had come to believe in a power greater than man, and she prayed for help. She knew the technology of her time, and she knew man was not going to be their greatest threat.

Touching her face, John said, "I will tell Grandmother."

An hour later, Shari and John stood outside in the bright spring sunlight. They heard Grandmother inside the cabin chanting prayers. John had his Colt and his shotgun, his knife, and his bow and arrows. They stood face-to-face, so close their toes touched. Their gazes locked as they both held the disk.

"They'll be waiting for us," Shari whispered.

"They are going to regret meeting me."

Shari pressed down on the disk, making blue light engulf them.

*****

Shari opened her eyes, expecting to be in the teleport room. But they weren't. She and John still stood outside in natural sunlight. There was no dome. There was no teleport terminal. There was no city. She saw mountains and smelled trees. They stood in a clearing, surrounded by a midsummer forest in full foliage.

"This does not look so bad," John said, releasing the disk.

"I don't know where we are." Apprehension tightened Shari's neck muscles. Something was very wrong. "We shouldn't be able to breathe outside the dome."

"Who told you that?"

"Artemis."

John arched a skeptical brown at her.

Shari blinked in self-incriminating disgust because contaminated air was an obvious lie. The presidents ruled with lies. She suspected most everything she believed was a falsehood.

"Stay where you are!" a male voice shouted from nearby trees.

John whipped his shotgun to his shoulder, and he pointed the barrel toward the edge of the pine, oak, and maple forest.

Shari saw a group of men stride out of the trees. They were dressed in old-fashioned clothing, denim pants, like John wore, and shirts of varied colors. Some wore hide shirts. They carried guns. Huge guns. Their guns were aimed at her and John.

She felt perspiration under her arms and wanted to take off her coat. Wherever they were, the weather was warm, and the situation frightened her. She hadn't anticipated any surprise like this. What was going on?

"Drop your weapons, or we'll kill you," a tall, muscular Negro man leading the approaching group demanded.

John lowered his shotgun. "There are too many to fight." He lifted his Colt by its handle and lowered it to the ground with his shotgun.

"Kick your weapons away," the man ordered. John did, and then one of the men took John's bow and arrows.

When the man, who Shari assumed was the leader, stood before her, she asked, "What is this place?"

"Freedom Land," the man answered.

"How did we get here?"

"Helaine."

"Where is she?"

"She's dead."

"Liar!"

The man stuck his hand into his jeans pocket and withdrew a colorful gold ornament. Shari stared at it. He held Helaine's necklace in his palm.

It was true.

Shari couldn't breathe. Her knees wobbled, and she felt sick. John grabbed her before she crumpled to the ground.

The men surrounding them pulled her and John apart, letting Shari sink onto the lush meadow grass.

"Do not hurt her," John warned as two men subdued him and tied his wrists behind his back.

Two other men approached Shari and picked her up. She struggled against them, but it was useless. "Let me go! Let me go!"

The big Negro man stepped up to Shari and withdrew a knife. "Hold her!"

"No!" John fought to get to Shari, but the men firmly held him back. He cursed violently when the big man pressed Shari's head down and yanked her hair forward while the other two men prevented her from moving.

With the tip of his knife, the big man dug into the back of Shari's skull. She screamed as blood dribbled down her cheeks.

"I will kill you, you bastard!" John yanked and bucked, struggling to get to Shari. But his captors held him.

With the tip of his bloody knife, the big man threw a small shiny blue object onto the grass beside Shari. One of the men holding Shari released her and stomped on the object, crushing it. The leader pulled a red handkerchief from his pants pocket and pressed it to the back of Shari's head.

"Now you're free," he said.

The men restraining Shari released her.

She knelt on the ground, holding the cloth to the back of her head, and stared up at the Negro leader. Her lips trembled as she asked, "What was that?"

"Your tracker."

"Tracker?" Shari gaped at the man. She didn't want to believe the ugly thoughts of despotism flooding her mind, but she saw the crushed truth in the grass.

The big man spit on the ground.

Tears welled in Shari's eyes as pain of another, harsher truth griped her. "Helaine's really dead?"

"Yes."

The leader extended his hand to Shari. She took it, and he helped her rise. "Here." He handed Shari Helaine's necklace. "She'd want you to have this."

"Thank you." Helaine. Dear Helaine. Shari gritted her teeth and wiped away tears as she brought the flag pendant to her lips and kissed her reverent mentor and friend goodbye. "Artemis?" she asked.

"Yes."

Damn him to the edge of all the known galaxies. "Why?" Shari had to know.

"Because she helped you escape."

The men holding John released him. He strode to Shari's side. "Are you all right?" When Shari nodded, John turned toward the Negro man. "What is going on here? Who are you?"

"A rebellion is what's going on, and my name is Jacob." Jacob's dark gaze flashed between John and Shari. "We must get out of this clearing. If you want to live, come with us."

Shari felt John place his hand on the small of her back. She glanced up at him. He tilted his head to the side and gestured for them to go. They had no choice.

The group, with Shari and John in the middle, walked single file into the forest. Shari followed John. He carried their coats as they walked beneath the canopy of trees that offered cooler air and some comfort. The forest smelled moist and fertile.

"We'll be safer in the trees," John said over his shoulder.

Shari doubted they were really safe, not with a rebellion waging. However, she realized, if Jacob and his followers meant her and John harm, they could have and would have killed them when they were captured. Her thoughts returned to Helaine with many questions. Shari suspected answers lie with the men she followed up the side of a mountain.

Several hours later, the path became rocky and steep, and a roaring sound reached Shari's ears. She and John followed Jacob around an outcropping of boulders, and Shari saw a twinkling waterfall. It gushed out of the mountain, and it was breathtaking. The sun caught the mist, coloring the water with a rainbow.

The line of men halted.

Shari's feet ached, and her throat felt so dry it hurt to swallow. She saw Jacob put his fingers in his mouth and give a shrill whistle.

"Look," Jacob said to Shari as he pointed toward a wall of bushes near the base of the waterfall.

Shari watched the bushes part and the mouth of a dark cave appear. The group headed toward the cave entrance. The roar of the waterfall hurt Shari's ears as they neared the cave.

"Quickly!" Jacob yelled.

Two men held the bushes open while Jacob led the group into the cave's mouth. The same two men closed the wall of bushes behind them and sealed them in darkness. Shari turned around and saw a faint light from an opening a good distance ahead. The other opening appeared too small to pass through. But it had to be large enough for a man to pass, or why would these men be in this...tunnel? It wasn't a cave. It was a passage.

Shari's eyes had barely adjusted to the dark when she heard the scrape of flint rocks and saw a spark flare before a torch burst into flame. She saw a man, dressed like the other men, step out from behind a rack of torches. He held the lit torch.

"Welcome back," the man said as he passed an unlit torch to Jacob.

The man who gave Jacob the unlit torch dropped flints into his pants pocket and touched his torch to Jacob's. Sparks flew as that torch ignited. Then the man passed out other torches and even gave one to John. Jacob used his torch to light other men's.

"Follow me," Jacob said, glancing at Shari and John.

Several yards inside the tunnel, the roar of the waterfall lessened, and Shari heard squeaking and the flap of wings. She glanced up and saw bats. Her whole body trembled in repulsion.

John put his arm around her. "If you do not bother them, they will not bother you."

"You're sure?"

John nodded.

"Let's go home," Jacob stated.

"It is going to be all right," John whispered when he released Shari, as they started forward.

"How do you know?" she asked.

"They are taking us to their hiding place."

When they reached the other end of the tunnel, the opening was barely large enough for a man to get through. But as they walked toward it, Shari smelled smoke and food cooking. Her stomach grumbled.

A few more steps around a rock protrusion and natural sunlight beamed ahead of them. It was so bright Shari shaded her eyes. She saw John do the same.

When they reached the other end of the tunnel, Shari's eyes adjusted to the sunlight, and she gasped. A mystical, round valley spread out before her. Trees ringed the valley surrounded by mountain peaks. A river flowed through the valley, looking like a ribbon of blue in a green nest.

The men guarding them rushed down a steep path, and Shari realized they were eager to be home. Jacob waited beside her and John.

"Watch your step," Jacob advised. Then he led them down a path toward the valley.

Down and around a large outcropping of granite, Jacob carefully guided them onward. On the other side of the outcropping,

Shari stopped short and stared because built on the bank of the river, she saw a village of log shelters. She saw a thriving civilization of men, women, and children.

"Children! Who are you people?" she asked Jacob.

"Those are our children. We're refugees from Artemis's dictatorship," Jacob answered. "We worked in the diamond mine. But we escaped."

"Diamond mine?" John asked.

"It's several days southwest of here. Diamonds are the dome city's power source," Jacob explained. "Artemis sends any dissidents to work in the mine."

"Slave labor," John responded with disgust.

"Oh my stars," Shari sighed. "How could I have been so stupid?"

"I take it you didn't know about the mine?" John asked.

Shari shook her head. "I thought the city was powered by sunlight."

"It is. Partially. But diamonds are the catalyst." Jacob pointed to the log dwellings. "Come. My family waits."

"Have you ever been to the dome city?" John asked Jacob as they continued.

"Yes, many times," Jacob answered. "I was a conveyance guard. I led the convoys that brought the diamonds from the mine to the city."

"How did they do that?" John asked.

"Underground railway. Most of us were of the underprivileged class and lived beneath the dome."

Shari and John exchanged knowing glances. Jacob could get them in and out of the city, and she knew John realized it too. Now Shari understood why Helaine had sent her and John here. Helaine had been thinking of helping her even during her final hours. Shari's heart swelled with love and appreciation for the woman who had been as close to her as a mother.

"Come, let's eat," Jacob said. "I will answer your questions after our bellies are full."

A female Negro child darted around a dwelling and ran toward them. "Papa!"

Jacob scooped up the girl of four or five years and set her on his shoulders. "This is my daughter, Liberty."

Shari stared as other children ran to their fathers. "So many children. How?"

Jacob chuckled. "The normal way."

"Just where are we?" John asked.

"In a valley in the mountains," Jacob quipped.

"I mean…"

"I know what you mean." Jacob slapped John on the back. "You're in what was once called Arkansas."

"Are there many more refugees?" John asked.

"Yes," Jacob answered as he walked toward the cabins.

Jacob led Shari and John through clusters of people. Men, women, and more children seated together outside their cabins, sitting in family groups around cooking fires. At a fire near the river, Jacob stopped and set his daughter down. A tall Negro woman rushed to him, a welcoming smile on her face.

"This is my wife, Nola," Jacob introduced the woman. Nola held a curly-haired baby about one-year-old on her hip, and a male child about three years old peeked from behind Nola's denim skirt.

"Welcome," Nola said. "I have hot food."

"This is my daughter, Nyla." Jacob rubbed the baby's head. "And my son, Josh." Jacob tickled the boy, who giggled and darted behind his mother's skirt.

Shari watched the children. She couldn't believe her eyes. She wondered how long Artemis and the other presidents had been lying about infertility. And more importantly, she wondered why they lied.

Jacob took his infant daughter from Nola. "Please sit," he invited Shari.

So she did. She sat on an unusual carved chair. John sat beside her on a matching footrest. As Nola served them wonderful-smelling food, Shari wondered where the furniture came from and how these people had built this settlement. In fact, how had they escaped Artemis in the first place?

Jacob sat across the fire on another mismatched, carved chair and bounced the baby girl on his knee while his son sat shyly beside him on a blanket. Jacob bowed his head. "We thank our creator for this food." Then he offered the baby a bite of his food before he shoveled a heaping spoonful into his own mouth. He saw Shari and John hesitating. "You must eat. You will need your strength if you are to rescue your son."

"You know about Danny?" John asked.

"Helaine told us."

John looked directly at Jacob. "I am sorry for my threat toward you earlier. I did not understand."

"I know that." Jacob fed the baby girl again before taking another huge bite. "Finish your meal. Then we will rest. It will soon be nightfall."

Shari and John exchanged relieved glances. They sat eating and watched Nola ladle more steaming food, from a metal kettle hanging over the cooking fire, into her children's wood bowls. These people had food and shelter, a safe village in a valley. She looked at the wood bowl in her hand and wondered where it came from, where the metal kettle came from. How had these people survived?

John was not shy. he dug into his food with a metal spoon. "Mmm, beef."

"Yes." Jacob accepted another bowl of food from Nola. "It is. The animals are wild. Sometimes, we are lucky and capture them." The baby girl fussed, obviously still hungry. Balancing his infant daughter, Jacob stirred the food in his bowl, blowing on it. He again gave his baby daughter the first bite.

"Let me take her," Nola said, lifting the baby from Jacob's arms. She sat by their son and fed the younger child. The baby chewed noisily, reaching for the bowl. "Patience, Nyla, there's plenty."

Jacob smiled at his baby daughter's antics.

Shari's heart contracted. A family. She saw families seated all around her. The future surrounded her. She swallowed the lump of joy in her throat. The food she ate tasted delicious. Beef and vegetables. Finally, she found her voice. She looked at Nola. "This food is very good. Thank you. Where do you get the vegetables?"

"You're welcome." Nola continued tending to her children. "We grow our own vegetables."

"That's incredible." Shari looked at the spoon in her hand. She lifted the bowl and looked at its painted design. "Where did you get this bowl? And the cooking kettle?"

Nola smiled. "Much of what we have we have scavenged for. There is a deserted city nearby. Anything else we need we make."

"Why don't you live in the city?" Shari didn't understand. Wouldn't the city be safer? Even a deserted city would certainly be more comfortable.

"Our guests need answers, Jacob," Nola said.

Jacob swallowed a mouthful. "We cannot live in the city because of the robots."

"But the robots serve us. They help us." Shari stared hard into Jacob's dark eyes. "At least in the dome they do."

"Outside the dome, the robots kill us."

"What the hell is a robot?" John demanded.

After the meal, while the cooking fires burnt to embers and stars glowed above the tree-covered mountains, John imagined the potential of this place, this time. Shari had gone inside Jacob's cabin with Nola. Shari was enthralled with the children, and that pleased John. She had the potential to be an excellent mother. He believed it would be so, with Danny and any other children they might have.

"Lost in thought?" Jacob interrupted.

"Yes. This place is not what I expected."

"Good." Jacob rose. "I'll be right back. It's almost time to gather for evening tribute." He walked away and entered his family's cabin. When he returned, he carried a small bundle.

Shari came to stand beside John, and Jacob's family surrounded their father.

John watched as Jacob unfurled the bundle and held it aloft. It was an American flag.

John watched with interest as the villagers left their fires and congregated in front of Jacob's cabin. They stood proudly and placed their right hands over their hearts, even the children. John hastily placed his hand over his own heart. And he felt pleased when Shari followed suit.

Together, the villagers recited, "We pledge allegiance to the flag of the United people of this land and to the freedom for which we fight. One people under God, indivisible, with liberty and justice for all."

Shit, it still existed. And it was beautiful. John reached out and squeezed Shari's hand. He cleared his throat as emotion swelled within him.

Shari looked up at him. "Are you all right?"

"Yes. Very much so."

Shari pointed to a worn flag flapping on a wood pole. "Is that not the flag of your time? Your country?" Shari inquired.

"It is."

"That's amazing."

"Yes. It is." John squeezed Shari's hand again.

"Good night one and all." Jacob concluded. "Sleep in peace." Then he turned to look at John. "John, you and Shari are welcome to spend the night in our home."

"Thank you. We would appreciate that." John placed his hand on the small of Shari's back and guided her into the little cabin after Jacob and his family.

The cabin had a fireplace, which John assumed was used during inclement weather, a table and four chairs, and hammock rope beds. When Nola settled the children, John heard the beds crackle with a sound resembling the crisp chorus of corn husks. Could it be possible?

Nola offered blankets and a woven grass mat to John and Shari.

"Thank you." Shari lay the mat on the earth-packed floor and spread the blankets. When John lay down, the mat crackled, and he knew, corn or a derivative was definitely possible. He cuddled with Shari beneath the blankets as everyone in the cabin settled for the night.

The sound of silence should have lulled John to sleep, but it did not. His thoughts were of Danny, and his stomach clenched. There were robots. And robots were killing machines.

John gritted his teeth as a deep sense of desperation enveloped him. How far away was Danny? What kind of horrors was his son experiencing? John bit his lip to keep his terror for his son from exploding from his chest. His worst fear had been confirmed. The future was a hellish place. The robots were why the people hid in this valley, surrounded by mountain peaks. So the robots could not find them.

Even with the superior weapons Jacob and his men carried, they could not kill the robots. It just did not seem real to John. Even a huge locomotive could be stopped. There had to be a way to kill robots. Or he could not save Danny.

Jacob had explained his people risked their lives just to raise their own produce and hunt meat. They lived in constant fear robots would find them. In a time of such vast technology, John wondered, why were the robots programmed to kill people?

John's mind whirled as he contemplated plan after plan to rescue Danny. According to Jacob, Danny had been here, in the future, for several months. The change of season proved that. This place, this time, was hard for him to accept, but the evidence lay before his eyes.

"John."

"Yes," John answered Jacob as Shari stirred beside him to wakefulness.

"Some of us are going to gather food. The produce grows wild outside the valley. Do you want to come?"

There was no light under the cabin's threshold. It was still dark. But of course, he would go. "Sure." John pulled away from Shari. He figured it was time to prove himself. He suspected Jacob and the other men were testing him. If he wanted their help, he had to earn it. He would expect no less.

Helaine had been one of them, but Shari was not. Jacob had not given John his weapons back. John knew not only him, but also, Shari had to prove themselves worthy of aid. Nothing was free in life. Not his time or Shari's.

"I'm coming too."

That is my eager wife, John thought. *Good girl.* "Come on."

John and Shari followed Jacob and the other men to the entrance of the tunnel. Their torches were lit, and each person was given a large cloth pouch.

John saw some of the men carrying their big-ass weapons. "Stay close. Your eyes will adjust." John took Shari's hand as they followed the others.

They came out the far side of the tunnel and walked single file through the forest down the mountain, moving as quietly as mice. Finally, they emerged in a large clearing. John inhaled deeply. That smell. It was appreciatively familiar. They stood on the edge of a field bearing tall plants with long leaves and tasseled tops. As the sun peeked over the horizon, John saw it. Sweet corn!

"I know what this is," he told Shari. "Watch me." He grabbed an ear on a plant and cracked it off. "Just feel for the cobs."

Under a radiant sunrise, they set to work, and soon the harvesters had their pouches full. John looked forward to the meal the fresh corn would make. After only minutes, he and Shari started walking toward the edge of the field. Their heavy pouches were slung over their shoulders.

"Run!" someone shouted.

John's gaze darted around. He and Shari were about to leave the cornfield and step into the clearing. "Stay here," he cautioned.

In the next instant, the deafening sound of multiple weapons firing filled the air. John pushed Shari to the ground. The air quickly filled with smoke, and in moments, it stank acridly of gunfire and scorched corn…and burnt flesh. Images of another war, his war, flashed before John's eyes. Nothing had changed. The cause was the same. People of the future still fought for freedom.

On the edge of the field, about one hundred feet from where John and Shari hunkered down, a huge metal monster floated above the ground. The damn thing was twenty feet tall. The monster had arms and legs like a man, but its head was square, and its eyes beamed light at the fleeing humans.

Two freedom fighters stood on the edge of the field, valiantly firing their weapons. The guns spewed out, reverberating shots in streams of blazing smoke. John saw bullets from the big-ass guns Jacob's men fired bounce off the monster's metal body, making a pinging sound. "Shit!"

"Run!" someone shouted.

"No. Stay down!" John held Shari to the ground. He saw a blast of light and heard a humming sound whiz past their hiding place. Then someone screamed.

The humming sound grew louder. John craned his neck and looked up. A metal monster flew in the air above them. It had rotary wings on its arms, and it was flying away. Dangling from the monster's metal clutches hung the limp body of a man. John watched the monster disappear with its captive.

John and Shari rose and made their way out of the field. Soon people gathered and huddled together. The woman who stood closest to Nola was crying. John saw Nola attempt to comfort the woman while Jacob spoke with several men.

John and Shari approached them. "Is there no way to fight those things?" John asked Jacob.

Jacob shook his head. "It got Myles. Myles was the man who handed you the torch at the tunnel entrance last night."

"Let us go after him." John could not understand why no one moved.

"No." Jacob shook his head. "We could never catch the robot. Besides, Myles is dead. And we have several wounded needing care."

CHAPTER 15

THE NEXT DAY, John and Jacob and four other men stood in front of Jacob's cabin, discussing a plan. John wished they would get on with it. He kept a lookout for Shari because he did not want her to come along. It was too dangerous.

"Where are you going?" Shari's voice stopped the men's conversation in its tracks. She walked out from behind the cabin.

Shit! John turned to face his wife. "How was your bath?" Nola was supposed to keep Shari occupied. It was apparent that the stall attempt had not worked.

"Refreshing. There's a hot spring nearby." Shari approached with her arms akimbo, eyeing him up and down.

He was trapped. She could see he wore his Colt. He had his knife in his boot, and he had a rope slung over his shoulder. The other men were armed with the big-ass guns Jacob had said were AK-47s. "Just going to gather food."

"Yesterday, someone died gathering food."

"Shari, please stay here."

"If you go, I go."

"It is too dangerous!" John saw Shari's eyes widen at his brusque tone. But it was too dangerous.

"From what I've seen, everything, every day, every time is dangerous here."

She was right, but he had to try. "Be reasonable. If something happens to me, you are Danny's only hope."

Shari walked up to him. She stood toe to toe with him, cupped his face with her hands, and beseeched him with her eyes. "Together forever, remember?"

"I cannot do what needs to be done if I am worried about you."

"John, I'm not blind. I know what you're going to do and that if you can find a way to terminate the robots, there's a better chance of getting Danny back."

John shook his head in resignation. Shari was right. Besides, he felt guilty trying to hide his actions from her. So he reached out to touch the side of her face. "Please. Stay here. I am afraid for you."

"I am afraid for you too, John. But we can't hesitate now. It's the way to Danny."

What could he do, hog-tie her to make her stay? She loved Danny as much as he did. She was right. "Just stay in the trees and be careful."

"I'll try."

It was all she could promise, and John accepted it.

The group left the valley in search of a robot.

On the edge of the woods, John cocked his gun and gave it to Shari. "If you must, aim for the robot's head. If you can, shoot it in the eyes. Jacob says it is from the eyes the monster shoots its killing beams."

Shari nodded. Then she reached up and grabbed John by the shirt collar. She pulled his head down and kissed him soundly on his lips. "You be careful."

John pressed his forehead against his wife's for a moment. God, he loved her. Then they turned and strode toward the tunnel and the cornfield. Jacob and his men walked ahead of John and Shari.

At the field, they separated into two groups. Some men went with John, some with Jacob.

"I will wait for your sign," John called out to Jacob before they moved into the field about one hundred feet apart. There they waited.

Minutes ticked by, feeling like hours. Still John and Shari and the men they waited with sat silently. Because the robot had discovered the cornfield the day before and had found prey, John and Jacob agreed it would return. But the waiting still felt torturous. John worried continuously about Shari. He hoped she would stay in the trees, where he had left her.

Several hours later, John heard the humming sound of the robot's rotary wings. Anticipation heated his blood. It was time for battle. He would fight again in a battle for life, liberty, and the pursuit of happiness, but hundreds of years after his last battle.

"John!" Jacob called.

It was time to put their plan into action. About fifty feet apart, John and Jacob stepped out of the cornfield, revealing themselves to the robot. As it came toward him, John swung the looped rope he carried and prepared to throw. He saw the lights from the robot's eyes focus on him.

The noose of his lariat grew wider and wider. "Now, Jacob!"

Jacob and the men with him rushed out of the field. They opened fire.

While the robot closed in on John, one of the men shot his AK-47 at the robot's face. The man had been chosen because he was an excellent marksman, and his shots peppered the robot's face. The bullets bounced off the robot, but one of the robot's eyes shattered, Its eye light and its weapon blinked out.

The robot discharged its other light beam weapon, but it missed the marksman. John released his lasso. It sailed through the air and settled around the robot's foot. John yanked the loop tight. Two other men bounded forward and grabbed the rope with John. All three men pulled, weighing the robot down.

Jacob and his men burst out of the field, rushing the robot. They charged like frustrated bulls. The robot fought the tether line John and his two helpers clung to. The robot wobbled in the air, and then crashed onto the field, smashing plants beneath its body. The air filled with dirt.

The robot fired haphazardly, missing John's group, unable to attack Jacob's men. The robot revved its rotary wings, attempting to fly, trying to cut its rope bond with its wings. John and the men with him bounced on and off the ground while the robot continued firing from its remaining eye.

Jacob and his group, although they were in front of the robot, were close enough that the robot's light beam weapon shot beyond them. They rushed forward, attempting to secure another rope line to any of the robot's extremities.

Reaching the robot ahead of his men, Jacob tied the rope he carried around the other foot of the thrashing machine. The men with him grabbed ahold of that rope just as the robot's right rotary wing bit into the line that held John and his group. The rope broke, but a piece remained tied to the robot's foot.

"Shit!" John ran and jumped, grasping the dangling piece of rope. He started climbing. He had to get to the robot's head. He heard Shari yelling, but he kept climbing. When he reached the robot's chest, he saw Shari run out of the trees. But there was no time for her now. He kept climbing.

The robot fought the line holding it, stomping around the cornfield, fluttering above it, firing, always firing. John and Jacob and his men lifted off the ground and whirled on their ropes. The bottom of their ropes whipped the tasseled tops of the corn plants, intermittently striking the ground. Below them, John saw Shari reaching for a whipping rope. One strike from a rope could kill her.

"No, Shari!" John yelled.

The robot tilted to the side and dove for the ground, attempting to crush John under its wing. Jacob and his men dangled precariously.

One of the men in Jacob's group fell to the ground. Then another man fell from Jacob's line. John saw Shari grab the whipping rope under Jacob's men and run toward a tree.

"Hold on! Hold on!" John shouted as he saw Shari tying the rope Jacob's men clung to around the trunk of a tree. The robot saw her too. It launched a light beam directly at her. The beam hit the ground beside the tree, missing Shari by inches. "Shari!"

The last man on Jacob's line fell, screaming all the way to the ground.

John dangled alone in front of the robot as the one-eyed monster leaned toward Jacob's rope. The robot's wing saw buzzed. Neck high on the monster, John braced his feet and pushed off, and he let go of his rope.

He flew backward. Drawing his Colt in midair, he aimed. John emptied his Colt into the robot's functioning eye as he fell.

He hit the ground hard, and he saw daylight go black.

*****

"John! John!"

He awoke slowly. Shari sat leaning over him. Tears ran down her face. "Shari."

"I thought you were dead." She tenderly touched his face.

"The robot?"

"Down. You got its other eye, and Jacob's men killed it." Shari sniffled and wiped her eyes on her shirt sleeve.

"Good shot," Jacob said, stepping up next to John. "Can you get up?"

"I think so." John extended his hand, and Jacob helped him rise. "The other men?"

"We think one man has a broken arm. But that's not bad!" Jacob slapped John on the back.

John saw the monster robot lying on the ground. Lightless. Motionless. Dead.

John leaned on Jacob as they walked toward the downed machine. The other men stood around it, congratulating one another. They shouted a cheer in unison.

"You killed it." Shari hugged John's side.

"Without its laser weapons, it's just a clumsy machine. We'll dismantle its head and smash its electronic brain just to make sure. Then we'll bury it to keep the other robots from finding it and us," Jacob said, slapping John on his back again as the other men set to work.

Back in the refugees' valley, John and Shari helped the wounded men. Shari tended cuts and bruises, while John set a broken arm.

After the man's arm was splinted, the man thanked John.

"It is what I do," John replied.

"I know that, Doc. But you care," the man said. "My name is Samuel, and I owe you."

John shook his head. "That is not necessary. Just take care of that arm."

"I will. I'll remember this." Samuel extended his free hand, and John shook it. "Doc, when my arm's better, will you teach me that rope-twirling trick?"

"Of course."

"I'd like to learn too," one of the other men said.

"I will teach anyone who wants to learn."

After the men separated to return to their families, John and Shari and Jacob stood outside Jacob's family's cabin. John rolled his shoulders, trying to relieve painful fatigue and stress.

"John, let me get a look at your face." Shari reached out and examined his cheek. "You have some bad scratches."

He placed his hand over hers, and then he winked at her. "Be gentle with me."

Shari snorted. Then she laughed. Then everyone laughed.

"That was one hell of a fight," Jacob commented. "The people are indebted to you, John."

John responded with a shrug.

"I need to care for John now." Shari gestured toward his bloodied face.

"I know just where you can do that," Jacob said. "You'll need a lantern. Follow me to the river. That's where my wife, Nola, and my children are. We've dammed a spot for bathing."

Jacob fetched towels off a line hung from his cabin to the next, and he handed the towels to Shari. Then he handed John a lantern that sat beside the cabin door. "Take your time. Supper will be ready when you get back. And, John…"

John paused.

"Thank you. It's good to have a doctor among us."

"You are welcome." Damn, it felt good to be appreciated.

"John, when you're ready, I'll help you get your son back," Jacob promised.

"I would be grateful, Jacob."

As John and Shari followed Jacob along a path, John heard women and children coming toward them before he saw them. They sounded happy. Several women with children stopped on the path when they saw him and Shari. Jacob stepped forward.

"All is well," Jacob said.

The children immediately began frolicking again. John smiled. These were normal children playing and chattering as they returned for hot meals. These people's resiliency reminded John of his own people, now centuries in the past. He felt proud of what he saw, here in the future, and he wanted to help these people win their war.

"Oh my God!" a Negro woman exclaimed when she saw Jacob.

"Come here, Nola," Jacob said to the pretty Negro woman.

They rushed together and embraced.

Shari hurried forward to the approaching women and children. "All the others are fine. They destroyed the robot!"

Nola looked up at Jacob. Her mouth fell open in surprise. "Really!"

"Really!" Jacob said.

The other women pushed closer, bombarding Shari with questions. Shari proudly told the others about the confrontation. "All is well."

"Daddy! Daddy!" a little girl chirped.

Jacob picked up the little girl, about four years old, and cuddled her.

"Here." Nola handed Shari a bottle.

"What's this?" Shari lifted the bottle into the lantern's light.

"Shampoo. From the abandoned city," Nola spoke over her shoulder as the group hurried off to see their husbands and fathers.

John reached out and took Shari's hand. He suddenly felt eager to be alone with his wife. His aches were forgotten as arousal tightened his groin.

At the dammed river, which was a hot spring, they quickly undressed. John saw Shari's nipples pucker in the cool evening air before she stepped in the water, and he knew she had lovemaking on her mind too. They stepped hand in hand into the steaming water and sank below the surface.

John quickly washed away the blood and grim on his body. When he stood, he saw Shari floating on her back, gazing up at the starry darkness overhead. The lantern light cast a gold illumination over Shari's beautiful body, and the sound of the manmade waterfall draining off the bathing pond soothed John's mind and heart. The fear that had dominated his thoughts since they entered the valley washed away in the hot water.

John swam up beside Shari and stood on his toes, looking down at her. Her breasts protruded from the water, gleaming wet and inviting. Shari's facial expression told him that she wanted him as much as he wanted her.

He reached out and tweaked one of Shari's nipples.

She lowered her legs and spread them wide. John reached out and cupped her womanhood. Shari sighed when he slipped his finger inside her. He felt her squeeze. He ached for this woman. His woman.

Shari launched herself into his arms. Their mouths met, and their tongues tasted each other's in a kiss as wet as the water surrounding them. Shari twined her arms around John's neck and pressed her hard nipples against his chest as she wrapped one of her legs around him.

John's manhood lay between them, fully erect. He pressed his erection against Shari's belly.

"Now, John."

"Are you ready?"

"Yes. Oh yes."

He stepped backward for firmer footing but did not hesitate. He placed his hands on her buttocks and lifted her open-legged body to press her down and impale her on his throbbing manhood.

In the weightlessness of the water, John thrust deep into his wife. Shari clung to his neck as she threw her head back and abandoned control of her body to him. He watched her breasts bounce with each of his thrusts.

John drove into her again and again, confirming their safety, their lives, their love. With the muscles of her womanhood, John felt Shari clench his manhood. He gritted his teeth. Soon. Soon.

Shari cried out when her pleasure burst within her, and John slipped his hand up her back and held her tightly against his chest. Then he thrust hard one more time and released his seed.

For several moments, they stood in the pool clutching each other. Shari pressed her face into the curve of John's neck and shoulder while their hearts drummed against each other.

"I love you, John."

"I love you, Shari."

"You could have died," Shari whispered.

"Sadly, some things are worth dying for."

"Yes."

"We will find Danny. Then past, present, and future, we will be a family."

"John, I want a baby."

John began thrusting inside his wife.

CHAPTER 16

THREE DAYS LATER, Shari and John stood with Jacob and Nola at the valley side of the tunnel entrance. John and Shari patiently waited, with their hands clasped and fingers entwined, while Nola and Jacob said goodbye. Nola and Jacob embraced several feet away and kissed.

Jacob was leaving to lead John and Shari to the dome city. They were going to get Danny.

Slowly, Jacob stepped away from his wife. "Anything you want from the abandoned city?"

"Maybe clothing for the children." Nola gave her husband a wobbly smile. "Do you have enough food? Weapons and ammo? Rope?"

Jacob nodded.

"I'll see you when we get back."

"Yes, you will."

Shari saw Nola wipe at tears after she turned, and Jacob walked away. The woman's courage and unselfishness constricted Shari's chest with gratitude. Nola could have insisted Jacob order someone else to lead them to the city. Jacob could be killed. Still, he chose to personally guide them.

"We appreciate what you're doing, what you're risking," John told Jacob.

"I figure we *all* owe you," Jacob replied.

"Why do you think that?"

"Mostly because you reminded us of something we should always remember," Jacob stated.

"What is that?"

"Fight together and overcome together. Besides, I have a son too," Jacob replied.

Shari prayed to whatever deity was listening that no one died. She planned to rescue Danny, and then she would do whatever she could to help the valley refugees.

Heavily burdened with backpacks, they walked south that day and the next day until they left the mountains and came to a wide river. Shari squinted to see the opposite riverbank.

Late that night, as they sat by a fire in camp, Jacob explained, "From here we'll head southeast. This river flows into a much larger river, and at that confluence is the dome city. That confluence is the dome city's water source."

"Does this much larger river lead to the ocean?" John asked.

"I've never been that far, but it's what I've been told. How do you know?"

"A hunch. And schooling years ago."

Shari heard stress in John's voice. She felt concerned and very curious. There was still a lot she didn't know about him, and so she aptly listened as John kept talking.

"When I was a boy, there was a war. The Union against the Confederacy. North against South. This place, Arkansas, was part of the Confederate South. Your much larger river was called the Mississippi."

"So in your time, there was fighting and killing?"

"Yes."

"What was your war about?" Jacob asked.

"Freeing the Negroes?"

Shari watched John watch Jacob. She knew John's next words were vitally important. "When I was a child, Negro people were slaves," John said.

Jacob was silent for several moments. Then he asked, "What side fought for the Negroes?"

"The Union. The North."

"Which side was your father's side?"

"My father fought for the Union. My mother's Indian people did not take sides. All I remember is that before the war, Negro people were slaves, and after the war, they were free. Before the war, Indian people were free. After the war, they were not."

"Your childhood wasn't happy, was it?" Jacob asked.

"No. My father died from his war wounds. The government took me from my mother for an education, I was told. I lost my mother because of my education."

Shari trembled. A chill whispered over her skin, not from the cool night air but from farther away. Perhaps from the deity John believed in. John's words caused an ache in her chest. She bit her lower lip. Poor John. He'd been alone. At least she'd had Helaine.

*****

It took them five days to fell trees and build a log raft. Once on the water, the current ran swiftly. The first few days were wonderful. The water was clean. Sweet-smelling green growth covered the banks. They never found a confluence. They just saw mile after mile of river.

But then the river changed. First came a bad smell. Then evidence of long-ago habitation appeared. The river grew more and more littered with debris. Some objects were small, like old gasoline vehicles, and some objects were crumbled short buildings, their roofs jutting above a snarl of trees and shrubs.

Homes, Shari guessed. The river had obviously changed course over the centuries. *What happened to the families who lived here?* Shari wondered.

They navigated with care.

"Shari." John pointed forward several dawns later on their downstream ride. "Look."

Shari saw the sun rise, and a city appear out of the morning mist while she sat on the floor of the raft. Her mouth fell agape as they passed beneath a huge bridge. On the faraway shore, taller crumbling buildings jutted skyward. A city.

"What is that stink?" she asked Jacob.

"Man's debris," he answered.

166

Her excitement dwindled as more towering buildings encroached on the river. She looked inside the buildings and saw floating refuse.

When the raft bumped against a creaking metal structure, John and Jacob disembarked and tightly secured the raft against the current.

"I wish I could walk across that bridge we passed under," Shari said.

"You can't. Sections of it are missing," Jacob said.

"That is one big bridge," John commented. "Give me your hand." He extended his palm to Shari.

"Where are we going?" Shari asked as she stepped onto the structure they were using as a dock.

"Into the city to get weapons and ammunition," Jacob answered.

"And clothing for the children," Shari reminded Jacob, feeling her excitement return and effervesce.

"We must be careful. Keep your eyes open." Jacob handed Shari and John ammunition belts. "Stay right beside me," he said. "There was a zoo here a long time ago, and there are dangerous animals roaming around."

John and Jacob hefted their weapons, and the small group set off, walking uphill.

Shari knew the city was deserted, but the skin on the back of her neck tingled as they walked through the metropolis. Their footsteps echoed on cracked concrete, and her heartbeat thumped in her ears.

The glassless windows of empty, decayed office buildings stared down at them, accusing them of intrusion. Vehicles sat helter-skelter in the streets. Shari thought it was as if the drivers had abandoned them in haste and ran for their lives. It felt strange to be in her time, in a city without a dome. She wondered what had really happened in the first hours after the catastrophe.

"It looks like all hell broke loose here," John said.

Shari sensed he was right.

As they passed a building with mannequins in plain view, Shari stared at them. All were naked, but for one. And she thought she saw the colored eyes of that mannequin move. Ridiculous! She kept walking.

"Still want to go shopping?" John teased. "That was the largest mercantile I have ever seen."

"Maybe." She smiled but felt strangely nervous. "After we get Danny, he might need some new clothing."

"How far to this weapons depot?" John asked Jacob.

"Just a few more blocks."

Good, Shari thought. She didn't like this city. She felt eyes watching, judging them. Soon they reached a squat building, where Jacob motioned them forward.

"This was a police station. There are weapons in the basement. It's where I got this one." He hefted his rifle.

"Some of the men and I come here when we can for ammunition and weapon parts."

Jacob led them through the police station, which was filled with smashed furniture. At a set of steps, he told them to wait. He descended and returned. "It's safe. Follow me and use the handrail."

As they descended, it became pitch-black and cold. Shari gripped the handrail like a lifeline. She heard flints strike and saw a spark. Suddenly paper flared, and Jacob lit a lamp. He pushed a door open, and Shari saw an arsenal.

She helped quickly gather what they needed.

She felt relieved when they turned to leave the arsenal. They were loaded down with three new assault weapons and so much ammunition Shari struggled to walk up the steps beneath the weight of the ammunition belts slug over her shoulders. But she felt protected.

When they reached street level, she stood panting.

"Are you all right?" John asked.

"Yes. I'm fine." She knew they would need every shell she carried when it came time to get Danny. She'd make it back to the river if she had to drag the belts.

Shari gritted her teeth and followed the men away from the police station. Her stomach grumbled. There was food on the raft, tempting her. The thought made her pick up her step.

The sun hung in the west as they walked back through the mercantile district of the city. They passed the store where Shari had seen the clothed mannequin. She looked. The mannequin wasn't there. "John?"

The growl of a beast caused Shari to whirl around in fright, and she searched for the source of the growl, and then a scream fractured the air. A human scream! Out of the mercantile a young woman bolted. She was the mannequin. Behind her charged a big, striped orange-and-black beast.

John and Jacob raised their weapons and fired, and the big cat dropped. But the woman kept running.

"Wait! Wait!" John called. He dropped his rifles and ammunition belts. Then he ran after the woman.

"John!" Shari dropped her ammo belts and took a step after John.

Jacob grabbed her arm. "Stay here. It's too dangerous. John will get her."

Shari wanted to follow John, but she knew she might endanger him in his pursuit. She swallowed her apprehension. He'd be back. "What is that thing?" She pointed at the large, dead creature.

"It was a tiger. I think." Jacob lay his burden down and withdrew a knife. "Now it's fresh meat and a fine skin. Keep watch, Shari."

As Jacob skinned the tiger, Shari tried to stay calm, but she couldn't. She stood guard while she worried about John. He'd been gone too long, for it had been hours.

The sun had long set by the time Jacob was done butchering the beast. Beneath the moonlight, Shari finally saw John walking toward her with the young woman she'd thought was a mannequin. The young woman was bound by John's rope.

Shari smiled. She knew John had lassoed the woman. He smiled at her before she flew into his arms.

He kissed the top of her head. "I am all right."

As Shari stepped away, she looked at the young woman. The woman appeared terrified, and Shari felt sympathy for her.

"John, let her go."

"She will run."

The young woman's sad eyes pleaded with Shari.

Shari remembered awakening in John's cabin. She recalled her fear. "Don't be afraid," Shari said to the young woman.

The woman, not much more than a girl, struggled against John's rope. "You can't make me leave here."

Shari and John looked at each other. The young woman spoke English. Shari wondered why this woman wanted to stay with the beasts. "We want to help you," Shari said.

"There must be others," John said to Jacob.

"Are there others like you?" Jacob asked the young woman.

She refused to answer.

"I promise you. We can help them too," Shari said.

John released the trembling woman. "Run if you want. Just know we will not hurt you or others."

The young woman hesitated. Her gaze darted over her captors, but she didn't flee. "Yes. There are others."

"I will go with her," John said. "Shari, help Jacob take the animal meat and the hide back to the river. I will meet you there."

The sun was rising while Shari paced near the raft. This time, John had been gone for far too many hours. Panic clawed at Shari's innards. She stared at the black bluffs across the river. The image of John fighting the robot flashed through her mind. She shook her head, refusing to think the thoughts plaguing her. John was strong, brave, and intelligent. Any moment he'd return. They'd rescue Danny, and they'd have their life together.

"Shari!"

She saw John striding toward her from out of the darkness. A group of about thirty young men and women walked with him. He'd found more refugees.

Shari charged up the street. She jumped into John's embrace and rained kisses on his face.

"I am all right." He held her close and stroked her hair.

"You're sure?"

"Yes. Yes." They hugged and laughed.

When John set Shari down, she turned toward the young people surrounding them. She suspected they ranged in age from sixteen to thirty. Male or female, they were all overly thin, wore tattered, dirty white clothing from the dome city, and had fearful expressions clouding their eyes. They also all had wounds on the back of their heads, where their trackers had recently been cut out.

Several of the young women were pregnant. One was very pregnant. She looked extremely uncomfortable.

Shari wished it was her in that condition.

"How long ago did you escape from the dome city?" Jacob asked the group in general.

One tall young man stepped forward. "A week. Are you really from Freedom Land?"

"We are," Jacob answered. "Is that where you are headed?"

The tall young man nodded.

"You're going the right way," Jacob told the group. "Just how common is knowledge of Freedom Land in this city?"

"Many know," the tall young man replied. "But many who know don't believe."

Jacob glanced at John. "I bet Artemis believes."

"We are in big trouble," Shari stated.

Suddenly, the uncomfortable-looking pregnant young woman doubled over and clutched her huge abdomen. Water dampened the earth between the young woman's feet. The tall young man rushed to the woman's side and wrapped his arm around her shoulders, supporting her. "Zella, are you all right?"

Zella straightened and looked into the worried eyes of the young man. "I think it's time, Tomas."

Tomas paled.

John stepped up to the couple. "It is all right. I am a physician. May I help you?"

Zella's gaze darted to Tomas. He looked more afraid than she did. Zella nodded, and John placed his hand on her huge abdomen. "I suggest we find a place for you to rest."

"The warehouse," Tomas pointed behind them to a vine-covered concrete building. "In the warehouse, we'll be safe. We've stayed there before."

171

John turned to Shari. "I need to deliver a baby. Will you help me?"

John, Shari, and Jacob followed the group of young people into the warehouse. John saw big, motorized machines. Metal, wood, and broken glass lay strewn all over the floor. They stepped over the refuse and cautiously followed the young people down into a basement. There the young people lit torches, and John saw litter kicked to the side, evidence they had stayed here before, perhaps many times.

Wood crates were haphazardly stacked up around a hole chopped in the concrete floor. The hole was filled with ashes. A hole had been opened in the ceiling above. The hole was blackened from smoke. Blankets lay nearby, and cooking utensils sat stacked on crates.

"Tomas, set up a partition with some of the crates," John said. "For Zella's privacy."

"Uh, sure." Tomas set to work, but his hands trembled as he stacked the crates, and then he dropped a crate on his foot. "Ouch!"

"You all right?" John asked.

"Yes, sir."

John nodded at Shari as she helped him settle Zella on blankets laid out behind the wall of crates Tomas and Jacob were still erecting.

When Tomas dropped another crate and almost fell over it, John stifled a laugh.

"Something is wrong with Tomas," Zella said as she rested on the makeshift bed.

"I know. He is going to be a father," John said with a smile. "You just rest easy, little mother." To distract Zella, John asked. "Any problems with your pregnancy?"

"Um, no." Zella watched Tomas knock a crate off the partition he had just set up. As Tomas placed the crate back on top of the others, Zella said, "Ours was a forced mating, but we fell in love. We couldn't let them take our baby."

"Of course not." John understood completely, but he held his tongue. Now he needed to help Zella. Then he would continue his search for Danny. Because of these young people, John knew his son was close. "Tomas, I need you to start a fire," John said.

Tomas stopped arranging crates to stare at John. "What?"

"A fire. I will need warm water to wash my hands and to bathe the baby after it is born. I also need boiled water to sterilize my knife to cut the umbilical cord," John said.

"I want to be with Zella when it happens," Tomas said.

"I know. There will be plenty of time." John wanted to reassure the father-to-be. However, he also just wanted to keep Tomas busy. Thoughts of Danny's birth entered John's mind and heart. "That is enough crates. Right now you need to fetch the water."

"I can do that. I know where some is."

"Good." John looked at Jacob and arched his brows in silent communication. Childbirth terrified men.

Jacob nodded in understanding. "I'll help you, Tomas."

Tomas said, "I know where there are buckets."

"Good, show me."

"We never stay in the same place two nights in a row."

"Wise. I'm a father myself," Jacob commented.

"Really?"

"Yes. Twice."

"How did you live through it?" Tomas asked.

"It wasn't easy. But you will too."

Behind the crate wall, John said to Zella, "Breath easy, this will all be over soon."

CHAPTER 17

HOURS LATER, PRIOR to dawn, buckets of water sat fetched and boiled. John's knife had been sterilized. The delivery blanket Zella had smuggled out of the dome city lay ready. However, Zella still struggled in hard labor. The baby had not turned.

Zella grew weaker with each passing hour. Tomas sat beside his wife and suffered with her. John knew what he had to do.

He rose and walked toward the group seated around the fire.

"Shari, Jacob, come with me."

Away from the young couple, John said, "The baby is breached. You are both going to have to help me. Jacob, I am going to turn the baby. I need you to hold Zella down. When the baby comes out, you take it, Shari."

"I need to wash my hands." Shari strode away.

Jacob nodded.

All three of them walked to Zella's side. Jacob knelt near Zella's head. John knelt at Zella's feet. Shari knelt beside John. John squeezed Zella's hand as his gaze searched her agonized face. "Zella, I need to turn your baby so it can be born." John knew if he did not help her, both mother and child would perish.

"Do...do it." Tears streaked down Zella's face.

John glanced at Tomas, who sat at his wife's right shoulder. The young man swallowed so hard John heard him. "All right, Tomas?"

"Yeah. Please help her."

"Zella, this is going to hurt," John said.

"Save my baby."

174

John spread Zella's knees as wide as possible, and he slowly inserted his right-hand fingers up Zella's birth canal. Her scream echoed inside the warehouse, making Tomas toppled over in a dead faint. After John turned the baby, it slithered in a bloody mucus from Zella's body. The baby's first cry brought cheers from those on the other side of the crates.

A few hours later, Tomas once again sat with Zella and their newborn daughter. They huddled together, adoring their baby. "How can I ever thank Dr. John?" Tomas asked Zella.

"Ask his friend. Jacob will know," Zella said as she kissed the top of her infant's freshly washed head.

"I will right now." Tomas leaned close and kissed the fuzzy dark hair on his daughter's head.

Tomas rose and strode around the crates. Jacob was not with the other young people by the fire, where the night's events had become a celebration. Food and water were being shared and laughter sounded.

"Congratulations!" the group chorused as Tomas approached.

"Thank you," Tomas said to his friends. "Where is the doctor? Where is Jacob?" Tomas's eyes searched the darkness of the cavernous basement.

"He and Shari have bedded," Jacob said as he strode out of the emptiness behind him. "Are Zella and the baby all right?" Jacob asked.

"Yes. Fine. Jacob, what can I do to show my…our appreciation?" Tomas asked.

Jacob stood silent for a few moments. "I will take all of you upstream to Freedom Land, but John and Shari need to go to the dome city. He needs a guide." Jacob stared into Tomas's eyes.

"Why do they want to go to the dome city?" Tomas asked.

"Because Artemis has their son."

Tomas's eyes grew wide. "I know a way in," he said.

A little later, in full light, the expanded group stood outside the warehouse near the dock. Tomas held his arm around Zella and their newborn daughter.

"Be careful," Zella begged Tomas.

Tomas kissed his wife. "I will. I'll see you in Freedom Land." Zella nodded, and Tomas released her, then he turned and walked away.

John and Shari stood several feet beyond. They watched the young family painfully separate. "I cannot let him do this," John said.

"I know," Shari agreed.

When Tomas reached them, John told him, "You do not have to do this."

"Yes. I do."

"Go with your family," Shari encouraged.

"I'm going to help you get your son back. Without you, I wouldn't have a daughter."

John slapped Tomas affectionately on the back. "Thank you."

"No need. My family will be safe in Freedom Land, and that's what I want. Maybe someday, we'll even be able to live beyond the sand in the mountains or at the great ocean." Tomas smiled.

"An ocean? Are you sure?" Shari asked.

"Yes. I know others who have seen it," Tomas proudly said.

John looked at Shari. Her eyes were round as coffee cups. "Can we get into the dome city from the ocean?"

"No. Others have tried to get out through water tubes, but the water tubes are too long and too small. We'll go in through the air ducts. It's how we escaped." Tomas turned and touched his fingers to his lips, and then he blew a kiss to Zella. She returned the gesture as she, holding her baby, stepped onto the raft with Jacob's group.

"Tomas, I have some military experience," John said as he watched Jacob and the other young men and women get on the raft. "It is too dangerous to use the same route twice."

"Yes, sir. But I know no other way."

Neither man said another word. They both turned and watched the raft being poled upstream. They watched until it disappeared from sight.

"What did you name you daughter?" John asked.

"Joan," Tomas answered. "It's as close to John as we could get."

John felt a lump clog his throat. He had to clear his throat before he could speak. "Thank you."

Tomas and Zella had given him the greatest compliment he had ever received. This place, this time, was not so bad.

John and Shari and Tomas hiked off, each with an AK-47 over their shoulder. As they walked, the men conversed. Tomas was interested in history.

"So you had telegraph communication?" Tomas asked.

"Yes."

"What did your people do before that?"

"Smoke signals," John said stoically. "One puff for run. Two puffs for come quick."

Tomas smiled. "Sure they did."

"My grandfather did."

"I read there were telephones."

"There were." John smiled. "I had me one."

"Ah, Doc. You're pullin' my leg."

John laughed. "My people enjoyed burning telegraph poles just to piss off white men."

"Sounds like fun, Doc."

"I believe it was."

*****

Two nights later, John and Tomas climbed a steep rocky escarpment. At the top, they lay on their stomachs as John stared in disbelief. On the other side of the bluff, he saw the massive dome city for the first time. It was miles wide in circumference, and the dome rose several hundred feet into the air. It appeared to be clear glass supported by glass beams.

The city inside the dome sat on a sandy, treeless wasteland. No wonder the inhabitants believed there was no life outside the dome. All the inhabitants could see, looking out, was miles and miles of sand. John wondered if the barren land around the city was an act of nature or deliberately made. He'd bet on the latter.

Beneath a half-moon, Tomas led John and Shari around the bluff to a ravine at the base of the bluff's west side. A whooshing sound echoed up the walls of the ravine. "What is that?" John asked.

"An air intake fan." At the base of the ravine, Tomas led them to a large boulder. He reached behind the boulder and pulled brush away from the opening of the duct, exposing large rotating blades.

The blades were as long as John was tall. "What powers the fan?" John asked.

"Electricity."

"That is what I thought." John knew about electricity. He had seen electrical power used in New York City.

"This gets a little difficult. I'm going to lodge a stone on the edge of the fan housing to stop the blades. When the fan stops, we crawl inside the duct. Be quick. The fan is powerful. It can push the rock away, and if you get caught between the fan and the boulder you're going to lose something." Tomas gestured decapitation.

"We understand," John acknowledged. He stared at Tomas. "Just how did you escape?"

"We triggered the gate at the other end, jammed the inner fan, and one of us stayed behind to unjam the fan and relock the gate," Tomas explained.

John looked down at the AK-47 lying across his lap. The big-ass gun was not going to solve major issues ahead. He glanced at Tomas. The two men held eye contact, for a moment, before Tomas rose and ripped more brush from between the boulder and the duct.

Then John turned to Shari. "I want you to stay here."

"No." She shook her head.

"Shari, listen to me." John grasped his wife's shoulders and looked sternly into her eyes.

"Why do you ask this of me, John?"

He placed his hand on her abdomen. "In case my child is growing inside you."

Shari's mouth fell open. "I..."

"You never thought of that, did you?"

"Yes. I did. As much as I want your baby, I need to help you get our existing son back. John, I know where they're keeping Danny. I need to go along to lead you. You have to know, if you leave me, I'll follow."

"You risk too much."

"As do you. Together forever."

John pulled her into his embrace. "All right, Shari. All right."

"Are you ready?" Tomas asked.

John and Shari both nodded.

John and Tomas set to work, straining, sweating as they moved the boulder mere inches away from the metal frame of the fan. The duct opening was still tight.

Tomas grabbed another rock, about twenty pounds, the size of a man's head. He grappled with the rock, quickly yanking his hands back to avoid the blades until he finally wedged the rock solidly against the frame of the duct. The next blade that came around struck the rock hard enough to send sparks flying. But the fan stopped.

Tomas bounded over the boulder, crawling between the blades and dropping inside the duct. "Hurry!"

"Go," John said. He helped Shari between the blades, and then he squeezed himself over a blade and into the duct. He landed partially on top of his wife. "Are you all right?"

"Yes."

John rolled off Shari as Tomas reached through the blades and grab the wedged rock. Tomas yanked the rock inside the duct with them, quickly jerking his body backward. The fan blade immediately twirled.

"Ugh!" Shari squeaked.

"What?" John asked, alarmed. "Are you hurt?"

Shari shook her head as she pointed to a long, dark smear on the floor and more smears on the sides of the duct. John knew what Shari saw. Bloodstains.

"Not all escapes are successful," Tomas said.

"People are overly brave when they are desperate," John stated. "What happens to those who do not make it?"

"Wild animals clean the refuse."

Shari gagged. She put her hand over her mouth. "That is inhumane."

Tomas nodded as he set the rock down inside the duct. "We'll need this rock for on the way out. Follow me." Then he rose. "Hold onto the back of my shirt so we don't get separated, and keep your hand on the wall to guide you. Most importantly, be quiet. The duct echoes."

A few feet inside the duct, the natural moonlight faded. Pitch blackness loomed ahead of them. John's heartbeat accelerated for battle. He had his knife in his boot, his Colt sat holstered at his waist, and one big-ass automatic pistol was in his hand. Even though he was fully armed, he doubted they had enough firepower to defeat the robots. He silently prayed for luck.

As they walked single file, Shari held onto the back of John's shirt. The air duct was as dark as the far side of the moon, but it smelled fresh. She'd lived in the city all her life, but she'd had no idea these ducts existed or that there was an ocean nearby. Of course, the city's air and water had to come from somewhere. What a moron she'd been.

Shari chided herself again because she had trusted Artemis. She remembered his speeches. He'd told the people someday life might begin again outside the dome. She remembered looking out at the desert of sand and wishing for a better future. She knew, after radiation, it took many years for trees to grow. And now there were forests! For how many generations had freedom lay just outside the dome, just beyond the sand?

"Stop," Tomas whispered. "John, feel the wall. Do you feel the notches carved into the concrete?"

Shari heard John's hand slid over the wall.

"Yes. I do."

Shari huddled closer to hear better.

"The first escapees made these marks. It means we're nearing the filter."

"What does the filter do?" John asked.

"It's a large pollutant-catching screen. We must crawl through it."

"Pollutant catching?" John questioned.

"The filters are bug catchers. The filters are changed regularly, but they're just for show. The radioactive pollutants are just another of Artemis's lies."

"Radioactive pollutants are?" John asked.

"Poisons," Tomas stated.

"I remember Artemis ordering days we could not go out under the dome," Shari whispered.

Tomas snorted. "Now you know why. Filter change. If the inhabitants knew the air outside had purified years ago, most people would want to venture out. Don't speak anymore after we clear the filter. It's best if we keep our arrival a surprise."

"Definitely," John agreed.

Shari shifted the weight of the heavy ammunition belt she carried. She thought of Danny's cherubic face and bubbly laughter. Someday she and John would show Danny that ocean.

"Here," Tomas said. "Reach out. You'll feel the filter."

John stepped forward, and Shari followed, extending her hand. And she felt the filter. It was soft. She pushed her fingers into it. It itched!

"Don't touch it any more than you have to, and don't touch your face," Tomas advised. "Take a deep breath and crawl as fast as you can through it. You can't breathe the substance the filter is made of."

She couldn't breathe! Alarm tightened Shari's chest. Danny! How could they get Danny out through this filter? He's just a little boy. He wouldn't understand.

"Here's the hole we came through. Kneel down," Tomas told them.

"Wait a moment." John quickly pulled his belt off. He buckled the belt around Shari's right wrist and held on to the loose end.

"Stay close, Shari," John whispered.

John placed his hand on her shoulder, and she knelt as he did. She took a deep breath when John started forward. Following on her hands and knees, Shari crawled as fast as she could. Pollutants! Yuck! She kept her eyes closed so she couldn't see what she crawled through.

As she scrambled out of the filter, John pulled her to her feet. She opened her eyes to see John's beloved face. She smiled as she breathed deeply.

Whoosh! Whoosh! Whoosh!

Shari heard the deadly sound of huge fan blades. A fan stood right in front of her, only a few feet away. From the other side, light flickered through the twirling blades and shadowed the filter behind them with flickering stripes. How were they going to get through this fan?

CHAPTER 18

SHARI'S GAZE DARTED to John. She saw him point to the floor of the large room, and she saw him lower his hand. She understood and sat. They were close, and she felt slightly nauseous with concern.

During all her other missions, she'd never been this anxious.

She saw Tomas point to the left side of the fan, and then she saw hinges. Tomas pointed to the right side of the fan and inclined his head. He silently mouthed, "The lock."

John nodded as he lifted his AK-47 to his shoulder, pretending to shoot the lock. Then he held his gun out as if blocking the fan.

Shari understood the plan. They'd be a weapon short, and that concerned her. However, what concerned her more was the noise the shot would make. She knew after dark the city people slept but not the robots.

Bile rose in the back of Shari's throat. Without a doubt, the shot would bring the robots. She rested her head on the wall. She swallowed several times. This was a bad time to feel ill. She stuck her fingers into her ears and closed her eyes, preparing for the loud shot.

The reverberation of the shot hurt her ears. The clamor of an alarm sounded, and Shari knew the real danger was on its way. The robots' reaction to the alarm would be swift.

Shari peeked beneath her lashes to see Tomas shove the barrel of his assault weapon into the rotating blades of the fan. The metal of the next fan blade screeched as the blade caught the AK-47 barrel and pushed it down, jamming the fan.

Her heart leaped from her chest into her throat as she bounded to her feet. They didn't have long. The robots were fast. John jumped out of the duct. Shari followed.

When Tomas bolted forward to jump, John held up his hand to stop the young man. "Go back!" he yelled.

Shari could barely hear John's words, but she knew what he'd said. She looked at Tomas and saw a stubborn expression form on his face. The younger man shook his head. "No!"

Shari watched the expression on John's face soften and change to one of supplication. "Go to your daughter! You have no weapon!" John shouted.

Tomas smiled as he gave John a sharp salute. John smiled and returned the gesture just before Tomas spun around and dove toward the dark filter.

Shari rolled her eyes. The male gender! They were strange creatures. She wanted to shoot both of them. She wanted to kiss both of them, especially John, because he was right. He could not let Tomas risk his life any further. She felt proud of her husband.

She jumped to the floor a few feet below her. They were on their own. That was as it should be. They were parents rescuing their son, and she was relieved she no longer felt nauseated.

"Let's go!" she yelled above the alarm's din.

Shari and John ran side by side. They ran so fast their feet barely touched the concrete floor. The massive, windowless room lay filled with huge, noisy machines. Shari believed these machines were life-support convertors. These machines changed foul air into breathable air. These were the machines Artemis used to restrict and dominate life under the dome.

When they ducked behind one of the convertors, Shari looked at John. She closed her eyes and swallowed before she could say what she needed to say.

John waited.

"John, if they find us, I'll be the one they'll want to capture because Artemis believes I'm a traitor."

"I will not leave you," John declared.

Shari shook her head. "If you must, you must. Danny needs his father."

John pulled her against his chest and kissed her. Then he gently pushed her away. "Follow me!"

Shari had no choice. She followed John.

They sprinted forward. They were beneath the city, and Shari knew they had to find a way to the surface. Then she could get her bearings, enabling them to find Danny.

As she and John continued darting from each floor-to-ceiling convertor, they stopped to listen, to check for robots, and to catch their breaths before they dashed onward.

After they'd sprinted a goodly distance, Shari saw an elevator bank of three lifts. She pointed. "Electric lifts!"

"We could get trapped! A stairway will be harder for the robots to use!"

Shari nodded. John was right. She knew a stairway should be close to the elevators. As she and John peeked around the corner of a convertor, the doors of the middle elevator opened.

Two robots stepped out. They were the kind of robots Shari believed helped people. These robots resembled humans. They were four-limbed, wore uniforms, and even had simulated hair.

However, Shari knew these robots were not here to help. They had come to investigate the alarm, and she saw each robot carrying a laser gun. Each gun incinerated flesh.

As the two robots walked forward in their stiff-legged gait, Shari and John raised their AK-47s. When the robots reached the corner of the convertor bank, Shari and John stepped out.

"This is for Danny!" John shot the robots in their metalheads. His assault weapon blew off the robots' too human-looking faces. The robots danced around helter-skelter for a few seconds, and then fell to the concrete floor, convulsing and finally going still.

Shari grabbed John's arm. "More will come!"

"Look for a way out of here!" John yelled.

They frantically scanned around them.

"There!" Shari pointed to a recessed door about fifty feet left of the elevators. The door was painted the same color as the walls, but Shari recognized the zigzag emblem on the portal. "Stairs!"

She bolted for it, and John followed her.

When they reached the door, Shari stood in front of it and commanded, "Door, open!"

The doorway slid wide, and she and John raced up the steps.

Although John's long legs could have carried him faster, he stayed beside Shari. They stopped on the third floor landing at another door. There were no steps beyond. They'd reached ground level.

John leaned over the stairwell railing and looked down. "No robots," he said.

"They'll find us." Shari breathed deeply while she stared at the door before them. When it opened, they might be free to continue searching for Danny, or they might be melted.

Shari looked at John. He and Danny were worth any risk she had to take. She was expendable. But John had to survive for Danny.

John's gaze held hers.

Shari saw love shining in John's dark eyes. Strangely, she had never been happier. "Let me go first."

"Why?"

"So I can see where we are."

John nodded.

The door panel slid wide. No robots waited. No deadly laser beams blasted. Nothing happened. Shari peered around John. They were at a walkway boarding depot. The electric walkway moved before them. They had come further than Shari thought.

"We must be in a residential area," she whispered. "The walkways are smaller to take people to and from their dwellings and their work sites."

They stepped out side by side, and the door slid shut behind them. There was no marking on the outside of the door. There was also no handle for them to get back in to the stairway. The door color blended perfectly with the exterior wall.

"Door, open," Shari tested. The door didn't function. She saw a keyhole and realized she and John stood in a maintenance alcove. She doubted the people who lived in this area even knew about the repair site.

She turned to John. "Lift me up."

"Be quick." John lifted her so she could see between the belt drive and the walkway structure.

Shari looked around. "I know where we are. We need to go to the sanatorium, the medical complex. They'll have Danny there in isolation."

"How far is it?" John asked.

"About a mile."

John stuck the barrel of his AK-47 into the belt drive. The walkway stalled, and he lifted Shari again and pushed her out. He scrambled after her, leaving behind his bent AK-47.

"Lead the way, Shari."

Staying in the darkness cast by shadows of the cloud height buildings, John and Shari darted toward Danny.

Apprehension tickled the back of John's neck. He knew their luck would not hold. He carried the last big-ass gun they had. He scanned the terrain as they moved between the monolith structures. This was one butt-ugly place. No trees. No bushes. No green anywhere. Everything was white. This place looked sterile and cold.

John looked up. The dome's support beams appeared to be constructed of crushed diamonds. The beams crisscrossed under the dome and ran to the ground. He suspected the diamond beams had something to do with the city's power. If those beams were blown up, even one, the dome might crack, and the city might be taken.

A few minutes later, John and Shari rested in the back of a walkway boarding depot. Shari leaned against John's shoulder. She looked exhausted. He wanted to pray again, this time not for Danny but for Shari. He put his arm around her.

Shari whispered, "The next building is the sanatorium. I'll take us to the back entrance."

John wanted to kiss her, but he did not. It did not seem right to touch Shari with love when his heart and mind were prepared to kill. He hoped only robots would fall, but he would not let people stop him either.

He checked his big-ass gun. Jacob had taught him how to use the lethal weapon, and John appreciated the hell out of it. But he still favored his Colt and knife. With those weapons, he intended to take his son home.

"If we get separated," John said, "go to the conveyance and find a way out."

"That goes for you too."

Shari had melted his frozen heart faster than March sunshine on icicles hanging on the south side of his barn. "Yes, my little mother hen."

"Please don't tease me, John. I've never been this uneasy about anything. But then, I've never loved a child before. And I do love Danny."

John caressed Shari's cheek. "That is one of many reasons why I love you." He saw tears in her eyes just before she turned and ran.

He followed her. They darted into the open and raced toward the rear entrance of the hospital.

"Door, open!" Shari yelled at the glass entryway. The portal slid wide.

Bracing his big-ass gun against his shoulder, John followed Shari inside. He quickly scanned the huge entrance lobby of the hospital. It was bigger than Fort Yates. He expected people to be milling around or those damn robots, but there was no one, not a visitor or a robot in sight. He felt relieved there were no people about because he knew no one could be accidentally hurt.

But no robots humming around did not seem right.

John and Shari hid behind a larger-than-life statue of Artemis. They waited and watched. John saw chairs and settees. He much preferred the waiting room at the Fort Yates infirmary.

Neither human nor robot entered the lobby. With his AK-47 still tight against his shoulder, John ran across the lobby after Shari. He never could have done this alone. His wife amazed him.

"Elevators." Shari pointed at a row of a dozen lifts.

"Shari, this feels wrong."

"I know, but we can't stop now." Shari then pointed to another zigzag sign. "Stairs."

"Slow down, Shari."

Cautiously they ascended the empty stairway. Four flights up, they stopped and leaned against a wall.

"John, we're at pediatrics. Danny will be on this level."

John nodded. He braced himself, preparing for all hell to break loose. "Door, open," he said.

The fourth-floor stairwell portal slid back, and John and Shari stepped out. John held his weapon ready to send any and all to hell and gone. But again there was no one. Battlefield intuition shot up John's spine as he and Shari crept down the pediatrics hallway.

John peered into rooms on the right, and Shari searched the left. There were no doors, and the rooms sat empty. He saw no toys, no comforting blankets, just empty white cribs. Where were those damn robots?

Finally, at the end of the hall, John saw Danny through a glass door. Why did Danny's room have a door? The door was closed. John recognized Danny's long dark hair as his son lay in a metal crib. He aimed his gun at the door. "Door, open," he ordered.

Nothing happened.

John noticed Danny's room door had a lock. He touched the door and found the lock secure. His combat intuition blared like a Civil War cavalry charge.

Artemis knew they were here. Danny was bait.

It was definitely fight-or-flight time. However, John was not fleeing without his son.

"John, look." Shari pointed to a yellow light over Danny's crib. "He's quarantined."

Quarantined? A quarantine made no sense. There were no childhood diseases in Shari's future world. Not even a chest cold or snotty nose. There was little illness of any kind.

John saw the yellow light over Danny's crib change to blue. "What the hell is that blue light?"

"That's a sleeping beam," Shari answered.

John braced his feet as he pulled his big-ass gun against his shoulder. "This is a trap."

John fired, shattering the door and setting an alarm off. He and Shari charged into the room. They bolted to the crib where Danny lay, still sound asleep, even after the ear-piercing gunfire and alarm.

Danny lay curled in a fetal position with his thumb in his mouth. He wore a long white gown. His toes peeked out the bottom of the gown. He had no blanket. Danny never slept without his favorite green blanket. John remembered Danny's blanket was hundreds of years behind them.

Without a doubt, Danny's time here had been traumatic. Anger as dangerous as a charging Brahma bull surged through John's veins. That bastard Artemis would pay for mistreating his son.

Shari scooped up Danny and whirled around. John stood with his big-ass gun aimed at the doorway.

John heard a humming sound approaching. He knew that sound. A robot! "Duck, Shari!"

She did.

A nursing robot carrying a laser pistol entered Danny's room.

"Shit!" John blew the damn robot's head off. The sound in the room echoed dynamite loud. The air fogged with floating debris.

Without a doubt, John knew Artemis had planned Danny's kidnapping. He was not a betting man, but he would bet his ranch Artemis did not expect his family to survive.

Artemis had ordered the robots to kill them.

John and Shari ran. Shari ran in the lead, carrying Danny. John covered their backs, blowing another robot to pieces at the other end of the pediatrics hallway. They darted toward the stairwell.

"Door, open!" Shari ordered.

The door to the stairs opened, and John shot still another mechanical monster before the door closed. They ran on. Their feet barely landed on the steps.

John suspected there would be more robots on the ground floor.

At ground level, John and Shari leaned against the wall, breathing deeply, listening. John looked at his son. Danny should be crying, frightened from the loud gunfire, but he still slept.

"He won't wake up!" Terror contorted Shari's face.

Panic gripped John as he gazed at his son's beloved face. Danny's breathing was deep and even. His skin color looked normal, but parental terror still enveloped John. What had they done to or given Danny to put him so deeply asleep?

"Halt!" a mechanical voice demanded.

John and Shari looked up. A robot, another very human-looking robot, stood on the landing above them. The robot had dark hair and blue eyes; and it wore a nursing uniform, white, of course. Both its pants and shirt glowed with cleanliness.

"Humans! What are you doing?"

"Escaping," John answered, raising his big-ass gun.

The robot leaped off the higher stairwell and landed on John, knocking him to the floor. Shari screamed.

John struggled against the robot. It was heavy, and his big-ass gun pressed hard against his chest. His punches were futile against the synthetic-covered metal monster. The robot put its hand around John's throat and squeezed.

Dropping his right hand to his side, John felt for his Colt. His fingers touched his gun belt. With one hand, he held the robot off his chest, and with his other hand, he fumbled for his pistol. He found his Colt handle as his vision darkened.

"John!" Shari screamed.

John felt the robot's weight lessen. Then he immediately felt the weight lean slightly off his chest, just enough for him to grasp his pistol. With his last ounce of strength, he yanked his Colt from his gun belt and pressed the pistol against the robot's head.

He fired.

The top half of the robot's head flew away in colored metal pieces, and the robot released John's throat. John sucked air. His vision cleared, and he saw Shari on top of the robot, pulling the machine's headless shoulders back. The robot twitched, and John fired again.

The robot fell to the floor, dumping Shari. John rolled on top of the metal monster and brought the handle of his Colt down again and again, smashing the stub of the robot's head flat as a flapjack. The robot finally lay still.

"John!" Shari yelled. "Let's go!"

John leaped off the robot as Shari picked up Danny.

They fled with their son.

The alarm still blared.

Outside the hospital, people stopped and stared, but no one interfered. And no one offered help either.

John and Shari ran toward the walkway. When Shari began to lag behind, struggling to carry Danny, John took his son from her before he grasped her arm.

Shari had more strength as John pulled her along.

"There." Shari pointed to a walkway depot entrance. "We're desperate, John. We have to."

John knew Shari was right. She could not run any further. And Danny needed care. "Go ahead," he said.

They went down the steps and entered the walkway depot. The depot sat empty. "The next transport will stop," Shari told John.

"Can Artemis trace you if we use this transport?"

Shari nodded. "By my thumbprint on the boarding meter, and there are cameras and sound."

The depot door shut.

Danny still lay motionless in John's arms. John silently prayed again. He needed courage to face the robots ahead, strength to get his family back to Freedom Land, and wisdom to outwit Artemis. Not even during the war, under fire on the battlefield, had John felt so helpless. Fear and ineptitude overwhelmed him.

What had the robots done to Danny?

Just before the walkway moved, the depot door opened again, and three teen-age boys stood at the entrance. They stared at the AK-47. They looked at Danny who lay over John's shoulder. They looked at Shari whose knees bent, barely able to keep her on her feet.

"Are you from Freedom Land?" the tallest of the three boys asked John, speaking barely loud enough for John to hear his question.

"Yes," John answered. He handed Danny back to Shari, and then he primed his big-ass gun.

The walkway depot door buzzed, indicating closure. Shari held the door open as she watched John. She saw John look at the boys. The boys looked at one another.

"Do you need help?" the tall boy quietly asked.

The buzzer sounded again.

"Yes," Shari answered. Her voice cracked with emotion and fatigue.

"We'll help you," the tall boy looked away from the depot camera as he whispered.

"Thank you," John said, also looking away from the camera.

"Sir, point your blaster at me. So the camera sees," the tall boy whispered again. "And say somethin' mean."

"Stick 'em up!" John boldly demanded, scowling to keep the smile off his face. "Get us out of here!"

Each boy raised his hands and feigned shocked expressions. Then each boy pressed his right thumb to the walkway boarding meter.

John waggled his big-ass gun at the boys and yelled, "Get out! Or die!"

The boys nodded and trembled as if frightened enough to pee their pants.

Shari let the depot door close.

"Freedom!" all three boys yelled as the walkway moved away from them.

The walkway gained speed. Faster and faster it took them. Shari saw John's eyes widened.

Light and darkness flashed across the walkway as Shari and John and Danny passed depot after depot.

"John, we should get off the walkway. Robots will be searching for us," Shari said.

"Anytime you are ready."

Shari pressed the emergency stop button. The walkway stopped so short it almost knocked John and Shari off their feet. John appreciated the magnetic pull that secured him and his family. The walkway was much more interesting on top than it had been beneath. This place did have some good features.

Another ear-piercing alarm blared!

"Shit!" John blasted the floor of the walkway behind himself and behind Shari. The floor released them. "Jump, Shari!"

They did.

Hours later, John and his family hid in the dome city under a water viaduct. The moon reigned full over the viaduct. While Danny and Shari slept, John contemplated what to do when the sun rose.

The dome would keep his family safe from inclement weather and safe from four-legged predators. Outside the dome, nature controlled the weather, and people had to fight animals. But people could shelter from the weather. People could fight and kill animals. And then people could eat the animals.

To John's way of thinking, people had the advantage over nature and predators.

John thought Artemis and his robots made no sense. He knew Artemis was far more dangerous than the worst storm or the worst beast. What did Artemis want?

His instinct told him the dome was a prison. People were slaves.

"Papa?"

"Danny. You are awake." John looked at Danny cuddled in Shari's arms. His son's eyes fluttered open. Danny's eyes looked deep brown and clear.

"Home?" Danny asked.

"Yes, Danny." John reached forward and rubbed his son's head. He touched the back of Danny's head and checked for a lump, a tracker, like Shari had worn, but he found none. At least Danny didn't have to suffer the pain of a tracker removal.

"We were lucky," Shari said, cuddling Danny.

"Maybe." John gazed at his wife over the top of his son's dark head. Still, John thought Danny's rescue should have been harder. There should have been more robots, better security. His survival instinct screamed an alert. Shit!

CHAPTER 19

JOHN DID NOT sleep. He watched Shari and Danny sleep. Danny lay nestled against Shari's breasts. She held him close, giving him her body warmth. She was his mother now. John's chest tightened with disquiet because he loved them so much, and his instincts warned him that even greater danger waited ahead for them. Artemis would not give up.

John intended to let Shari and Danny sleep for as long as he could. He would wake them only when he had to, in a few hours. His main concern was how to get them out of the dome city. How did he do that?

He knew they must not get on the walkway again. If his suspicion about Danny's rescue was right, Artemis had robots waiting for them at the end of all lines. What was that bastard planning?

John and Jacob had discussed an immanent revolt. After what he had seen, as soon as he got Shari and Danny to safety, it was revolution time.

He listened and watched for an attack. Just beyond where they hid, lay darkness and very probably Artemis's traps. He intended to fight the robots with Jacob.

Later that night, Shari awoke, and she told him, "Whatever you're thinking, John, we won't go without you."

"I do not see an option. Shari, listen to me."

She vehemently shook her head. "We will not separate." She hugged Danny closer and glowered at John over their son's dark head.

John inhaled, ready for an impending argument.

Suddenly, the night air smelled different. The air moved as it was disturbed. A bird flew away from the viaduct. John jumped to his feet. He pushed Shari and Danny to the ground before he pulled his big-ass rifle to his shoulder. "I am armed!"

"Papa! Papa!" Danny wailed.

From out of the darkness a voice said, "Doc, you need to come with us."

"Who is there?"

"Don't shoot. It's Samuel, Doc. You set my arm. Jacob told me to get you out of here."

"Show yourself!" John demanded. He held his big-ass rifle tightly against his shoulder, ready to fire.

Four men walked out of the night.

When they neared, John recognized Samuel, and he saw Samuel's arm still lay in the sling he had put on the man. The other three men carried big-ass weapons, blankets, and ropes. And they all beamed toothy white smiles from soot-covered faces.

"You got your son, Doc!" Samuel said. "We all hoped you would."

John lowered his weapon. "It is good to see you, Samuel."

Samuel and the others walked closer. "Jacob thought you might need help gettin' out of here," Samuel said.

"Yes. We do. Did Jacob make it back with the group of refugees?"

"He did. He's a good man."

"He is." John knew he owed Jacob more than he could ever repay. "That was quite a surprise entrance you made."

"It's a lot easier gettin' in the dome than it is gettin' out," Samuel said.

"How did you get in?"

"Diversion and explosives, Doc."

"What kind of an explosive?"

"It's called C-4. I found it at the arsenal in the abandoned police station. Just a little makes one hell of a bang."

"I am certain it does."

Samuel pointed up. "Daylight is comin'. We better get movin'. The robots will be comin'. Why don't you help your wife?"

196

Shari accepted John's hand to rise, and then he took a yawning Danny from her.

"Let's get you folks outa' here."

"We are so glad to see you," Shari said as she followed Samuel, John, and Danny away from the viaduct.

"Hungy," Danny said. Then he sneezed, smiled, and stuck his thumb into his mouth.

Samuel stopped. "How about some granola, Danny?" he asked.

He turned around and approached John and his family. First he dropped a blanket over Shari's shoulders. Then he opened a tin and offered the contents to Danny. "Have some granola. It's dried grain, nuts, and raisins."

"Go ahead," John told Danny.

Danny stuck his hand into the tin and started devouring the granola. Gratitude and relief swamped John. He owed these brave men, and he intended to reciprocate their kindness. "Thank you. That was some entrance," John said as he patted Samuel on the back.

"My wife made that granola." Samuel beamed with pride.

"How is your arm?"

"Good, Doc. Now let's get you and your family outta here before we meet any robots."

"Do we have to go through the filter?" John asked.

"Nah. Not anymore," Samuel said, grinning from ear to ear like a boy with a new toy. "Follow me."

Samuel led them to the next towering diamond support beam, where he halted and pointed at the base of the dome. "Watch this." He tapped on the dome. Two taps then three.

John looked out, through the thick glass, and saw pink dawn peeking over the horizon. Then he saw the heads and bodies of three men appear on the outside of the dome, men he remembered from Freedom Land.

"Cover the boy, ma'am, and stay back until it blows, and then you and the boy go first," Samuel said, pointing toward the side of the dome.

Shari sat with Danny on her lap. The toddler faced her with his head on her chest and his little legs wrapped around her waist. Danny put his thumb in his mouth, secure in his mother's arms.

John knelt in front of them, leaning protectively over Shari and Danny.

Peeking over his shoulder, John saw Samuel walk forward and pull a length of what looked like smooth rope from around his waist. He stuck the rope securely to the side of the dome with a putty substance before he walked back to John and his family.

Samuel lit the smooth rope with a sulfur stick. The rope fizzled as it burned toward the putty. Boom!

"Gotta move folks!" Samuel called out. "Robots are comin' to fix the hole!"

Through dirty air, John followed Samuel as he led his family away from the dome.

When they reached fresh air, Samuel turned to John. "You and your family run. Keep going."

"I want to stay and help," John offered.

"No, Doc. It's best you go. Your services are too valuable to risk."

"You go too, Samuel. You're not such a good shot with one arm. We'll stay," one of the other men advised. The others nodded.

John glanced at Shari and Danny. His sense of duty urged him to stay and fight with the men who had rescued his family, but his common sense reasoned it was best he leave. Taking Danny from Shari, John set out with Samuel.

They made it halfway across the sand barrier before they heard gunfire.

"Papa?" Danny asked, pointing back the way they had come. "Notty bots come!"

Standing side by side, John and Shari glanced at each other. "It is all right, son. The other men will stop them." Danny clung to his father, and John's heart ached as he hugged his child. What had they done to his baby boy? "The naughty robots cannot hurt you anymore."

They turned and hurried away. They walked until they reached the forest.

When they stopped to rest and drink water from a metal jug, John tied the ends of the blanket Samuel had given Shari around his shoulders and waist. Shari set Danny inside the blanket pouch. From there, John carried his son on his back. As the group headed north toward Freedom Land, John felt a sense of going home.

It was late that night before the group stopped to make camp in a grove of pine trees, which bordered a swiftly flowing creek. They made no campfire. They were still too close to the city. The moon hung brightly above them, and the air that surrounded them offered the scent of green foliage.

"How's my big boy?" Shari asked as she took Danny from his father.

"Hungy!" Danny announced.

"I bet you are." Shari hugged Danny and fondled his dark hair. She hoped the men had more food. Her stomach grumbled as she worried about Danny. When was the last time he had eaten?

"I am going to reconnoiter the area," John said. "One of the men will stand guard."

Shari crooned to Danny as she carried him toward a blanket John had spread on the ground. As she set Danny on the blanket, Shari got a strong whiff of urine. "Oh, dear. Mama has to do something about your bottom."

"Mama!" Danny chirped.

Shari's heart danced with joy. "Yes, Danny. I'm your mama." She laid Danny in the middle of the blanket and set to work stripping off his sodden diaper. She dropped the offending garment in the grass. She was about to tear off a piece of blanket for a fresh diaper, when Samuel approached.

"Ma'am, Jacob's wife sent these." Samuel extended a cloth bundle.

"Thank you, Samuel." Shari reached up and gladly accepted the offering. She untied the string closer and dumped the contents on the blanket. "Oh my stars!" She smiled in delight and blinked back tears of gratitude when she saw toddler-size clothing and several clean cloth diapers. "Oh, Nola, you are a true friend."

"I have food too, ma'am." Samuel turned his back as he rummaged through another bundle. He turned toward them and handed Danny a piece of dried meat. Danny chattered in delight as he sucked on the jerky.

"Thank you, Samuel."

"Ah, it's no never mind, ma'am. The doc took good care of me. I'm just repayin' the favor."

Shari didn't debate with the man. She knew she would only embarrass him, and she was too appreciative to do that. She began tending Danny on the blanket. "I will have to think of something very special to do for Nola," she told Samuel as she looked through the clean garments in the bundle.

"You and the doc already have. I'll be fetching water now, ma'am." Samuel bobbed his head before he sauntered off.

Actually, Shari thought she liked the future she and John had returned to. It was totally altered from what she had known and surprisingly different from what she expected. There truly was freedom here. It just had to be secured. She believed the people of Freedom Land could do that.

Shari watched one of the other men cut up chunks of dried meat. Shari's mouth watered. "What can I do to help?"

"Well, ma'am. You can cut up these vegetables," the man said.

"Of course." Shari sat on the blanket, eagerly performing her task. While she worked and waited for John, she also waited for the men who had stayed to fight the robots. She prayed to whatever deity was listening that they all make it back to Freedom Land.

A few hours later, after a simple meal of cold jerky and raw vegetables, Shari lay on a blanket with Danny cuddled against her. John sat nearby with Samuel. The other men stood guard around the camp.

Samuel asked, "Doc, did you check the boy for a tracker?"

"Yes. There was none."

"That's good," Samuel said. "But that's unusual. I thought for sure they'd put one on your son."

"I will watch him carefully."

Apprehension curled around Shari's heart. She had no doubt Artemis was capable of anything.

The next morning, Shari awoke to feel Danny's warm body snuggled next to her, and she heard him grunting. He was trying to have a bowel movement. She smiled and lay still, not wanting to disturb him.

She looked over Danny's head and saw John again sitting with Samuel and the other men. The variety of male voices told her all the men were present. Her prayers had been answered.

Now they could go home to Freedom Land.

Danny grunted again, straining to pass his feces. Shari rubbed his head. "What's the matter, Danny?" She knew he was having trouble cleansing his bowels. "Don't strain so hard, sweetie. It will come." Again she wondered what he had eaten while he was held captive. She was sure his bowel movement was irregular because of the change of nutrition. Still, Danny had been in the future for several months. His system should have adjusted.

"Do you want to get up and have something to eat with Papa and his friends?" Perhaps something to eat would help him move his system. The thought of hot, cooked food tempted her stomach, and she heard her gut rumble. She was hungry a lot lately.

Shari picked Danny up, still wrapped in the blanket, and carried him to John.

"How is my boy?" John asked as Shari sat down on a log next to him. Danny stretched out his arms toward his father, and John accepted his son to cuddle him.

"He has a little constipation problem," Shari said.

"I can take care of that. What do you say we look for berries today?" John gazed into his son's cherubic face. Danny stuck his thumb in his mouth and nodded. "Then that is what we will do."

John looked at Shari and reached out to touch her hand. "I am sure it is the food Danny has been eating. Some fresh fruit will help." John tickled his son's belly, and Danny giggled, then he curled up on John's lap.

"Ma'am," Samuel said, "would you care for some hard-boiled eggs and dried beef?"

"Real eggs?"

"Yes, ma'am."

"Since it's spring. These are duck eggs," Samuel said. "They got big yolks."

"Yes, please, Samuel. Danny are you hungry?" Shari asked. She was surprised when Danny shook his head and stayed snuggled with John.

"Oh, I think you can eat a little," John encouraged. Danny shook his head again as he sucked his thumb. "All right. We will find you some berries later."

John was good for his word. He found berries a couple of hours later in a gulley they passed. John picked plump, juicy blue berries that stained his fingers.

Danny gobbled the berries down.

"He will relieve himself soon. Then he will feel better," John assured Shari.

That night they camped in a cave, the delicious smell of roasting wild birds and boiling roots filled the air. "Eat, son," John encouraged Danny. "Mmmm. Good pheasant. You like this." Danny shook his head and just sucked his thumb.

Shari tried bribery with sweet yams. "Danny, if you eat, we'll play." Still, Danny refused.

The worried parents exchanged anguished glances.

Danny tried again that night to have a bowel movement. He could not relieve himself, and he cried. John rubbed his son's tummy while Shari stroked his head. Finally, Danny slept, lying between John and Shari.

"If he does not move his bowels in the morning, I will make him a laxative. I hate to do that. But I am concerned he is going to become ill if I do not," John said.

Shari nodded in the cave's shadowy darkness. She knew Danny had to be starving. She had every faith John could make Danny feel better.

However, Danny still couldn't relieve himself the next morning. His whimpers tore at Shari's heart. The other men all tried to cheer the toddler, but Danny just wanted to be held.

John went in search of a plant he said would help.

The group patiently waited in the cave's safety.

When John returned before midday, he carried two different types of plants. One had no leaves. It had long, spike-like arms. "This is aloe," he said, showing Shari the plant as she held Danny, who wore tear streaks down his chubby cheeks. "This is rhubarb."

It was a tall plant with large leaves and stalks of green with red veins.

Shari watched as John cleaned the plants. He chopped several of the rhubarb stalks into small pieces, split the spike-like arms of the aloe and squeezed out a gooey substance into a kettle. With a small amount of water, he boiled the concoction. "I wish I had something to sweeten this," John commented as he worked.

"I have something for you, Doc," Samuel offered. "How about some honey?"

"Perfect."

When Danny awoke, he had a sweet drink waiting for him. The toddler eagerly drank it down, confirming Shari's belief that he really was hungry. So why didn't he want to eat?

"We can stay here for the day, Doc," Samuel said.

"No. Let us move on. Waiting here will not help Danny."

"Sure, Doc."

The group set out. Once again, John carried Danny in the blanket pouch on his back. Shari attempted to play with Danny as they walked, but the toddler acted listless and whiney. That just wasn't Danny's normal behavior. Shari could tell John worried too because she saw his clenched teeth grind beneath his cheek.

The group walked longer that day to make up time. At dusk, they stopped near a stream to camp. As the men gathered wood for a fire and secured the area, Shari placed rocks in a circle for the cooking fire. Danny followed her around, picking up pebbles in his attempt to help. Shari felt so proud of him.

When Danny bent and picked up a rock, the tooting sound of him passing gas reached Shari's ears. "What a big boy you are," she encouraged. Exercise would help Danny. "Can you bring Mama another rock?"

John smiled as he worked nearby, tying dried sticks to the wire Samuel was hanging. The sticks would rattle, if a robot touched the balustrade, and alarm the camp.

Shari and John both watched as Danny squatted on the ground. Danny closed his eyes, wrinkled his chubby face, and strained in an attempt to pass feces. Soon the stench of Danny's bowel movement filled the small clearing.

Danny stood and smiled at Shari. "Hungy, Mama." Danny giggled.

The tough, rugged men of Freedom Land burst into guffaws.

"I know, sweetie. I know."

Shari laid Danny on the blanket and set to work changing his diaper. "Whew, you stink, little man." Then she saw what was in Danny's diaper. "John!"

A moment later, John knelt beside his son. In Danny's feces-filled diaper laid a small blue tracker. John's face turned red as his blood rushed to his head. "Artemis will regret this. He will suffer before I—"

"John!" Shari stopped John before he said words Danny shouldn't hear, but she totally agreed. Artemis would suffer!

CHAPTER 20

WHISTLES AND CHEERS filled the air as John, Shari, and Danny and the men of the rescue troupe arrived in Freedom Land. Hugs and kisses followed as John and his family met Jacob's family in the middle of the crowd.

"Good to see you." Jacob slapped John on his back.

"Thank you for sending Samuel and his men." John's gratitude filled his voice. He did not think they would have made it back without Samuel and his men. What could he ever do to repay them?

Jacob tousled Danny's hair. "Hello, young man."

"Lo," Danny whispered, shyly eyeing Jacob's children.

John's chest swelled against his ribs. He felt so proud of Danny. The boy had been through so much, but he was still curious.

Tomas walked forward with his wife and newborn daughter, and John and Shari greeted them.

"How is the baby?" John asked.

"Great. Just great." Tomas extended his hand, and John shook it. "Thanks again."

John looked around at the beaming faces of the villagers and said what he feared, "Jacob, I think we have been followed." The words tasted bitter and sounded vile as they came from his mouth. Guilt sat heavily on his shoulders because he knew even unintentionally that he had endangered the people who had helped him.

"Damn!" Jacob exclaimed.

"Artemis made my boy swallow a tracker. It came out in his poop two days ago." John gritted his teeth as he watched the children scamper around.

"Down. Down." Danny squirmed, pointing at Jacob's children. Obviously, Danny's moment of shyness was over.

John stood his son on the ground, and Jacob's daughter came forward and took Danny's hand, leading him away to play.

"He'll be fine," Nola assured Shari, who looked on nervously.

"Let him go," John said, knowing Danny's mood and actions had returned to normal. He wanted to run and play and probably get into mischief. For the brief time, before the robots came, John wanted his son to enjoy freedom.

"Play nice," Shari told Danny.

"How long do we have?" Jacob asked John.

"I do not think much time."

Samuel walked up and concurred.

"Then it's war," Jacob said.

Samuel began calling the adults of Freedom Land to a meeting. The other men who had been in the rescue party helped Samuel summon everyone. When the people were amassed, Jacob stepped onto a tree stump and addressed the populace.

"My friends! The rescue party was followed. Doc's son was forced to swallow a tracker. The boy has passed it and will be fine, but we must prepare for an invasion." A rumble of concern rippled through the people. "There is no time to go for more guns or ammunition. We must fight with what we have. The invasion could occur anytime. We must fortify at once. Women and children must go to the woods."

Jacob turned to John. "The people have always known someday we would be found. This is not your fault, John."

"I still feel responsible and will fight with you."

Shari stepped closer and wrapped her arm around John's waist. "It's only right."

"John, you've renewed our courage. When they come, we'll be ready." Jacob extended his hand to John, and the two men shook. "Any advice you have will be welcome."

"Do you know what a catapult is?"

After the sun set that night, John sat next to Shari, hidden behind a huge oak tree on the edge of the village. Jacob and Nola and many others also hid nearby. Everyone except the children, who were concealed in the forest that ringed the edge of the camp, were ready for an attack. The Freedom Land children were guarded by Tomas's wife and some of the other younger mothers.

Fires burned in the camp as if everyone rested for the night, but no one slept. Each man had his guns and ammunition ready. Each woman was ready to load the big-ass rifles and provide first aid. The Freedom Landers were prepared for an invasion.

John held Shari close to reassure her and to keep her warm. His chest felt tight with concern. So much could go wrong. So many could die.

"The lookouts were a good idea," Shari whispered. Beneath the moonlight, John saw her crane her neck and look up at the men perched high in the treetops, ready to sound an alarm.

John looked up. "An old Indian trick," he whispered. Shari pinched his side. "Ouch." John chuckled quietly. "You are so fierce. Those robots better watch out." Shari squeezed his side. He loved her so much, and he wished she had gone with Tomas's wife, but Shari had refused as he knew she would.

"I love you, John," Shari whispered. John pinched her buttock, making her squeak in surprise. "Don't start something we can't finish." He heard the smile in her voice.

John breathed deeply, inhaling Shari's scent. He really wanted to make love to her, but that had to wait until after they won the coming battle.

He forced his thoughts back to the attack ahead. John hoped they had enough fighting supplies. Guns and ammo and ropes were essential to their defense, as was the makeshift wagon wheel catapult loaded with boulders that sat a short distance in front of the trees.

Everyone waited in the darkness, and John knew the hearts of these people beat in unison. He felt proud to be with them.

The sound of rocks thumping to the ground echoed through the forest. It was the signal! The lookouts in the trees had spotted robots approaching and dropped the rocks.

"Go," John said to Shari. "Be safe." Then he heard Nola scramble from her nearby hiding place. Two mothers fighting for their children. He prayed to whatever Great Spirit was listening that all would survive.

John strained his eyes for one more glimpse of his wife, but she had been absorbed into the forest darkness. Shari and Nola had an important task to perform.

First John heard the humming sound of robots, and then he spotted the robots' lights off in the distant sky. He hoped Artemis was with his monster machines. But he doubted it. John wanted to kill Artemis up close and personally. He watched the robots fly closer, and he fingered the rope in his hand. His lasso lay ready.

John trusted the Freedom Landers to wait for the signal. Soon. Soon.

As four of the heinous machines passed over Jacob's hiding place, Jacob yelled, "Now!"

John heard the creak of wood and the screech of metal as Shari and Nola released the catapult's bound arm. The arm rose and flung the rocks in the basket through the air. The pinging sounds of rocks hitting robotic metal reverberated through the valley. The boulders striking the clustered robots knocked them to the floor of the valley.

Then all hell broke loose. Men in the trees, hanging from ropes, swung out of the trees and dropped fishing nets over the downed robots. The robots thrashed about, fighting the restraint.

John knew the nets wouldn't last long. "Iiieee!" he yelled his war cry as he ran forward.

Men on the ground charged forward with big-ass guns.

The robots' laser lights radically bounced off tree trunks and into the sky. Blasts of gunfire blared, and the smell of spent ammunition stung fighters' noses.

One by one the robots' lights blinked out, until the forest stood dark again.

Then villagers' torches flared, and men burst out of the woods. Soon crunching metal echoed through the valley as men pounced like dark wraiths onto the robots and smashed the robots' heads with rocks and clubs. They worked in groups. Each group concentrated on a robot.

The attack ended as fast as it began.

Each group leader called out the status of his group. No one was killed. No one was hurt. More torches burst to life and dirt-smeared faces appeared. White smiles spread. Shouts of joy rose to the tops of the trees as everyone rejoiced.

"Shari! Shari!" John called. He heard no reply. "Shari!"

Suddenly a robot rose into the air. It had no light shining from its eyes or on its body. John saw it wobbled above the refugees' heads as it flew away. Everyone stared up at the crippled robot. The men raised their weapons, but then they halted because everyone saw an unconscious woman in the robot's clutches.

John gasped when the moon's light revealed the woman was Shari. "No!"

"Why is it taking Shari?" Jacob asked.

John knew. Because Artemis ordered the damn monsters to take her. Dead or alive, Artemis wanted revenge.

CHAPTER 21

SHARI FIRST HEARD the humming, clicking mechanical sound of robots, and then she smelled the sterile sheet covering her body, and next she tasted sticky cellulose tape over her mouth. Then she remembered the attack and the robot she thought was terminated, but wasn't.

There was only one place she could be, the sanatorium. She gritted her teeth, inhaling slowly. She had to think before she reacted.

She kept her eyes closed. It was best if the robots didn't know she was awake. Gingerly she tried to move her arms but couldn't. Her legs were strapped down too.

John and Danny? The others? What had happened to them? Shari bit the inside of her cheek to keep her panic in check. She felt a single tear leak from her right eye.

"So you're awake."

Shari opened her eyes.

Artemis stood by her bed. She glared at him as he reached forward and yanked the tape off her lips.

"I'm going to make you sorry you brought me back here," she promised.

Artemis rolled back his gray-haired head and laughed. "I doubt that."

Shari yanked at her restraints. "John will come for me, and he'll kill you if I haven't."

Artemis leaned over her and slapped the cellulose back over her mouth. "No, you won't. And if he comes, he'll die."

Shari yanked her restraints again, cursing Artemis beneath the binding over her mouth.

"Calm down, or I'll have you sedated."

Inhaling slowly through her nose, Shari stared her hatred at the dictator.

"I'll tell you what you will do. First, you'll abort the embryo you're carrying and then—"

"No!"

"Yes. You're pregnant. And I can't have that. Besides, I want my child to be female, and the embryo of that barbaric man is male."

Shari thrashed violently. She didn't know she had conceived. Now Artemis intended to kill her baby! John's son!

"Then…you'll be impregnated with my sperm."

Shari screamed against the cellulose tape.

Artemis opened his white shirt, surprising Shari. She quieted and stared at the clear artificial shell covering what should have been Artemis's chest. She saw a mechanical heart beating beneath the shell. Her gaze darted to the dictator's face.

"I'm dying, and I don't want to. I'm afraid I made too many trips to the past, and I've caught some nasty disease. In the middle ages I believe. No matter. After you bear the infant from my sperm, I'll have my mind transplanted into the child. I will be able to reproduce myself over and over again. I will live forever."

Artemis was insane! Shari's stomach rolled, and she gagged behind the binding over her mouth. Artemis reached out and yanked the tape off her mouth again.

Shari rolled on her side and vomited on the floor.

"Disgusting!" Artemis sneered. "Bot! Clean up!" Then Artemis whirled around and strode from the room.

*****

Several hours later, Shari awoke again. *Hum. Hum. Click. Click.* Oh no. It wasn't a bad dream. She really was in the dome city and in the sanatorium. And a robot was coming!

Shari tried to move her arms. She was restrained. She tried to move her legs. Her legs were restrained too. She was trapped like an animal. Whatever she did, it had to be now. Her baby, John's baby, must live.

As the robot came closer, Shari feigned sleep. She heard the robot enter her room. She felt cold metal fingers touch her arm, checking her temperature and heart rate. It was now or never.

She bit the inside of her lip and let blood run out the side of her mouth. Opening her eyes, she gagged. "Help." She gagged again. Biting herself deeper, Shari spit more blood, and then she bucked convulsively.

Then Shari suddenly stilled and lay motionless as if she had fainted. She held her breath. The robot immediately released her restraints.

Shari bolted upright and shoved her fingers into the robot's eyes, and she pushed the robot's eyes into its mechanical brain before she shoved it away.

The robot fell back, screeching and jerking from damaged wiring. The robot dropped the syringe it held onto the floor. Shari jumped from the bed. She grabbed the syringe before she charged out the sanatorium room. As she ran, she slipped the metal-tipped syringe inside the trousers she still wore.

She heard an alarm sound, and she knew robots would come from everywhere. They did. Shari darted and ducked. She hit and kicked, but she didn't get far. She screamed as the robots captured her.

Within minutes, she was back in the same sanatorium room, back on the same bed, and struggling against two robots trying to strap her down and make her helpless once more. The robots ignored her as tears ran down her face.

"Stop it!" Artemis stepped in the doorway. As he walked forward, he said, "Stop it or die."

Shari stilled.

The two robots held her motionless, powerless, and desperate.

"I rule here and I will rule everywhere. I have already killed some of the world leaders to gain control. There are other cities, you know, many others. No one can stop me!" Artemis bragged.

"No," Shari whimpered. "Please don't do this."

Artemis slapped Shari across the face, making her ears ring.

"Give me a syringe," Artemis ordered a robot.

One of the robots turned to hand Artemis a syringe.

When the robot extended the syringe toward Artemis, its hold on Shari lessened. Shari bolted upright groping for the sedative-filled syringe. She managed to yank the syringe from the robot before she was flat on her back once more.

A robot took the syringe from her.

Shari saw Artemis grow red in the face. "If you try anything like that again, I'm going to kill you!" He hit her again and again and again.

CHAPTER 22

BEFORE DAWN, THREE days after the attack on the village, John and Jacob, with Samuel and Tomas, crab-crawled across the sand toward the west side of the dome city. John had planned this attack with the diligence of General Grant, and he had come bearing enough weaponry to kill bear.

From the arsenal in the abandoned city, John had an egg basket full of rectangular C-4 blocks, which Samuel had become fond of using. If the South had been this prepared, the Confederacy would have beaten the Union.

Several methods of Lakota torture flashed through John's mind as he neared the base of the dome. He intended to use those torture methods on Artemis.

John had been a man of healing, a man of peace, when he had fought slavery. It had not even been his fight, but he made it his fight because he knew what slavery did to mankind.

This fight was again for freedom, but this time it was personal. John fought to save his wife, and he justifiably anticipated killing Artemis for hurting Danny.

"That way," John whispered to Jacob as he pointed along the edge of the dome. "Plant it about one hundred feet from me."

"I got it," Jacob confirmed. "Samuel, stay with John."

John watched Jacob and Tomas crawl away. Soon he saw Jacob and Tomas placing their explosives.

John knew another group was setting charges at the diamond mine, intending to destroy the energy source of the city. He hoped the mine group would be successful, but whether the mine group's mission was accomplished or not, John was going to get Shari.

When pebbles landed on the ground near him, John understood Jacob's charge was placed, and his men were safely away.

"It's our turn. Are you ready, Doc?" Samuel asked John.

"Yes. More than ready."

"Move slowly. We don't know how stable this C-4 shit is. It's old as the hills. Gently attach the blasting cap to the fuse cord," Samuel instructed.

With steady hands, John did as Samuel said.

"Now gently push the cap into the putty, and then press the putty to the dome."

"I wish you did not have to be here to instruct me," John said.

"Shut up, Doc. You're the one who shouldn't be here. It ain't your war, and it ain't your fault my arm's broke."

"Shut up, Samuel. You would bitch if you were hung with a new rope."

"No need to compliment me, Doc."

John chuckled as he firmly pushed the explosive putty against the glass dome. He and Samuel smiled at each other. Energy coursed through John's veins, he looked forward to the detonation.

Samuel stood, smiling. "Grab the wheel, Doc."

John grasped a handle on the fuse cord wheel, just as Samuel did. Then crouching low, the two men slowly walked, unrolling the cord as they moved away from the dome. John looked over his shoulder and saw the sun turning the horizon gold.

They set the empty wheel down a good distance from the dome because they were ready to poke the bear.

John reached into his pocket for a sulfur stick.

"Light that Lucifer, Doc," Samuel encouraged. "I'm lookin' forward to this."

John struck a sulfur stick and set the flame to the cord. Then he and Samuel ran as if their asses were on fire, and they needed a water trough. They dropped to the sand and watched the sparks sizzle along the cord toward the C-4 pressed against the dome.

With every foot of fuse that burned, John felt his heart drum faster. Faster! Faster! He wanted his wife. Just before the flame reached the C-4 on the dome, John pressed his hands over his ears and pressed his face into the sand.

Boom!

Glass and sand flew high into the air, raining down everywhere.

"Go!" John bounded to his feet and rushed toward the huge hole in the dome. The robots could not repair this damage quickly.

Glass bits crunched beneath John's boots as he entered the city. He saw people in white clothing running frantically toward white dwellings. He heard those people scream, and he saw them wearing expressions of panic and stupor.

John suspected it had been like that for the innocents of his time when Sherman burned Richmond on his march to the sea.

He wanted to help the people, but he could not take the time. He had to find Shari.

Behind him, John heard Jacob shout, "People, stop! Breathe! The air is good! The air is good!"

As John ran past another cluster of people, he heard Tomas shout, "Fight! Fight for freedom!"

John's long legs carried him in the direction of the city's capitol building, toward Artemis's stronghold. He saw it ahead. It was just as Jacob had described, a glass and gold pyramid.

Jacob had said the capitol was where citizens under government watch were housed. It was the jail. It was the first place he would look for Shari.

Behind him, John heard fewer screams, less terror. He knew if the people incited and joined the freedom force, victory would be attained.

As he ran, John heard the whooshing sound of blades and glanced over his shoulder to see a flying robot approaching. He ducked between two buildings. While he watched the robot near, he saw three young people, two women and a man, running on the walkway.

John saw the robot bear down on the people.

Shit! John knew the innocent people expected the robot to aid them. His conscience told him to warn them, but his heart told him to be quiet, not to draw attention to himself. He could not do it. "Hide! Hide, people!"

The robot fired at the young people, just as John knew it would. No humans were safe this day. The robot's laser hit the walkway, and debris flew into the air, making one young woman fall. John cursed when he saw both women cower, and then the man leaned over them, protecting them.

"Run! Hide!" John yelled. But the citizens were too frightened or confused to move.

John bounded out of his hiding place when the robot turned to fire his eye lasers again. Pulling his Colt, John aimed at the robot's head and fired. His first shot hit the robot in the top of its forehead, doing little damage, but his shot brought the robot's attention around to him.

He fired again and again. His shots blew out the robot's eyes. As the robot flailed, John lassoed it, and then he quickly tied the rope to the edge of the moving walkway. His rope held the robot, pulling it firmly toward the floor of the city.

John watched the metal monster crash onto the walkway.

The damaged walkway stalled.

As the robot floundered, the young women still cowered, but the young man stood and stared.

John fired his Colt into the air, drawing the young people's attention. "Help me!" John shouted. "Crush the robot!"

John rushed to the young man's side and picked up a large chunk of metal walkway debris. He smashed the robot's head. "Hit it! Hit it!" he yelled.

The young man, a tall, handsome blond, grabbed fist-sized chunks of debris and pounded the robot's head repeatedly. Then the young women began to help, and soon the robot lay motionless.

"Thank you for saving us," one of the young women said to John. Color returned to her pale face as she trembled. The other young woman nodded but didn't say a word. She just stared at the downed robot.

The young man turned to John and looked him up and down. "You are not from here."

John chuckled. "Is it my hair or my clothes?"

The young man, still part boy, did not understand John's jest. "You carry weapons. How did you come here?" the young man asked, still obviously perplexed.

"That is not important now. Listen to me… There is life beyond the dome. The air is good! But you must fight for your freedom. If you do not fight, then flee."

"There is good air?" one of the women asked.

"Yes." John struggled with his patience. He had to move on to find Shari. "And trees and water. And babies."

"Babies?" the other young woman asked.

"Conceived naturally," John stated.

"Naturally," the young man said. "You mean sexually?"

"Yes."

The young man smiled in boyish delight, making John laugh. "All in a place called Freedom Land."

"Then the rumor is true?" the young man said.

"Very true. There are other men here, willing to help you escape and lead you to Freedom Land."

"We want to go!" the young man proclaimed.

"Good. Go that way. There is a hole in the dome." John pointed westward, where the dome's hole gaped.

"But why are you not fleeing?" a young woman asked.

"I must find my wife."

"Wife?" the young man said in disbelief.

"Yes. Shari. I have come to rescue her. I believe she is in the capitol with Artemis." John saw a strange expression, one of surprise, even reluctance, cross the faces of the young people. Especially, the young man's. Shit!

"We know who Shari is," one of the women said.

"Yes," the young man added. "She is a famed time traveler. Shari is not in the capitol."

"Where is she?" John demanded, his fear and frustration making him growl his words. He took several deep breaths to calm himself. He was out of patience.

"In the sanatorium." The young man pointed toward the building.

"You mean the medical place?"

All three young people nodded.

Panic gripped John's heart. He shook his head. Stop! Think! "Why?"

"She is to be impregnated. It was to be mine. I am Thorne 06031913," the young man answered.

Without thought, John grabbed the young man by the front of his snowy-white shirt and lifted him off the ground. Murderous intent filled John's mind. "Did you touch her?" he snarled.

"No! No!" Thorne croaked. "I gave no specimen! Artemis is with her."

John's breathing slowly regulated. His vision cleared of bloodlust as he realized why the robot had fired on these young people. Artemis wanted Thorne dead. Why?

As John's haze of fury subsided, he released the young man. "Go! Get out of here!" he ordered.

"I will help you find her," Thorne offered.

John shook his head. "Get these young women to safety. There is life waiting for you." *At least the young man had courage,* John thought. "If you want to help, help in Freedom Land."

"I will find help for you sooner than that," Thorne said, extending his hand to John. "Watch for smoke signals."

John laughed as he accepted the young man's hand. Thorne seemed a descent young man. But John knew he could only count on himself to save his family. That belief went back for many generations.

As the three young people ran toward their freedom, John marched toward the sanatorium.

CHAPTER 23

IN THE SANATORIUM, Shari lay on an operating table. She was naked from the waist. her legs were raised and restrained in stirrups, and she was bound and gagged again.

She watched a medical robot arrange sterilized instruments needed to abort her child. Shari felt sick, but she knew she couldn't vomit for she'd drown in her own regurgitation. She was so frightened sweat dampened her armpits.

Rolling her head to the side, she saw Artemis walking toward her. Shari struggled in terror. "Please don't," she begged beneath the cellulose over her mouth.

She knew Artemis couldn't understand her words, but her desperation was evident. Artemis shook his head.

"You're lucky I didn't beat the bastard from your womb. The only reason I stopped was my concern that if I damaged you, you might not be able to produce my child. That's also why I'm having your womb scraped clean instead of giving you a drug-induced abortion. You have to remain fertile. Robot! Do it now!"

As the robot moved toward Shari, the glass door to the operating room exploded. Shards of glass hit Shari's shins, nicking her with tiny cuts. An alarm blared!

And then Shari saw John! He stood in the shattered operating room threshold, holding an AK-47 to his shoulder.

Artemis whirled around, and Shari saw his back was peppered with glass shards.

Blood dripped from a small cut on Shari's shin, but it didn't matter because John was here. Shari thought she had never seen anything as glorious as her husband in warrior mode running toward her.

She heard John yell a terrifying war cry as he brought his AK-47 to his shoulder. She watched him fire repeatedly, blowing apart the medical robot. It fell to the floor, cut in half and screeching. John blasted the robot again as he jumped over it.

Then John pointed the AK-47 at Artemis. "Do you want to be buried or burned?" he asked as he aimed the weapon.

Shari saw two robots rush into the room. She screamed a warning against the cellulose covering her mouth. She saw John spin around, and then she saw him blow the heads off both robots. The robots collided and fumbled about, bouncing off the nearest wall before they dropped to the floor, convulsing as their circuits sparked.

Shari heard more explosions detonate inside the sanatorium and outside the building too. Artemis whirled around and ran.

Shari's hope sparked anew. Maybe the freedom fighters were taking over the city. Maybe Jacob and other freedom fighters were destroying Artemis's stronghold. She knew one certainty that was always true: anything was possible with hope.

She watched John stride to the table where she lay. When he reached her, he tenderly ran his hand down the side of her face before pulling the cellulose off her mouth. "Shari?"

"John!"

"What was it doing?" John asked as he opened the metal cuffs restraining Shari's hands.

He eyed her raised legs and looked at her bruises while he freed her legs. "Shari, what was that thing going to do to you?"

Shari bolted upright and threw herself in to John's arms. "It was going to kill our unborn baby."

"Our baby?"

"Yes."

John's body shook as he held her tightly against him. "Did it?"

"No."

"Thank you, Great Spirit." John pulled back and looked at her face. "He beat you."

"Yes." She did not care that her face bore the black and blue marks of Artemis's anger. "But I am still with child."

John looked into her eyes as he removed the clasps on her ankles, and as he did, Shari saw moisture in his gaze.

"John, I am fine." Shari saw another robot appear in the doorway. "John!"

He spun around and blew that robot to pieces, like he did the others. Then he lowered her legs onto the bed. "There are large bruises covering your entire body."

Shari nodded. "I will heal."

"This is not over until Artemis is dead."

"I know."

John helped Shari down from the table. "Can you stand?"

He pulled a blanket from beneath the table and gently wrapped it around her.

"Yes, with help."

John pulled her into his arms again and held her for a moment. "Oh, my love, you have suffered so much."

Against John's chest, Shari said, "John, he wanted to beat the baby from me, but he didn't fearing damage to my womb. He wanted to impregnate me with his sperm, and then he planned to transplant his brain into the baby because he's dying, and he wants to live forever. But, John, the beating was a good thing because it stopped him from doing the abortion until my body was strong enough to endure it."

John tightened his arms around his wife.

Shari groaned. "Easy, John. He hurt my ribs."

John eased his hold. "We need to go."

"Yes. Please. Get me out of here."

"Just lean on me."

They carefully made their way through the halls. As they passed a room, Shari saw white clothing lying on a bed. "John, stop. Let's put the clothing on so we look like everyone else." She pointed to the clean garments.

They stepped into the room, and as John helped her put on the garments, he asked, "When did you know you were pregnant?"

"I didn't. Artemis told me."

John lifted her chin with his finger and gazed into her eyes. "We have been blessed."

Shari nodded and closed her eyes as John's lips met hers.

It was a brief kiss before they pulled apart. "Where's Danny?" Shari asked.

"With Nola."

"Let's hurry home."

They used a back stairway to descend.

On the bottom floor, John and Shari cautiously headed for the front of the hospital. John glanced around as they walked through the huge lobby. No one even looked at them. Once outside, they darted behind a water fountain that looked like Artemis.

"Look there." John pointed off in the distance, at the top of a rise.

"What is that?" Shari asked as she squinted at swirling smoke.

"A smoke signal. We have to move fast."

Shari nodded, hoping she could continue to run because she felt herself growing weaker and dizzier. The robot must have given her something.

John supported her weight as they rushed past the sanatorium's walkway depot entrance. Even with John's support, Shari stumbled. John scooped her into his arms.

As John carried her, Shari counted on Artemis's cowardice to keep him hidden until dark. Then they might have a chance to make it out of the city.

"You need to rest," John said.

"I know. At least we should find some cover."

Shari leaned feebly against John's shoulder as they slowed their pace.

Suddenly laser blasts hit the ground on either side of them. John stopped short. He stepped in front of Shari.

Shari cursed herself, not because of her weakness but for being a fool. Artemis had let them escape. He'd set a trap, and they had run right into it.

Artemis had manipulated her like a puppet on a string. No! She refused to let that happen. She was a freedom fighter! She knew what she had to do this time.

"What do you want?" John called out.

"That should be obvious." Artemis's voice came from a speaker system mounted on a building nearby.

"John, save yourself." Shari forced herself to stand tall next to him.

"Stay back, Shari," John said, stepping in front of her. He raised his arms in surrender.

Shari heard a bark of laughter through the speakers.

"Now you will both die," Artemis sneered.

A laser blast hit John in midthigh, toppling him forward. Shari screamed when she saw John's pants catch fire. She dropped beside John and smacked out the flames even though her hands burned.

With the flames smothered on John's leg, Shari pushed against his side. "Let me go, John."

"No."

The pain in John's voice hurt her more than the pain in her hands or her heart. There was no escape this time. There was only surrender or death.

Artemis's sadistic laughter mocked them as he said, "Do you want to be buried or burned?"

"I'll come with you, Artemis!" Shari yelled.

"No." John tried to shield her with his body.

Shari pushed at John's shoulder. "I must!"

"No!"

She looked toward the sky and saw Artemis flying above them. Four robots flew with the dictator, and all the robots carried laser weapons. Shari suspected Artemis would kill John first so she'd have to watch.

Suddenly AK-47 shots reverberated all around them as bullets whizzed over her and John's heads. She saw John smile.

Was he insane?

"The cavalry has arrived," John said.

"I'll kill you yet, you bitch!" Artemis yelled.

Robots fired laser blasts at the rebels who fired their AK-47s from behind nearby structures. With lassoes the rebels pulled down the robots protecting Artemis, forcing him to flee.

"Shari, we must get away from the tunnel!" John jumped up and pulled Shari to her feet.

More blasts and bullets flew over their heads. John limped forward, pulling Shari away from the walkway. But he surprised her when he pulled her into the lasers and bullets. What was he doing?

"John?"

They would definitely die now!

Shari saw John drop his gun and pull his knife from his boot, and she realized he was out of ammunition. Her first thought was of Danny. At least Danny was safe with Grandmother.

Suddenly the walkway tunnel ahead of them exploded. The force of the blast threw John and Shari backward. They landed hard several yards from the walkway entrance.

Shari lay still, afraid to breathe. Slowly she inhaled. She hurt so badly she feared moving! So many times they should have died. John's Great Spirit must have great plans for them.

"Doc?" Jacob called out.

"I am here!"

The smoke of the walkway explosion began to clear, and through the haze, Shari saw John rise not far from her. In gratitude, she said, "Thank you, Great Spirit."

*****

"Shari!"

"John!" Shari answered.

He hobbled toward her. His leg burned as the salt in his sweat scored his wound, but he continued walking to Shari. John knew they had to finish this revolt today while they had the advantage. The trouble was, which way did Artemis go?

"Jacob!" John called out.

"Here, John!" Out of the dark, blown tunnel strode Jacob and a band of freedom fighters. Samuel walked beside a dirt-covered Thorne. Samuel wore a grin from ear to ear.

That was a good sign.

"The diamond mine?" John asked. Because the tunnel was dark, he suspected the mine was dark too. The miners had been successful in their mission. The explosions had knocked out the city's power.

"Downed too," Samuel proudly said.

"Damn, good job, Samuel!" John said as he hugged Shari. "Are you hurt, wife?"

"No, I don't think so." John helped Shari rise and gently touched her limbs. "Nothing is broken, John."

John smiled. His white teeth sparkled from his dirty face. "The freedom fighters blew 'em to hell and gone."

Jacob and Samuel walked up to John, and Samuel slapped John on the back. "Hello, ma'am," Samuel said. "I hope you ain't hurt, are you?"

"The baby?" John softly asked.

"We are both fine." Shari lay her head against John's chest.

"She is fine," John stated.

Then a loud, noisy collapsing belch came out of the dusty walkway tunnel. "That's the end," Samuel said, smiling his own dirty-faced smile.

Jacob's wife, Nola, came forward, from where Shari didn't know, and Nola put her arm around Shari's shoulders. "Come with me," she invited.

As Nola led a shaking Shari away, John, Jacob, and Samuel turned in the direction of the collapsed walkway. "Where are they going?" Shari asked.

"To make sure all the monsters are dead," Nola answered.

*****

John held his knife in one hand, and with his other hand, he felt his way down the collapsed tunnel, leading the others behind him.

He came to a turn and listened cautiously because it was an excellent place for an ambush.

The lights blinked on as he looked around the corner, and a laser blast whizzed by his shoulder. Another robot! Where the hell was it? John could not see much in the debris filled tunnel. No matter, he would finish off this final monster. Then he had to go after Artemis!

John saw the tunnel divided ahead. He pointed at Jacob and made a beckoning sign. Jacob nodded, and the men split up. John took a deep breath, and he and Jacob crept around the corner. Immediately a laser blast hit Jacob in his thigh, and Jacob went down. "Go!" Jacob hissed. "I am okay. Go kill it."

Another laser blast hit John in his throwing wrist. It stung like a son of a bitch! He felt blood drip from the wound. Shit! He inhaled his frustration and continued onward.

The lights went out! It was as dark as Hades again in the tunnel, but John's eyes quickly adjusted to the darkness, and the air was clearing. He had to put an end to this robot before it could kill his friends.

John heard a slight noise. It sounded like a footfall. What the hell? He aimed and threw his knife at the sound.

Immediately, he heard a gurgling noise.

The light in the tunnel flashed dimly, and then it blinked out again. In the moment of light, John saw where his knife had landed. Artemis stood a few yards before him, and John's blade stuck out of the dictator's neck. Artemis still stood! How was that possible? How the hell could the man still be alive with a knife in his neck?

The tunnel light blinked on again, and this time the light stayed lit. John saw Artemis drop to the tunnel floor.

John strode to Artemis's body, and as he stood over Artemis, John saw the man's eyes glow. Now John knew how Artemis was still alive. He was still alive because he was no longer a man. John reacted. He leaped on top of Artemis. However, to John's surprise, he found the robotic dictator still amazingly strong.

Pulling his knife from Artemis's neck, John stabbed Artemis in the chest. John's knife did not puncture Artemis's metal shell. Artemis's eyes grew brighter. John stabbed harder into the metal shell.

The sharpness of John's knife finally punctured Artemis's metal body, but the monster man still struggled. This was impossible!

John saw, during their struggle, they had reversed the direction of their stances. He saw a spot of light at the mouth of the tunnel. He saw Jacob standing in the light.

Silently praying, John faced the light at the opening. It took all his strength to slowly maneuver Artemis so the robotic man's back was to Jacob and the tunnel opening.

John trembled. His grip on his knife was slipping from the blood running over his hand.

John saw Artemis's eyes brighten. He knew Artemis was prepared to fire his eye lasers. Shit!

Suddenly a laser blast came out of the dark tunnel and hit Artemis in the back. During that instant, John stopped pushing and yanked the dictator's head back. John slices across Artemis's throat. Blood spurted! Finally, Artemis's strength subsided, and he toppled over. He lay still as his eyes turned black.

John looked down. The dictator's chest was deeply punctured, and John saw inside Artemis lay a mechanical heart. Artemis's metal heart beat no more. The dictator's once mortal soul sank into hell.

"Doc! Doc!"

"Here!" John answered. He sat on the floor and panted in pain. He saw Jacob running toward him before his eyes blurred.

John saw who carried the big-ass gun that saved him. It was Jacob! Tomas ran with Jacob. Behind Tomas ran Thorne. Shari ran behind Jacob and Tomas with Thorne.

John tried to rise, but then he gave it up. It was over. He stayed on the tunnel floor as his whole body seemed to float above raging flames.

Shit!

Strangely, he felt at peace.

Tomas reached John first. "You okay, Doc?"

"Never better."

Shari reached him and collapsed beside him. She threw her arms around his neck and wept. As best he could, John held her close to his side.

"Wow, Doc?" Tomas said. "That was a close one."

John looked up at Tomas and smiled. "Yes. How...did...you know where I was?" John gasped, barely holding onto consciousness.

"Well, I come across this young man." Tomas gestured toward Thorne. "He was stopping Shari from running into the depot to follow you. She told us what was going on." Tomas slapped Thorne on the back as the young man looked uncomfortable. "While Samuel went to help others in need, Shari and Thorne brought me here. We all figured you might need some help. So...how you doing, Doc?"

John grimaced. "Dandy," he answered. John felt Shari's warm wet tears fall on his face as she stroked his cheek. He reached out and took her hand, lifting it to his lips. He kissed her knuckles. "Thank you, wife."

EPILOGUE

A WEEK LATER, Shari and John sat gazing into the flames of a comforting campfire in Freedom Land. Now not so stiff and sore, they cuddled together. The refugee camp had quadrupled in size, and everyone wore a smile.

Childish giggles filled the air, making Shari look up. Jacob's daughter ran toward them with Danny in hot pursuit.

"He's got a bug!" Nyla called out.

John grabbed Danny as he bolted by. "And what do you think you are doing with that bug?"

Danny squirmed in his father's arms.

"I get, Nyla," Danny giggled.

Nyla stopped and turned around, only to walk back to Shari and John. Danny held out the bug, and Nyla squealed. Then she looked at John and Shari. "I'm not scared. The bug is dead. It's just a game."

John let Danny go, and the boy raced off after Nyla. Shari sighed and leaned against John's good shoulder. He wrapped his arm around her and kissed her. When he pulled back, she sighed contently. She truly felt blessed by all deities because she now believed.

"Are you happy?" John asked.

"More than I ever dreamed." Shari closed her eyes and sighed.

"We have a decision to make."

She looked at John. "I know."

Shari wondered about their decision. Should they decide to return to the past or stay in her time? Both had benefits. Whatever John wanted, she would do because it really didn't matter. Home was where her heart was, and that was with the man at her side. She looked at Danny joyously playing, and then she laid her hand on her stomach. "What do you think?"

"I think we should build our cabin soon. We cannot continue to rely on Jacob's and Nola's generosity."

Shari turned her head, and her eyes meet John's and held. Her gaze filled with moisture. She surprised herself as she realized what she wanted. She wanted to stay in her time. "I want to stay here in Freedom Land."

John smiled down at her. "I do too. They need a doctor here."

Twin tears rolled down Shari's face. "How did you know what I wanted?"

"The way you just looked at Danny and touched your stomach." John kissed the tip of Shari's nose. "Our family is expanding." He laid his hand gently on her still flat abdomen. "Danny and our baby will have more freedom here than they will in my time. Although we better build a big house because I want a place I can make love to you anytime I want."

"Me too."

Their lips met in a promise for their family's future. The world's future. Together forever.

The End

ABOUT THE AUTHOR

GERI HAWTHORNE WAS born and raised in North Dakota. History and science fiction have always been interests of hers, and it seemed natural to her to combine them in her writing. She has been active in journalism since high school and college. *Time Quest* is her debut novel.